Pure Mania

BY THE SAME AUTHOR

The Assault on Culture: Utopian Currents from Lettrisme
to Class War (Aporia Press & Unpopular Books, 1988)

The Festival of Plagiarism (Sabotage Editions, 1989)

EDITED BY STEWART HOME

Plagiarism: Art as Commodity, and Strategies for its
Negation (Aporia Press, 1987)

The Art Strike Handbook (Sabotage Editions, 1989)

Pure Mania

Stewart Home

Polygon
EDINBURGH

©Stewart Home 1989
First published in 1989 by Polygon
22 George Square, Edinburgh

Typeset on the Telos Text Composition System,
and printed and bound in Great Britain by
Redwood Press Limited, Trowbridge, Wiltshire

British Library Cataloguing
  in Publication Data
Home, Stewart
  Pure Mania
  I. Title
  823'.914 [F]

ISBN   0 7486 6035 6

One

PAUL JOHNSON LOOKED DESPAIRINGLY INTO his coffee. He felt out of place as all around him tea-swilling proletarians washed down their greasy lunches with that most 'British' of drinks. Christ, Tracy would kill him if she knew where he was and what he was doing. Tracy, he cursed the day he'd met her. And yet, he knew he'd never meet another girl who could take her place. There'd been plenty of girls before her but after meeting Tracy he realised they'd meant less than nothing. Tracy had told him to abandon his career as a performance artist and he'd obeyed. She'd had him dangling on a string since the day they'd met.

That was four long years ago now. Paul had been part of the entertainment hired for the hen party thrown by the girl who was about to become Tracy's sister-in-law. He'd gone through his usual act. The female revellers were asked one at a time to come up onto the stage and take a snip at his clothes with a large pair of tailor's scissors. It took an hour before the last stitch of clothing had been removed and he was revealed in his naked glory. After this, an assistant had covered him with whipped cream and a lottery was held to choose four lucky girls who would get up on stage and lick it off. Tracy had been one of those four. But while the others licked as if there was no tomorrow, Tracy held back. It was only after most of the cream had been eaten that she began to lick his ear. After a minute she'd stopped and whispered 'Imagine your ear is a cunt'. Then she'd started licking again and Paul had imagined. Pretty soon he'd become oblivious to the other women running their tongues over his naked flesh. Oblivious to the audience he was paid to entertain.

1

That night Tracy took him back to her flat in Poplar. He realised how beautiful she was as they sat holding hands on a District Line train. Hers wasn't the shallow beauty which could be captured in a photograph, or even by a skilled painter. Ordinary girls who could be made to look beautiful in a still shot were ten a penny. What Tracy had was a mobility of expression. And it wasn't just her facial expressions. Her hands, arms, whole body moved to emphasise whatever point she was making.

When they made love Paul came to an even greater appreciation of her body. Tracy exercised regularly and was very careful about her diet. Her muscles were lithe and well toned. He ate her snatch and she tasted beautiful. Tracy followed a strict raw food diet: nothing cooked, no meat, no dairy products. There were no poisons in her body, nothing sour or unpleasant. A doctor would have said she was underweight, a herbalist would pass her as having reached the peak of physical perfection.

In the past Paul had treated girls as objects, he'd used them and abused them. But Tracy was different. Her beauty arose from her ability to express herself. She couldn't be treated as an object because of this very expressiveness. And so Paul found their relationship difficult. It was easier for him to treat Tracy as a superior than as an equal. But every now and then he'd rebel against this state of affairs. Christ, in his time he could have had any bird he wanted. But that was before he'd met Tracy. Now there was no point in even thinking about this because a relationship with Tracy was all he desired.

Paul had tried to assert himself again that morning. He'd done so because he was bloody worried. It was only a matter of time before the cops caught up with them. And when that happened it would be several years before he saw Tracy again. In view of these facts, Paul didn't consider it unfair to demand that he move permanently into his girlfriend's flat. He simply wanted to make up for the time he knew he was going to lose – and in advance.

2

He had already spent more than half the week at Tracy's pad. There was plenty of space, the place was clean and bright – quite the opposite of his squat just down the road in Bow.

Paul picked up his coffee and sipped guiltily. Tracy had an inflexible eco-vegan line against the consumption of cash crops. And here he was sitting in a cafe they'd fire-bombed just six months previously. The establishment had only recently re-opened. Cars shot by on the Blackwall Tunnel Approach. The Bromley Snack Bar emptied as lunchtime drew to a close. Factory hands and council workers left for an afternoon of physical toil. Paul ordered another coffee and began to relax. He'd never felt happy among working men. Now they'd gone, he only had the waitresses' grim smiles to contend with.

As his second coffee arrived, Paul told the waitress he was just going next door to buy some cigarettes. She shrugged. He'd done a runner from the cafe before and she knew he was about to do it again. She didn't have the heart to report the matter to the police. There was something a little bit pathetic about Paul. He'd done too much speed in his youth and you could see the toll it had taken on him. He was so underweight that his looks were often unfavourably compared to those of a corpse. His six two frame, drainpipe jeans and undersize denim jacket added to the impression that he'd long ago joined the ranks of the living dead. His head was shaved at the sides and closely cropped on top. The haircut didn't suit him. The waitress sighed as she reflected there was very little you could do to help those who inflicted pain on themselves. At least she could spare this lost soul the agony of a trip to a magistrate's court. Paul made his exit, ambled up the road and under the subway.

If Tracy ever found out he'd been drinking coffee, she'd do her nut. But, Paul reflected, she would at least appreciate the fact he'd not paid for the beverage. He reached the tube station. The ticket inspector's booth was empty. He jumped a westbound train. He was only taking it one stop.

Like Tracy's flat on the **Teviot**, Paul's squat was set off the beaten track. It was an odd set up – a Victorian terrace running down one side of a street, surrounded by the tower blocks which had been built to replace housing stock destroyed during the Blitz. The street's main claim to fame was that Alan Farquhar of the **Very Cross Brigade** had lived in the terrace between serving his time for terrorist offences and extending an overseas holiday when his post-Angry Brigade drug smuggling activities came to the attention of the British authorities.

Back in '88 the council had slapped a preservation order on the terrace. The houses, dating from 1870, were allegedly one of the few local examples of **Victorian architecture** to have survived site clearance in the 1950s. Paul couldn't understand why anyone would want to save them. He'd much rather live in a nice modern flat with central heating, double glazing and furniture from **Habitat**.

Tracy rarely visited Paul's squat. This was hardly surprising, since he shared it with two sorts, Catfish and Chickenfeed, who had once been leading lights in the legendary **Hoxton Hillbillies**. During the mid-eighties the lads had lived in the notorious pre-sort squat on **Hackney Road**. The Hillbillies had never had a kitchen. They'd demolished their own toilet one night after deciding that such contraptions were bourgeois. Dogs were allowed to shit all over the house, while the human inhabitants used a broken washing machine which had been turned on its side for purposes of defecation. Anyone who wanted a piss simply did so out of the window – preferably on a passing pedestrian. Having reached their mid-twenties the former Hillbillies had mellowed. They now had both kitchen and flush toilet. But out of nostalgia for their previous lifestyle they refused to clean either.

Paul lay on his bed, dreaming up schemes to please Tracy. If he thought of something which would really

4

demonstrate how much he loved her, then perhaps she'd let him move into her flat. For some reason Paul remembered a story he'd once heard. It concerned a prophet who'd predicted a wave of bombings in Brazil. The events duly occurred and when the cops rounded up the culprits, their leader turned out to be the psychic who'd predicted the terrorist outrages. Paul thought about the story and eventually remembered where he'd heard it. A journalist called Edward Case had related it on a late night radio show. Paul had been told by a friend that Case had taken to drinking in the Cubitt Arms on the Isle of Dogs. Presumably he'd moved into one of the **Wimpey Homes** on the Manchester Road.

Paul took the Docklands Light Railway from Devons Road. The pub was closed when he tried the door and so he walked to Island Gardens and sat in the park starring across the Thames to the Naval College at Greenwich. His thoughts took an unpleasant turn. Paul disliked sailors and the sea. He was a confirmed heterosexual and the idea of long journeys locked in a confined space with nothing but the company of men was anathema to him. And yet when Tracy told him to imagine that he had a cunt, it really turned him on. Once she had finger fucked him and he'd begged her not to stop. Afterwards she'd suggested he was gay.

They'd finger fucked several times since then but never with such spectacular results. Tracy had once suggested that Paul try to imagine what it was like to have sex with another man. He'd not really succeeded and the fact that he'd even made the attempt put him into a deep depression for several days. Paul did not feel at ease in the exclusive company of men. As far as possible he avoided public toilets. He was unsure whether he feared some pervert might make a play for him, or whether Tracy was right and he, himself, might unexpectedly make a pass at another man.

The landlord was unlocking the doors when Paul returned to the Cubitt Arms. Paul ordered a pint and sipped at it. He didn't have to wait long for Edward Case to show up. Paul recognised him instantly, he'd seen him on telly. Case ordered a double whisky. Paul strolled up to the bar as the landlord fixed the drink.

'Evening' Paul mouthed. 'I saw your Channel Four special on the New Vulgarity in Pub Culture last week. It left me deeply depressed – what on earth can we do to stop the erosion of our national heritage?'

'There's an answer,' Case sighed as he stretched his six three frame, 'but they won't let you breathe a word of it on TV. It's quite logical really. As I demonstrated, pubs tend to be owned by breweries, and the major British breweries are being taken over by the international megabrewers of lager who run down the quality of the real ales which were reintroduced in the seventies after the CAMRA campaign. This decline in quality has led to a drop in ale consumption. Lager realizes a better profit than ale, and so the multinationals are aiming to phase out the traditional British beverages in favour of the piss-weak brews they're importing from the continent. Equally serious is the **lager culture** these breweries are introducing into our pubs. Ale drinking is no longer the pub-goer's chief concern. Rather, pubs are aiming at providing an integrated lifestyle for young people, so money can be made from sales of food and the loose change poured into jukeboxes and one armed bandits. You can say that much on TV but they won't let you breathe a word of the very obvious solution.'

'Which is?' Paul demanded.

'A strong government which will represent the interests of the British people and their culture in the face of incursions from multinational capitalism and the **world Zionist conspiracy**. It's not simply a question of the erosion of our pub culture, it's four-be-twos corrupting our youth with multi-cultural schooling. We need a government which is prepared to kick multinational interests out of Britain and confiscate their assets. A government which will return to traditional values and instil in the British

6

people a love of order. Give them back their sense of purpose, restore the racial purity which is the birthright of every Aryan nation. It's time to return to the era of gunboat diplomacy. Put teeth back in the old bulldog and give young people something to believe in. The Jewish conspirators have but one intention, to destroy the White Race and everything it holds dear. They are evil, cunning, and more than willing to sell the birthrights of our people on the international market. What we need is a rigidly centralised economy guided by the strong hand of a National Socialist government. If only **Enoch** was Prime Minister, he wouldn't sell the British people down the river to the EEC!'

'But that sounds like fascism!' Paul protested.

'It is, it is!' Case retorted. 'But you've got to understand fascism has been given bad press, you've been brainwashed by the rantings of lefty teachers and a liberal media. Think about it, don't you think it's a good thing to eliminate socially undesirable elements from society? Wouldn't you prefer a world without queers, a society where you weren't continually looking out for your arse?'

'I dunno,' Paul replied, 'my girlfriend says if I just expressed my true feelings then I'd get on much better with fairies.'

'Of course you would, once you'd killed a few you'd have a far more relaxed attitude towards them! Come home with me and I'll introduce you to the glories of my sweet Nordic culture. Come, let's satiate ourselves with the joys of rape, pillage and plunder!'

PAUL HAD BEEN RIGHT. CASE had one of those **Wimpey** homes on the Manchester Road. Christ, they depressed him. They reminded him of the Goldsworth Park Estate in Woking where his brother lived. Goldsworth Park at the time building work had been completed was the largest private housing estate in Europe. Being located in one of the greyest London suburbs, prices were somewhat lower than on the Isle Of Dogs. Instead of yuppies, the place was full of newly weds who'd been banged up in first homes they hoped to move out of very quickly. Paul hated Woking and had never been back since leaving home at the age of seventeen. **Aleister Crowley** was right when he described the place as the funereal antechamber to Waterloo. There was something fundamentally evil about the town and its inhabitants. Tory to its core, the only thing it was ripe for was destruction.

Case poured his guest a **Hundred Pipers** before excusing himself. Paul lounged on the leather sofa. The furnishings were expensive but betrayed a lack of taste. Social realist pictures, fur rugs, leather, chrome and glass furniture. Case was a self-made man trying to hide the fact that most of the decor he'd known as a child had been purchased in **Woolworths**. There were no heirlooms here. All the furniture was new. But Edward's ideas on aesthetics had very obviously been handed down to him by his parents. They were a caricature of what the poor imagined the tastes of the wealthy to be. It was pathetic really. Case reminded Paul of his own dad. The two had a lot in common – right down to the large and largely unread collection of **Book of the Month Club** leatherbound classics.

Upstairs Case was grooming himself in the bathroom. It had been a long time, too long in fact, and Case was not going to let another opportunity pass him by. The recent divorce had been humiliating. An ordinary man would have been destroyed by such an ordeal. To have one's own wife stand up in court and denounce you as a homosexual was not a pleasant experience. Particularly if it put paid to your long laid plans to establish an Aryan Youth League.

And more so if the allegations were not true. It was not as if Case could have licked and fucked lovely male

8

arses when he was sober. No, he had only slipped when drunk – as he was now – and even then the bum fucks had usually occurred during the course of a pagan ritual. Case considered queers to be an aberration against the natural order. To prove to himself that he was indeed heterosexual, he had refrained from gay sex for at least two months.

Edward was very proud of the original SS uniform he'd slipped into. He felt it lent him an air of dignity. He'd bought it in the mid sixties from a Stepney based plumber who was deserting the National Socialist Movement for the **Liberal Party** – and it had cost him a bomb. He had a peculiarly strong love of the boots and leather gun belt which he polished with fetishistic care every Sunday. A few of the boys he'd picked up had laughed at his idea of sartorial elegance. He'd had to punish them severely before dumping parts of their bodies on various suburban golf courses. Case believed that any true Aryan could not fail to succumb to his charms as he goose-stepped to marching songs in his Nazi gear.

Paul was standing by the bookcase, leafing through a translation of **Mein Kampf** — when Case made his entrance. Edward preferred to stick to the original, despite the fact that his German nightclass had been far from a success. He had obtained the English edition for the benefit of those guests who were willing to own up to limitations in their schooling.

'Forget that.' Edward barked. 'I'll put on an original recording of the Nuremberg rallies!'

Hitler's voice boomed out of **Wharfedale** speakers and Case goose-stepped on the spot, swinging his arms and muttering 'Jawohl, mein Fuhrer'. As the speech reached a crescendo Edward pulled Paul against him and pushed the boy down against his crotch. He took out his cock and ordered Paul to swallow it. Paul obeyed, simultaneously horrified and fascinated. As he sucked his revulsion turned to pleasure. The action activated million-year-old genetic impulses buried at the centre of his cortex. When Case shot off a wad of liquid DNA both men experienced the thrill of orgasm as a return to the primitive unity of the swamps.

After this, Paul found himself spread across the sofa with his pants and trousers around his ankles and Edward's tongue lashing into his arse. Then Case was kissing the small of Paul's back and pulling himself up the younger man's body. Paul could feel the old Nazi's hard-on against his legs and gasped with pleasure when the cock was eased into his sphincter. Case was pressing his lips against the young man's shoulders and into the back of his neck. The pounding in Paul's arse metamorphosed into an orgasm that hit him like a wave. It was as if years of longing and repression had been swept away. The encounter left Paul both exhausted and satisfied. He was tingling all over and could not lift his face from the stuffed leather in which he'd buried it during the act of coitus. Normally he was a five-times-a-night man. But after this single fuck he felt as though it was enough to satisfy him for the rest of his life.

PAUL WASN'T SURE HOW LONG he lay on the sofa. Case had showered and changed his clothes and was suggesting that Paul go and clean himself up. When Paul went up to the bathroom he found the water had been run. Normally he liked to sit in the bath as it ran, testing to see how much heat he could take, but this time it seemed right that he should plunge into into the tub. He switched off the light and sank back, thrilling at the feel of the water around his arse.

Paul's first sexual encounter had taken place in a bath. He'd been drunk and got into the tub fully clothed, intending to run the water. The girl he was visiting rushed in and prevented him getting a soaking. She'd done this by pushing him back into the bath, unzipping his fly and taking his cock out of his pants. Judy, the girl in question, was known locally as Deep Throat. It had not surprised

Paul when she'd taken his stiffening member into her mouth and proceeded to suck, chew and swallow it. He'd come in her mouth, which she didn't seem to mind.

After that, she'd dragged him into her bedroom and they'd pulled each others' clothes off. Judy had shoved Paul's face into her snatch and he'd licked at it for a few minutes before hauling himself up her body. He'd entered her and come very quickly. That first time he was shocked at the swiftness with which they reached the peak from which man and woman can never jointly return. It was a disappointment, a let down, a pleasure which very suddenly faded.

Paul wanted to lie on the bed and doze. Judy hauled him up and threw his clothes at him before hurriedly pulling on her own gear. Graham, her boyfriend, was downstairs. To this day, Paul didn't know whether Graham had guessed what they were up to. Either way the event had never been mentioned again. Graham had remained friendly until Paul moved out of Woking the following year. He'd not seen them since then but he'd heard they were still living together.

When Paul came down from the bathroom, Case poured him a strong coffee. Both men were sobering up. Paul was silent, brooding, unsure what to make of his recent experience.

'What's on your mind?' Case enquired.

'I. . . well I. . . I'm not. . . Am I gay?'

Paul was sipping his coffee. Christ, it was his second of the day. Tracy would murder him if she found out. And yet, this time he'd something of an excuse. He needed to clear his mind. He had to process his recent experience and his brain just refused to do that while the effects of the alcohol he'd drunk lingered on in his body.

He knew Tracy was the only person he really loved – but doing it with a man had been so different, so exciting. Perhaps he was a bisexual. He'd heard that was common. But somehow this didn't fit with his mental

11

picture of himself. He needed to convince himself he was still straight. He didn't feel he'd changed in any way. And yet, he felt the knowledge he now had – that he'd done it and enjoyed doing it with a man – should somehow make him feel different.

'No,' Case assured him, 'you're not queer. We were both drunk. People often do things out of character when they're drunk. You know that.'

Paul's reaction made Case think of his own youth. He'd been screwing boys in his **Scout** troop long before he'd first made it with a girl. He supposed this boy's response to their recent encounter was not dissimilar to his own on first making it with a woman. Case had never felt comfortable in the company of women. That first time, when he was eighteen, had been a shock. He was on a camping holiday with three other cub reporters. He'd noticed the woman the minute she walked into the bar. She'd met his gaze, smiled and walked over to him. Case bought her a drink. Then they'd gone back to his tent, leaving his companions in the pub.

He hadn't needed to tell her he'd not been with a woman before. She guided him through everything he had to do. Afterwards she told him she was thirty-six and married to a successful but dreadfully pretentious **artist**. She remained with the painter on the condition that she could go off once a year for two weeks, during which time she did what she liked with no questions asked when she returned home. Her husband was well aware of her penchant for picking up younger men. In particular she was attracted to **virgins**. Her husband had been a virgin when she'd met him. Case had never learned the woman's name, and after that night he'd never seen her again.

'Well, I suppose I'm straight. But how can I be sure?' Paul was demanding.

'Look at me.' Case was gesturing with his hands. 'Do I look like a fairy? I was married for twelve years and am

12

only very recently divorced. What about you, you've got a girlfriend haven't you?'

'Yeah.' Paul didn't sound fully convinced this entitled him to heterosexual status.

'Well, there you are, we're both confirmed heterosexuals!' Case insisted.

Paul lowered his eyelids and stared at the floor. There was something about this man. If he looked at him for too long he was afraid he'd get a hard-on. Paul was still frightened by what he'd been through. Not so much by the act itself as by the fact it seemed more than likely to happen again. He'd never been unfaithful to Tracy. But perhaps it was okay when it was with a man.

'What's it now?' Case enquired.

'The girlfriend' Paul replied.

'Having trouble with her?'

'Yeah. I don't think she realizes how much I love her. That's why I wanted to see you. I thought you'd be able to dream up some way I could make her understand how much she means to me.'

'I don't see how.'

'Well, she's a militant vegan, a radical ecologist, a campaigner against the use of tea, coffee and all other cash crops. You probably know that debt repayments from **Third World** countries to the First World far outstrip the aid the West sends to feed the hungry. Well, Tracy, that's my girlfriend, believes that instead of growing cash crops to export to the West, the Third World should be growing the food it needs for itself. So she campaigns against people drinking tea and coffee, and I thought that if I could help her get some media coverage for her cause then that'd show how much I love her.'

'Now I see where I come in!' Case beamed at Paul. 'I think I can help you out and get myself a good story at the same time.'

Case was going through all the angles in his head. He figured it'd be easy to get this kid to do something illegal.

13

It might take a bit of thinking through but if he could come up with something vicious enough and then tip off the cops, it would make a great scoop. He smiled as he thought of the **Class Justice** renegades he'd led into five-year jail sentences when he'd assisted them in orchestrating their **Yuppies Out of the East End** campaign. And if he could just stir up enough lawlessness, it would create the perfect conditions for the growth of a popular fascist movement.

'Would you be prepared to break the law?' Case enquired.

'I'm not sure.' Paul had done plenty that was illegal to help Tracy with her campaign but he'd have to be certain he could trust Case before he'd admit that. He wanted to test the man before confiding in him to any great degree.

Case could see the boy wasn't going to be the pushover he'd first imagined. Nevertheless, there was potential which was worth pursuing. Even with legal activities he could get some good stories and use the publicity to win over the boy's trust. Once you got someone hooked on the **media**, on getting their face into it, they started needing heavier and heavier doses of publicity. And the price to be paid for that fix was corruption.

Case would get his way with this boy in the end. After all, he'd already been up his arse and now he had him drinking coffee – an activity which the boy's beloved girlfriend opposed with the mindless militancy of a liberal. 'Another coffee?' Case enquired.

'Oh no, I couldn't!' Paul replied.

'Don't be polite. I can see you enjoyed the one you just had. Besides it would do you good. Get the alcohol out of your system. If we're going to have a serious talk about **an anti-cashcrop campaign** then you'll need to clear your head. Go on, just another cup.'

Paul acquiesced. He supposed one cup wouldn't make much difference to the world economy. And he was having it to keep Case happy. Drinking this cup of coffee would assist in the abolition of the cash crop economy. It was a

14

sacrifice on his part. A little offering to the great god of publicity.

'Have you got any ideas?' Case enquired as he poured Paul's second coffee.

'Ideas?' Paul repeated.

'You know,' Case encouraged, 'ideas about what you can do to get publicity.'

'Well,' Paul replied, 'I thought I could do this event called **Haircuts For Peace.** It's not exactly about the cash crop problem but it fits in with Tracy's broader ecological concerns. I'd hold this party where everyone could come along and cut each other's hair. I'd collect all the hair and burn it in Downing Street as a protest against war. Burning hair smells like burning bodies, it's really disgusting.'

'Not bad.' Case tapped his nose with an index finger. 'Have you thought of including pubic hair in this? That would generate media interest.'

Pubic hair made Paul think of Tracy. He'd only been seeing her a few weeks when she'd commented on how much he liked her snatch. They'd often do a sixty-nine, Paul always underneath licking Tracy's minge, her crotch pushed right into his face. Tracy performed a respectable blow job but she was no Deep Throat. She sucked and chewed but never swallowed. And coming in her mouth was unacceptable behaviour. Paul had only done this once, and although nothing had been said he could tell she wasn't pleased. She'd not blown him for weeks after that. Fortunately, she'd still been happy to wrap her legs around his neck and let him eat her snatch.

'Pubic hair's good.' Paul replied. 'Perhaps we could include nail clippings too.'

'So where's this event to be held?' Case demanded.

'There's a derelict house near Vauxhall tube, I was thinking of that.'

'Good, do you know how to organise publicity?'

15

'No, not really.'

Case tossed Paul a book called **Using The Media.** 'You can have that. It explains how to write a press release and everything else you'll need to know. You won't have to work too hard since I'm already on your side and that guarantees a write-up in the **Globe** – and I should be able to swing some television coverage.'

'I'm surprised to find you so helpful, now that I know you're a Nazi. Ecology and peace seem the antithesis of your political convictions.'

'Not at all!' Case retorted. 'Fascists believe in ecology too. The White Race needs a clean and unpolluted land in which to live.'

Actually Case felt little sympathy for ecological concerns. He was mainly interested in power. Although, like **Hitler,** he was a vegetarian, this was strictly out of reverence for the founding father of National Socialism. Case felt no compunction when it came to butchering any person or animal which got in his way. He realised Paul was testing him and came up with answers which would win the boy to his side.

It was true that certain Strasserite sects were concerned with ecology. But Case had no time for their rabid anti-industrialism. When the opportunity arose he would eliminate their type from the National Socialist Movement. Hitler had known well enough where such peoples' sympathies lay. He'd hit the nail on the head when he'd said 'Scratch a brownshirt and underneath you find a red'. And Adolf knew how to deal with such scum. He'd wiped them out in the glorious **Night Of The Long Knives.**

'So you think we can work together?' Paul enquired.

'I'm sure of it!' Case replied.

There was a smile on the journalist's face. In a few minutes he'd phone for a taxi to take the boy home, in the meantime he was enjoying his company. The youth's corruption had begun. Case was determined to meet Tracy and seduce her. It took two to make a relationship and he could see that in this instance the partnership wasn't working very well. Judging by the boy, the girl would be in a pretty distressed state. Case was going to enjoy sending these bastards to hell, or at the very least prison. The divorce had depressed him, this project was just the thing to lift his spirits.

Two

THE TEVIOT WAS SITUATED ON the most north-easterly fringe of Poplar. The estate was one of innumerable post-war developments which stretched from the original east city gate for twenty miles into what had formerly been unspoilt Essex countryside. Despite their numerical supremacy, the modern blocks failed to dominate the psychogeography of the area. A handful of Victorian pubs stood as monuments to the traditions of dead generations which still dominated the lives of the living. Unless such vestiges of a fallen empire were wiped from the face of London, the city would remain forever a mausoleum.

The Teviot had been designed as a low-density development. It consisted of both low and high-rise dwellings. To its east lay the Blackwall Tunnel Northern Approach; its accident-prone lanes were verged with pavement for just half a mile before being replaced by hard shoulder. To the west lay the electrified Docklands Light Railway. Limehouse Cut, a canal, ran across the estate's northern boundary; East India Dock Road formed another natural barrier to the south. With only two minor roads serving as exits from the estate, the inhabitants were hemmed in and they knew it.

Tracy Smith had moved to the estate five years ago. At that time the council had just appointed a new Estate Officer to fill the voids from the two years the job had lain vacant. The officer lasted less than a year. Estate officers never lasted long on the Teviot. The voids always built up faster than the council could find someone to fill the job – thus adding to the high rate of homelessness in the area. Tracy lived in one of four identical blocks built on the northern tip of the estate. At the time of their construction they'd won architectural awards but were now officially designated as hard to heat due to condensation, damp and ill-fitting windows.

Tracy had a maisonette on the seventh and eighth floors of **David House**. The neighbours on either side had water pouring into their homes whenever it rained. The block had been built in the fifties and in this case the architects deserved praise for the stylish continental design. If the block had been properly maintained, people would have been clamouring to live in it instead of moaning or – if they could find somewhere to go – moving out. Limehouse Cut to the north was not much to look at, but before the construction of Canary Wharf back in '89, you'd been able to look south across the estate to a stretch of the Thames.

Tracy was sitting at the kitchen table. An untouched beansprout salad lay in front of her. Tracy's thoughts were elsewhere. She was thinking about Paul. She'd always loved him but felt he didn't really appreciate the fact. As a result he was forever dreaming up new schemes to prove to her how much she meant to him. She knew already. Had seen him on a bender the one time she'd tried to end their relationship.

The endless bottles of **Hundred Pipers** had been bad enough. To make matters worse, Paul had insisted on drinking them in her flat. She'd tried asking Paul to leave but he always refused. He was bigger and stronger than Tracy, so short of calling the cops there wasn't a lot she could do.

Then he'd started trashing cars. Tracy would have approved of this activity had it not been for the technique he'd developed to do it. His method was to punch a hole into a car windscreen, pour in petrol and then drop in a lighted match. Several times the flames had whooshed up and singed his face, hair and shirt before he'd had time to make his getaway. Paul told Tracy he didn't care if he lived or died. He couldn't imagine a future without her.

Tracy loved Paul and hadn't the heart to watch him

destroy himself. She just needed some space for herself and she'd had more of this while going steady with him than when she'd tried to end the relationship. Not only did Paul come round as often as ever, he'd inevitably be abusive and drunk. The minute he ran out of swear words he'd burst into tears. Eventually his behaviour forced Tracy to relent on her decision to chuck him.

For a while things seemed to get better. But recently Tracy had felt an intense need for extra head space. She knew she had to ring some changes in her relationship with Paul. Her problem was knowing how to set about doing this.

Tracy shifted her weight and got up from her chair. She was sick of being indoors. The argument she'd had with Paul was the last straw. She put on a jacket and headed for Swaton Road. It was quicker walking over to Paul's squat than trying to find a public telephone which worked and calling him up. She didn't mind the ten minute walk but the return trip would be a drag if he was out. Twenty minutes of her time gone with nothing to show for it. Tracy knew the exercise was good for her but she wasn't in the mood to look for silver linings.

Catfish answered the door and, of course, Paul wasn't in. She was invited in anyway and for some reason accepted. The place stank but Tracy's mood was so black she didn't notice. Chickenfeed was brewing a pot of herb tea. The two sorts weren't quite toilet trained but they were heading in the right direction.

Chickenfeed offered Tracy a steaming mug of mint tea. She accepted gratefully. Sipping at the soothing brew, she sank back into a chair which had been rescued from one too many skips. Tracy decided she was glad Paul wasn't in. What was the point of having it out with him? They never managed to resolve anything.

'Got something on yer mind Trace?' Catfish enquired as Chickenfeed slipped out of the room.

'Yes and no.' she replied.

'Well, it don't bother me if you don't wanna talk about it, I'm quite happy to talk about myself instead.'

'What you been up to?' Tracy asked.

'Well, apart from a systematic glueing of the locks on every McDonalds I come across, my new band has started gigging.'

'Where you played?' Tracy was genuinely interested. She was fond of Catfish and knew music meant a lot to him. She'd liked his previous band, **The Dispossessed**. She knew he was determined to make a better go of the music scene with his new group **Alienation**. The Dispossessed had built quite a reputation for themselves on the far left fringes of the hardcore scene. They'd been dominated by a couple of Trots and consequently disintegrated when their SWP-supporting bass player went NF. Catfish had always been an anarchoid and under the influence of Chickenfeed his new group were using humour to make their political point.

'We've played the Crowns a couple of times and the Finsbury Brewer once. We're hoping to play tonight. The **Stockbrokers** and the **Conservatives** are playing on the IOD. We figured we'd gatecrash the gig, boot the headliners off stage and give their yuppie followers the shock of their lives.'

'Sounds good!' Tracy enthused. 'I think I'll come along.'

'You do that, we could do with as many friends as possible in the audience.'

UPSTAIRS CHICKENFEED WAS TAPPING AWAY on his word processor. His fingers moved deftly over the keyboard as he knocked out his four thousand words for that day. Occasionally his right hand would move over to a glass of **Hundred Pipers**. Like most writers, Chickenfeed would imbibe steadily while 'creating'. The whisky loosened him up and helped get the verbal diarrhoea flowing. After much tapping Chickenfeed felt satisfied with the day's output. He scrolled back the screen to where he'd begun his current session, lit up a joint and 'felt' the words hit him as he read back through the draft.

He knew instinctively he was onto yet another winner. This new story **Casual** would provide him with his break into the commercial market. His writing had been of the generic, and unsaleable, boy-in-a-bedroom variety until he'd had one of those flashes of inspiration common to men of genius. He'd decided to produce an updated survey of the territory **Richard Allen** explored in the early and mid seventies. Allen had written **Skinhead, Suedehead, Boot Boys, Knuckle Girls** and fourteen other novels in a teenage sex and violence mould. Chickenfeed, working under the pen name Kelvin Callahan, had established himself as a cult writer with stories such as **Mob Violence**, **Vegan** and **Hip Hop**, which had been snatched up by the underground press. A commercial publisher had taken note and ordered a novel.

Chickenfeed wrote to a strict formula. He read and reread Allen's novels taking note of key phrases and narrative techniques. Then he set to work on his own book, incorporating the Allen style but updating it, referring to fashionable brand names and the latest trends. The novel was more or less finished, all he needed to do was add some authentic background material and one spectacular incident to make success a certainty rather than just a faint hope.

Chickenfeed sucked on his joint. He hoped he was going to get that spectacular incident tonight. He'd persuaded Alienation to invade the stage during a Yuppie gig. All he had to do was turn up, watch the events as they unfolded and then write up the fight. Chickenfeed hated using his imagination. He preferred to fictionalise events which had actually taken place, or else just rip off incidents from other peoples' plots. Like all professional writers, his livelihood depended on being able to produce the required number of words. He felt nothing but contempt for dilettantes who wanked off over their artistic integrity.

Chickenfeed didn't want to waste time thinking about

what he was producing. He simply sat down at his word processor and let his fingers tap out the first thought that came into his head. He didn't give a fuck about literature, all he wanted to do was earn a living.

Chickenfeed sincerely believed there wasn't a novel in existence which couldn't have been better written as a short story. But artistic integrity didn't pay bills and the medium was a money spinner for anyone who hit the bestseller lists. It was this and this alone which made Chickenfeed conform along with the best of them. This which had transformed his life into an exercise in knocking out 4000 words a day.

The money he made from his short stories was less than a bread and butter income. He was in line for a seven figure credit rating if his novel became a success. Of course, he'd have to knock out five or six books a year if he was going to get the flat in **Mayfair** which he'd promised himself. So far, all he'd got from writing was pulling power. Until he became a cult figure he'd not had much luck with the birds. Now all he had to do was snap his fingers in a trendy club and some beat dolly would come running. He wondered how the hell writing had become such a glamorous profession. Then he pushed the thought from his mind.

Chickenfeed was imagining what it was like to have money as well as notoriety. It wasn't just a matter of being able to buy the things he wanted. Once he was rich the middle classes would respect him. This pathological trait would enable him to enact his revenge on the people of **Chelmsford**. He'd a chip on his shoulder about growing up in that suburban hellhole. Plenty of kids got away from the place by moving to London. But they didn't generally become rich and remain unrespectable. Once he had money he'd take the occasional trip back to his home town, just to make the locals eat shit.

Chickenfeed sucked a final drag from his joint and crushed the roach into an ashtray. He drained his glass and poured another **Hundred Pipers** with tonic mix. He was about to curse himself for drifting off into such a useless train of thought when inspiration struck again. As a writer he simply couldn't afford to waste material. He'd work a novelist into his plot and have him fantasise about success within the profession. If it was good enough for Richard Allen then it was good enough for him. He tried to recall the name of the writer in **Skinhead Farewell**. He couldn't, so he pulled the book from a shelf and flicked through. The name was Dick Arlen, a one letter change from the Allen pen-name.

Chickenfeed was writing as Kelvin Callahan. He wanted something similar. His first attempt was Melvin Carlahan. He rejected this. Tried again. Kevin would do for Kelvin. Callahan was an Irish name. Callan was too. The names were reasonably similar. Kevin Callan. Chickenfeed liked that. It was a wonderful name for a writer.

He pushed the ashtray and the crushed roaches it contained to the back of his desk. No Allen hero would smoke dope. 'Drugs was for hippies.' Chickenfeed made a note of the phrase. He'd use it later. Of course, all the bikers in the Hell's Angels novels smoked weed. But that was a different genre. **Casual** was to conform to the Allen stereotype of respectable working-class hooligan. Chickenfeed made a mental note to rough out the plot for a novel about drug addiction and homosexuality. He smiled grimly when he was struck by the thought that he could write it using Callan as a pen name.

Chickenfeed saved the text he'd been working on. Once the data had been safely stored he created a new file. He typed in the name Kevin Callan and began to recreate his recent train of thought in computer screen transcription.

THE MOULDERS ARMS WAS CRAMMED with Thursday night spenders. Yuppies got paid monthly. Their credit card ratings made any day of the week a good time for a splurge. On the Isle Of Dogs, the Yuppie's big social night was Thursday. On Friday they'd all get in their BMWs and head for the country. Thursday was the night on which the rich vermin who'd sent docklands property prices skyrocketting condescended to go 'native'.

Personally Chickenfeed, Catfish, and Tracy, could not understand why anyone in their right mind would buy a place in East London when for less money you could find something better in the **Elephant and Castle** or **Peckham**. The yuppies inhabited a senseless world of mindless viciousness dominated by balance sheets and share prices; to attempt a rational explanation of their behaviour was futile.

Do-gooders might point to some flaw in the toilet training of the Rolex watch brigade to explain its lemminglike capacity for self-destruction. But ultimately such explanations don't hold water. The entire population of the Western World has been warped from a lifetime of sexual repression. Fortunately it is still only a minority who put monetarist ecconomics above personal relationships and environmental concerns.

The truth is that yuppies are fundamentally evil, being more committed to a fetishistic pursuit of the almighty quid in the cesspool of a 'free' market economy than the polymorphous pleasures of orgasmic human unity.

Onstage **The Conservatives** were running through their set. They'd just finished their controversial pro-Powellite number **Rivers Of Blood** and were launching into their soon-to-be-released debut single **Free Trade.** The response was enthusiastic. Couples dancing cheek to cheek disentangled themselves so they could applaud. Even those snogging against the back wall of the pub broke off from such activities to demonstrate their appreciation.

The group were organised around a simple guitar, bass, vocal and drum set-up. Minimal and not very effective. The ideals they sung about were those of the audience. The music reflected this, simplistic plodding which amongst

25

themselves they managed to pass off as energetic flash. The 'sound' reminded Catfish of early **Jam**, just crappy R'n'B with poor lyrics. In '77 the **Jam** had been the voice of conservative youth, with their frontman mouthing off about voting Tory at the next election. And, grey suburbanite that he was, **Weller** had remained deeply conservative right the way through his later labourite posturings.

Catfish glanced around. Most of the yuppies were drinking wine. His mates stood out a mile in their black and red M **and** S castoffs, pints of lager or Hundred Pipers and tonic in their hands. Christine, Alienation's vocalist, appeared nervous. Alan and Wayne, bass and drums respectively, were looking forward to the aggro. Christine was the only member of the band without a lengthy gigging experience and Catfish put her nervousness down to this.

'When we gonna make a break for the stage?' Alan was demanding.

'Not yet, wait till the Stockbrokers come on.' Chickenfeed replied.

Although he was not a member of the band, Chickenfeed had taken full command of the situation. The others trusted his judgement. He'd written most of their lyrics and helped out with their image. He'd even got them to sign an exclusive management contract with him.

In the past Chickenfeed had played bass in various no-hope bands. However, he'd eventually come to the conclusion that he was not much of a musician. On the handful of occasions he'd been up on stage with a group he'd found it frustrating that the singer got ninety-five per cent of the audience's attention. He'd have taken up singing himself if he'd not been painfully aware that his voice was barely up to backing vocal standards. It was nearly five years since he'd swapped his plectrum for a pen, and more recently a computer keyboard. However, in moments of reflection, Chickenfeed would admit to himself that he still harboured musical ambitions.

The Conservatives had done one encore. The enthusiastic applause was loud enough to merit a second. But **The Stockbrokers'** roadies marched onto the stage before the Conservatives completed their exit. Their movements were hurried as they set to work switching the gear around, removing the support band's amps and drums and packing them into a corner at the side of the stage. The gig was running late and if the headliners were to play a full set there wouldn't be much of a break between bands.

Backstage Peter Conduit was psyching himself up for an hour under the glamorous glare of the spotlight. Tonight, especially, he was prepared to sing his heart out. Conduit was thirty and until two years ago he really had been a stockbroker. His investments from that time provided enough income to keep him in the style to which he was accustomed. He picked up the odd bob or two from his work with the band, but he followed his new career out of love of the job – or at least the adulation which accompanied it – rather than the pittance that some claimed was its major reward. The other members of the band had been stockbrokers too. Peter suspected that for the rest of them music was little more than a hobby. Something to keep them busy after their early retirement. An exciting way of earning cocaine money.

Despite the group's lack of commitment, Peter was determined to make their musical career a chart-topping success. They'd built up a solid reputation on the wine bar circuit. From this, Peter had almost single-handedly created an exciting new scene. There were now nearly thirty bands following in the Stockbrokers' wake. **Dow Jones, Financial Services, Euro Dollar, Wall Street, The Shares, New Issue** and a score of other groups owed more than a passing debt to the Stockbrokers.

The Stockbrokers had been gigging regularly for over a year. None of their imitators had been around for more than three months. Although one or two, such as **Dividend**, were genuinely committed to yuppie musical ideals, most of the groups were just cynics who saw this new scene as a short cut to a recording contract.

The Conservatives were the first band to be signed up – and they'd only been together two months. Conduit was determined to hold out until the right deal came along. The Stockbrokers could afford to wait. Every last member of the band really had made a fortune in the city. They were whizzkids who'd reached the peak of their profession in their mid-twenties.

Peter despised the Conservatives. They all claimed to be over thirty and yet he knew for a fact that Matthew, their singer, was a mere twenty-six. He also knew why the group had accepted the first record deal they'd been offered. Although they worked in the City, none of them were quite as successful as they claimed. Each was a humble clerk on a low income and they had mortgages, joint ones, on cut-price properties in undesirable suburbs. Not one of them had the killer instinct of a genuine city slicker.

Peter booked the Conservatives as support because their lowest common denominator appeal emphasised the exclusiveness of his own brand of boogie. Tonight it was particularly important to make a good impression. Journalists from all the major music papers were in attendance. In the past, music journalists had been intimidated by the upper class atmosphere of the wine bars the Stockbrokers would play. That was why most of the press write ups for yuppie rock had appeared in **Tatler**, **Ritz** and other upper crust publications. But, by playing on yuppie home ground, the band were able to pull a reasonable audience in a pub. And a humble pub was just the right place to lure those elusive music critics.

The band were already on stage, playing an instrumental. Peter adjusted his carnation, picked up his umbrella and put on his bowler hat. The instrumental came to an end. Peter strolled into the spotlight amd was greeted by a wave of applause. The band launched straight into **House Slave**, their most popular song:

> Let me take you home and bathe you in my
> money,
> Treat you like a puppy dog and then abuse
> your body,
> I'll cater for your material needs if you'll say
> you love me,
> All you need to do is get on your knees and
> plate me.

Peter sang the opening verse with as much energy as traditional British reserve allows. The fans went for it. Well-heeled members of the audience were on their knees puckering their mouths in simulation of an activity which Conduit had no intention of engaging in while news journalists were around to witness it.

Peter often wished he could imitate the manic stage act of the American singer **Iggy Pop**, who'd indulged in fellatio with members of his audience. Conduit's public school breeding had conditioned him against such public displays of his sexuality. The kneeling men with puckered mouths knew that for a handful of them fantasy could become reality after the show.

'Isn't it about time we stormed the stage?' Catfish was attempting to issue a command.

'Wait for their last number. It'll have more impact then.' Chickenfeed insisted.

'I dunno how much more of this godawful music I can stand. It sounds like a bad version of the Jam, and I didn't think anyone could sound worse than Weller's mob.'

'Your music'll sound that much better once everyone's suffered this.' Chickenfeed patted Catfish on the shoulder as he spoke.

'Look at 'em,' Catfish gestured at the audience by flinging his arms out from his chest. 'They're actually enjoying it. They've got no taste whatsoever.'

'Don't worry!' Chickenfeed reassured him. 'Look over there.' He pointed at the gaggle of journalists huddled around the bar. 'They're not enjoying it. But they're gonna love it when you crash the stage. It'll give them something decent to write about in next week's papers. Music journalists are always desperate for a story. They're only here because they've been told this is the new trend. You're here to prove that sorts and deja vu are where it's really at. Stay cool and you'll get your name and face splashed all over next week's editions. Play the new number **Storm The Yuppie Homes**.'

Catfish smiled grimly. He could see Chickenfeed had it all sewn up. The song was exactly what was needed. Christ, he must have been slow not to realise why Chickenfeed had made them work so hard on that new song. Now he got it, and he was going to give it everything he had.

Chickenfeed ordered another round of drinks for the band. He was determined to wean Christine, Alan and Wayne off lagerade, so this time it was **Hundred Pipers** all round. If they'd been doing a complete set he wouldn't have allowed them to drink as much alcohol as he had tonight. Although he swore by booze for writing, it was generally a bad idea to let a musician get drunk before a work session.

Tonight would be an exception. There wasn't going to be time to loosen up with a soundcheck. The band wouldn't be able to ease themselves into things by kicking off with a number they knew back to front. On top of that they'd be using strange instruments nabbed from another band. Tonight Chickenfeed worked as hard at feeding them alcohol as on any other night he'd have struggled at keeping them on the wagon. He figured the aggro as they invaded the stage would sober them up just the right amount. The booze was the fuel which would rocket the group to fame and provide Chickenfeed with his ticket to Mayfair.

At last the Stockbrokers announced their final number:

England Forever. They didn't need to say it was the end of the set. With the exception of a few journalists and the bar staff, everyone in the Moulders Arms knew they always finished with this Powellite anthem. Chickenfeed motioned with his arms. Alienation and their followers cut through the pub in a flying wedge scattering yuppies as they went. Chickenfeed leapt onto the stage and launched himself at Peter Conduit. The singer was knocked backwards. This prevented him from completing the final syllable of the word 're-pat-ri-ate', which the group used instead of a 'one, two, three, four,' count in on this particular number.

Catfish came in right behind Chickenfeed and headed for the guitarist. He clenched his fist and heard the satisfying crunch of splintering bone as it smashed into the bastard's nose. Then he jabbed a left hook into the shitbag's excuse for a mouth. The guitarist staggered backwards, spitting out gouts of blood and the occasional piece of broken tooth.

The journalists at the bar began to take an interest in the evening's proceedings. Pens were whipped from coat pockets and biro scribblings were made across rapidly covered notepad pages.

Chickenfeed finished the singer off with a kick to the groin. Christine was complaining bitterly that she should have been left to take on her opposite number just as the rest of the band had.

'You're a sexist bastard!' she was screaming at Chickenfeed. 'I could have taken him out any day of the week.'

'Look, I'm sorry,' Chickenfeed mumbled. 'But for the time being just get on with the act. You can have it out with me afterwards.'

'Alright!' Christine spat. 'But I'm gonna fuckin' murder you later.'

Chickenfeed only just managed to keep a smile off his face. It had worked out just as he'd planned. He'd never once doubted Christine's ability to punch out the opposition. In the aggro stakes Alan was the only one

31

who gave him anything to worry about, but fortunately the bass player had been backed up by a load of mates. What had worried Chickenfeed were the bouts of stage fright his lead singer had been suffering. Thanks to the ploy he'd just pulled, Christine was no longer nervous. She was so fucking angry every last ounce of emotion would go into her singing.

Alienation's followers stood guard around the stage as the group tuned up. Catfish turned the reverb right up on 'his' amp.

'We're Alienation,' Christine announced, 'and this is called Storm The Yuppie Homes.'

'Eins, zwei, drei, vier.' Alan's count in was in German, just as Chickenfeed had instructed.

The riff was dead simple and ultra fast: eight beats of E, followed by four beats of D and four beats of A. When it came down to it even Catfish would admit that it was a **Gloria** ripoff. What gave it more power than the **Van Morrison** song was the fact that the bass run lasted twice as long as Catfish's guitar sequence and ended with two strummed powerchords. Alan also hardened the sound by playing all the beats with adrenalin-pumped fury. The drums were an explosion of noise and the guitar was all distortion. Christine's voice was as clear and angry as a tolling bell. You could make out every word:

Storm the yuppie homes, go swarming through their doors,
Storm the yuppie homes in a war to end all wars,
Storm the yuppie homes, East London unite!'

Catfish's and Alan's voices came in hard as they played seven extra beats on the E:

Hackney, Mile End, I.O.D.!

The Stockbrokers' yuppie fans were horrified. This was a direct assault on their lifestyle. The music journalists lapped it up. The sound was crude. Both it and the lyrics lacked any trace of subtlety, but then rock 'n' roll had always had more to do with energy than finesse. **Alienation** oozed sex, anger and excitement, all vital ingredients which had been lacking from the Stockbrokers' set.

Several journalists were checking their notepads to make sure they'd got the name of the group. Even as they did so, Chickenfeed was handing out embossed cards bearing the band's logo and a contact number.

The song lasted a mere one minute and twenty seconds. That was all it took to clear the pub of yuppie scum. Even the landlord was smiling. He'd scowled when the violence broke out but made no intervention. He'd avoided involvement for his own safety. Now that he'd seen and enjoyed Alienation's act he was glad he'd left well alone. After all the dreary music he'd put up with in his time, he was overjoyed to hear something with a bit of life in it.

'Don't forget the name – Alienation!' Christine screamed as the band left the stage.

The feedback from the amps they'd neglected to turn off soon built up to a pitch which covered the moans of the four Stockbrokers lying in states of grievous injury at the foot of the stage.

The landlord rushed out from behind the bar and offered free drinks all round if the group would just do something about the white noise. Catfish was onstage turning off amps before you could say, 'mine's a treble **Hundred Pipers** with soda mix.'

'Well,' the landlord was pontificating, 'I can't say I approve of your methods – but, and it's a big but, it achieved the required results. That yuppie music was fucking abominable. I made a few bob on the bar from the audience's expensive taste in thirst-quenchers, but you've made me realise that putting up with their pathetic excuse for talent isn't worth the profits. You name the date you want a gig here and its yours.'

The music journalists had their ears pinned right back. It was a rare occasion indeed when a group could capture the loyalties of a publican.

'What about next Friday?' Chickenfeed suggested. 'I'm sure these people,' he gestured at the journalists, 'will be happy to supply all the required publicity in next week's music papers.'

'Sure, if the band are prepared to give me an interview now and do a photo session tomorrow!' one of the journalists replied.

'No problem!' Christine, Catfish and Chickenfeed replied in chorus.

Three

TRACY WASN'T SURE WHY SHE'D agreed to visit Edward
Case. Edward had instigated the meeting by relaying an
invitation for a chat via Paul. Case had expressed an interest
in the Green Movement and was apparently eager to give
it publicity. He'd certainly worked wonders with Paul's
Haircuts For Peace event. He'd written a pre-event feature
on the protest for **The Globe**. Chickenfeed had told her that
since the piece had been printed their phone hadn't stopped
ringing.

It seemed like a week for publicity. There'd been news
stories and features on Alienation in all the music papers.
Spins described the group as 'a clenched fist rammed hard
into the flabby belly of what rock has become.'

Harmony said that 'out of the grand melee which is
British déjà vu will emerge the rockers to inspire a sixth
generation of youth revolt.'

With such publicity a large crowd for their gig at
the Moulders Arms that evening was guaranteed. Tracy
was going to see Case and then make her way to the
concert.

Edward was working on news coverage of the **Haircuts
For Peace** event when the doorbell rang. He liked to work
on stories in advance. He was prepared to do a minimal
amount of revision after the fact, but only if absolutely
necessary. He'd talked the whole thing through with Paul
and if everything went according to plan his piece would
be as accurate as the reportage of any other journalist. Of
course, he made the odd exaggeration here, numerous gross
distortions there, but he was a newshound not a historian.
What his employers required was a good story – and he'd
lie to his back teeth if that was what it took to supply it.

He opened the door and ushered the girl into his living room, introducing himself at the same time. She was five feet six with brown eyes and closely cropped dark hair. At first glance she looked about seventeen and appeared plain verging on ugly. Case made a more studied appraisal, her eyes were pretty and she had a nice smile. She was beginning to go wrinkly. Her nervous manner and lack of figure had misled him. She was somewhere in her late twenties. A good four or five years older than her boyfriend.

'. . .beansprouts, they're pure energy.' She talked thirteen to the dozen and Case missed most of what she said as he poured two **Hundred Pipers**.

'Mix?' Case enquired.

'No, straight.' she replied 'Soda isn't good for you. Too many impurities. Whisky is okay, it's natural, I think it's fine having the odd shot on a raw food diet. Much better than ale or lager.'

'I can't abide the taste of lager,' Case informed her. 'I'd drink ale if you could get a decent brand in London. But there's nothing doing so I stick with **Hundred Pipers**.'

'It's my favourite brand too,' Tracy told him. 'My first boyfriend turned me on to it. It must be ten years ago now. When I first moved to London, I went to **Middlesex Polytechnic** to take a Humanities degree but I only lasted a term. It was deadly boring. But while I was there I did get to meet Gerald, my first boyfriend. We lasted about a year and a half. We eventually broke up because he couldn't handle the fact that I didn't like wearing makeup. He wanted me to be a doll he could show off to his friends. He thought I'd come round eventually and be the woman he wanted. It took a year and a half for him to realise my feminist politics really meant something to me. When he saw I wasn't going to change he packed me in.'

'Where are you from originally?' Case enquired, once he was able to get a word in.

'Wendons Ambo in Essex. I left when I was eighteen. My family live in Norwich now. Well, my mother anyway.

36

My father died in a car crash shortly after I left home. I think my mother was rather glad to see the back of him. They never really got on. She's remarried now. I've got two step-brothers and a step-sister, as well as three younger sisters and an older brother from Mum's marriage to Dad – oh, and a half brother from her second marriage.'

'And where did you meet Paul?' Case asked.

'Oh, at my step-sister-in-law-to-be's hen party. He'd been hired as a stripper; he claimed it was performance art. Meeting me put paid to his artistic pretensions. We argued it through for a few weeks and I eventually convinced him that art is an ideology of class, gender and racial oppression.

'I can't stand all that garbage about universal human values,' Tracy continued. 'That's why I packed in my Humanities degree. It was when I was doing the degree that I came to realise what a con art is. All that talk about high culture rising above the conditions of the society in which it's produced is just nonsense. The idea that there's a universal human condition is one of the many ways in which the dominant culture attempts to pass off patriarchy and capitalism as the unalterable lot of womankind.

'By looking to history,' Tracy was enjoying her rant, 'and other cultures, we can see that the concept of universals is a product of western civilisation. These ideas have no grounding in any so-called reality. Literature, classical music, museum art, all reflect the interests of our white male ruling class. It makes me sick when when I see those so called art critics putting down ordinary people for not appreciating fine art. They would throw up their hands in horror if working-class people suddenly took an interest in art. That would destroy its elite status. Art has nothing to do with the lives of most people. It's all about middle-class guilt and male anxiety. Neither of them are healthy. They're not things I can identify with.'

'I too have always believed in the value of a popular folk culture,' Case reassured her. And to get her mind off

37

what he found to be a tedious subject he asked if she'd like another **Hundred Pipers**.

'Please!' Tracy shot back.

'Tell me about your boyfriend Paul. He's a nice lad, very much in love with you. I feel he's got a lot of talent but is a bit lacking in ambition. I'd like to help him.'

Paul had told Case enough for the journalist to realise things weren't going very well between him and his girlfriend. Case was manoeuvering Tracy onto the subject as a seduction ploy. Both partners in a relationship which is going badly are inclined to wander. Case had already proved this point when he'd exposed Paul's latent homosexuality.

Case was using his most tried and trusted chat-up technique of getting his potential bedmate on the subject of an awkward or failed love relationship. Being suitably sympathetic and understanding. Never arguing when they suggested all the difficulties in the relationship stemmed from some problem in the personal make-up of their partner, even though it always takes two to fall apart. Edward was an old hand at manoeuvering strangers into his bed. He knew from experience that anyone whose love life was going through a rough patch was an easy target. Case had not fallen for Tracy, at least not yet. Her attraction was chiefly that she was Paul's girlfriend. Edward liked seeing couples break up.

'Paul doesn't understand how trapped he makes me feel.' Tracy was thinking about the first time they'd made it. It was always wildest the first time she did it with someone. Of course she could more or less recapture this peak with the right kind of drugs. Alcohol loosened her up but too much and she'd not be much use to anyone. Dope or mushrooms were best.

Case was smiling indulgently. He could see Tracy drifting off on long trains of thought. He wouldn't push her. He'd just let her say whatever she wanted and in her own time. He wasn't going to butt in.

'You see,' Tracy continued, 'Paul thinks he has to keep proving how much he loves me. He thinks that if he shows me how much I mean to him I'll love him back just as much and let him move in with me.'

'Uh huh.' Case's voice was a whisper.

'But Paul's behaviour ends up making me feel trapped. It's not that I don't love him. It's just that I need some space. He doesn't understand that I sometimes have to spend a little time on my own.'

'My wife was exactly the same,' Case confessed 'Eventually she divorced me. She wouldn't believe that I made my Sunday afternoon trips to the country on my own. She didn't understand that I needed a bit of time to myself and insisted I must be having an affair. In the end I felt it was best not to contest the divorce, although it broke my heart to lose her.'

'That's just it!' Tracy exclaimed 'I don't want to lose Paul but he's driving me away. I don't know how much longer I can stand the situation. Nothing ever gets resolved.'

Case put his hand on the girl's knee, faking a slight tremor. There was nothing false about Tracy's trembling. Edward knelt in front of the girl. He pushed her pinafore dress up her thighs and kissed her bare legs. He pushed the covering a little more and Tracy shifted in her seat. The dress went up around her waist, revealing that she wasn't wearing any knickers.

Case continued kissing Tracy's legs. First the left and then the right. He was shifting his body and his mouth inched upward as he did so. Tracy's legs slipped apart and Case found himself licking at her moist love hole. Tracy moaned, leaned forward and pulled off her dress. Then she pulled off the white T-shirt she'd been wearing underneath. She wasn't wearing a bra. She was naked except for a pair of eighteen hole **Doctor Marten** boots.

Tracy pulled on Case's jacket collar. He kissed her belly and then a breast as she hauled him upwards. Their mouths met and Tracy's tongue darted into the space between

39

Edward's lips. Her left hand had slipped into the waistband of his trousers. Her right hand was fumbling at his flies. Case kicked off his shoes. His trousers came down, and then his briefs. Tracy's tongue was still in his mouth. He pulled away for a minute so that he could take off his jacket. Tracy unbuttoned his shirt.

Case wriggled free of the shirt and eased himself back down Tracy's body. His mouth found her love hole, the sex juice anointing his lips. Edward grabbed Tracy's boots. Somehow he managed to continue working miracles with his tongue while simultaneously removing her DM's.

Tracy reached forward, slipping her hands under Case's arms. She pulled him upwards and once again their mouths met. Tracy stood up, pulling Edward up with her. She could taste her own sex juice as Case's tongue slid into her mouth. She reached down with a hand and fingered her love button. Then she tugged urgently on Edward's cock. She pulled his manhood towards her moist fuck hole. Edward held back. Tracy freed her mouth.

'For Christ's sake fuck me!' she hissed.

Edward eased the first half inch of his member into her love hole. Stopped. Pushed forward another half inch and then pulled back the same distance.

'Fuck me you bastard, fuck me!' Tracy's voice was low, urgent and carried a slight tremble.

Edward remained still.

'For Christ's sake!' Tracy screamed as she pulled Case down onto the deep shag carpet.

Edward thrust forward and began to pound out the primitive rhythm of the swamps. The beat quickened and Tracy croaked the word 'Bastard' on an out-breath as she clawed her nails down Case's back.

Edward smiled grimly. He knew the score and how he was supposed to respond. He'd read the reply often enough in books, and tried to utter it in response to other girls – and boys. Until this evening he'd never succeeded.

'Bitch!' He spat the word on an out-breath.

Tracy was thrashing beneath him, rocking so hard that he was flipped over. His cock slid out of her. Case was on his back with Tracy on top of him. She arched up. Her back straightened as he re-entered her. Edward reached up with his hands and curled them round her shoulders. He was thrusting up with his pelvis and trying to pull Tracy down against his chest. She kept pulling back, breaking free of his grip and rocking more and more wildly. The forcefulness of her grunts increased. The final three as she reached orgasm were powerful enough to make the walls vibrate.

Tracy let out a long sigh and the words 'You lovely bastard,' were emitted with it. She sank down against Edward's body and he locked his arms around her in a vice-like grip. He could feel liquid genetics boiling through his cock as he thrust forward and then pulled back in a strong and steady rhythm. Tracy's grunts were at least two octaves higher than Edward's low rumble. This time they came together. For a second they both registered a blank across the movie screens in their skulls. It was as if there'd been a power cut and everything had blacked out, followed by a burst of white which they both imagined to be a genetically encoded memory of the first star exploding. They'd reached that peak from which man and woman can never jointly return.

They lay panting for a long time. Edward's cock had gone limp but it was still inside Tracy. Her breath was fiery against his cheek, his breath warmed her skin. Tracy wriggled. Edward's limp member plopped out of her love hole. She slid off his chest, rolled over and sank into the deep shag carpet.

Her hand found Edward's and gripped it. He turned over and kissed her cheek. It was then that he registered just how skinny she was. It came as a slight shock. She had nothing out front and nothing at the back. Her bones showed clearly against her skin. Still, there was something about her, and Edward couldn't be too critical since he didn't have the world's biggest prick.

For five minutes they lay on the floor panting. After that Edward began to feel self-conscious about his nakedness. He pulled himself into a foetal position before getting onto his feet and marching up to the bathroom where he proceeded to clean up. Tracy poured herself another Hundred Pipers and swallowed it in two large gulps. When Edward came down he was wearing a fresh set of clothes. He told Tracy he'd run a bath for her.

Tracy lay in the warm water and reflected upon her sudden and unexpected coupling with Edward. She'd have to tell Paul. But she'd do it gently. Make a few hints so that it would gradually dawn on him. She wanted to see both of them, Case and Paul. It was funny, she didn't want to bin Paul. In fact, if anything, her infidelity had strengthened her feelings towards him.

Case poured himself yet another Hundred Pipers and added the remains of a bottle of soda. He was always very cool and calculated during the course of a seduction. He rarely put a foot, or indeed a hand or dick, wrong – but when it came to post-coital socialising he was a nervous wreck. His confidence did not return until he'd got his clothes on. He supposed it had something to do with his undersized cock, not that anyone had commented on it for years. No woman had ever made complaints. It was only the boys in the showers at school who'd mocked him over the pea-sized patheticness of his endowment. But their taunts had remained with him through the years. As a result he'd never been able to enjoy orgies or group sex.

Case stood up when Tracy made her entrance. She was still naked and she flung her arms around his neck, kissed him on the mouth and whispered, 'I love you.'

'I love you too.' Case replied, hoping he didn't mean it.

Seducing Johnson's girlfriend was part of his strategy for the boy's humiliation. Falling in love with her had never been a part of the plan.

Tracy kissed him again, then moved over to her clothes

which Case had folded neatly over a chair.

'I've got to get going. I promised to go and see a band,' Tracy explained as she pulled on her T-shirt.

'Will I see you again?' Case asked nervously.

'Of course, silly!' Tracy replied 'The concert's only up the road. I'll come back afterwards. You'll wait in for me?'

'Of course!' Case could feel his confidence returning. 'We could also talk over the topic you came here to discuss. . .'

'Publicity for the deep ecology and anti-cashcrop movements.' Tracy had pulled on her dress and was tying up her boots.

'I've thought of a good way to get front page coverage, but it's illegal.'

'What is it?' Tracy demanded.

'Well, if you were prepared to attack cafes and leave anti-cashcrop leaflets behind you.'

'Sounds great. We'll plan the first raid when I get back.'

Tracy took Case in her arms and their lips met. Tracy's tongue was in Case's mouth, seeking unknown pleasures. Their bodies locked together for a few brief minutes.

'I love you, I love you, I love you,' Tracy whispered.

'And I love you too.' Case replied.

'I love you but I'm already late,' Tracy sighed as she broke away from the journalist's embrace.

'I'll be waiting for you.' Case whispered as she left.

THE LOCAL FIRE INSPECTOR WOULD have suffered a coronary if he'd seen the number of Friday night spenders packed into the Moulders Arms. **Spins**, **Disc** and **Harmony** had all given Alienation multi-page coverage that week. It was the publicity boost which every new group requires to make success a guarantee rather than just a faint hope. Most of those present had yet to hear Alienation's music. To the majority this was a mere detail. The fans had already been won over by the reports they'd read in the music press. Alienation were said to be the next big thing. Hundreds of kids were present who wanted an in now. In a few months they'd be able to boast of being trend-setters.

A minority came for the spectacle. They were fanatics whose sole interest was violence. These kids didn't give a fuck about trends. They simply wanted to see a repeat of last week's trouble. Aggro wasn't enough to satisfy their blood-lust, these perverts liked their violence spiked with media attention.

The **Blood Shadows** had come with a view to starting the trouble which so many expected. If Alienation could make a name for themselves by jumping on stage during another group's set, then the Blood Shadows figured they could do the same. And if the band they pulled this trick on had made headlines by way of similar antics then the scandal would be all the greater.

Jim, the Blood Shadows' singer and guitarist, was hoping this was his big break. The band, a three piece, had been together for two years, but they rarely got the chance to play in front of a paying audience because the lyrical content of songs such as **White Power**, **Master Race** and **Kill The Reds** had resulted in a fascist tag being applied to them. Most of London's music venues were controlled by front wheels who took a dim view of Jim's rabid anti-Zionist stance.

Jim had a feeling for violence. He liked nothing better than an aggro. The thud of a steel toe-capped DM landing in someone else's groin did something for his soul. He had a bent for creating mayhem and took a grim satisfaction in proving his superiority to the opposition. Tonight he was tooled up with a lead filled cosh.

Steve the bassist had a pair of knuckle dusters, while Tony the drummer was carrying a blade. The Blood Shadows had Big John and Mad Mick Hawkins, their two loyal followers, with them. John had always sworn by the power of his bare knuckles. Hawkins was referred to by the group as their secret weapon. Once Mick got into a physical confrontation he wasn't happy until he throttled his opponent into unconsciousness. Often even this wasn't enough. It was a regular feature of Friday and Saturday nights that Mick's mates would have to pull him away from some hapless bastard to keep a murder rap off his shoulders.

Tracy walked in while the support band were playing. Until two nights ago they'd been called the **Skulls**. They'd dressed in black and their music was pure Gothic Punk. Impressed with Alienation's sudden success they'd changed their name to **Contradiction** for tonight's show.

For this gig their faces were covered by ski masks. They'd not had time to get new hair cuts, but had replaced their **chelsea boots** with Doctor Marten shoes. Each musician was wearing a red armband. Although they hadn't had time to write any new tunes they'd speeded up the tempo of their songs and changed some of the lyrics. The number they'd just announced as their last had been called **The Death Box** until a few hours ago. Tonight it had new words and was introduced as **Winston Silcott Had The Right Idea**.

The Skulls had played with Alienation before. They were friends of Alan's. That's how they'd got the gig tonight. Tracy wasn't impressed by their act. Rather than pay attention to the fag end of their set she fought her way to the bar and ordered a **Hundred Pipers**.

Paul spotted her as she was pushing her way through the crowd with the whisky in her hand. The band had stopped playing and by a combination of shouting and waving he caught Tracy's attention. She made her way over to him. He squeezed up on the bench he was sharing with Catfish and Chickenfeed. Tracy eased herself in beside him.

'How did it go with Case?' Paul enquired.

45

'Well, very well!' Tracy told him 'You hadn't warned me how handsome he was.'

'Did you get some publicity ideas sorted out?'

'Yes.' Tracy told him 'But I'm amazed you'll allow me to visit such a handsome man on my own.'

'Well, that's what Case wanted so I suppose it was best. Tell me about the ideas for publicity.'

'We thought we'd attack some cafes and leave anti-cashcrop leaflets behind. I'm going to enjoy working with Edward, he's such an attractive man.'

'So you've got a date fixed to work out the details?'

'Yes, I'm going back tonight after the gig.' Tracy told him.

'Good, I'm glad you've got it together. You know how keen I am to assist you with your campaign against cash crops and the destruction of the environment.'

'I almost feel like you're pushing me into the arms of another man.'

'I don't feel I have to push. I know you're always on the lookout for people who can lend their expertise to your campaigns. After all, it was you who turned me on to green issues. Now we make a great team and we can both get a lot out of Case.'

'Will he be at your **Haircuts For Peace** event on Sunday?'

'Yes, he's promised to come,' Paul informed her.

'Well, don't hog him all to yourself.' Tracy dug her arm into Paul's ribs.

'Of course not!' Paul replied 'You know I'm trying to help you out with your campaign.'

Tracy decided Paul wasn't going to take the hint about her sudden and unexpected intimacy with Case. She gave up trying to tell him about it. It could wait for another day. While they'd been talking Catfish had left their table and was now up on stage.

Christine announced Alienation's first song as **Towards A Gay Communism**. The tune wasn't bad but

Chickenfeed's lyrics were pure hackwork. The title had come from a chapter in **Mario Mieli's Homosexuality and Liberation**. The chorus was a slightly modified version of a sentence Mieli quoted from **Larry Mitchell**. 'There's more to be learned from wearing a dress for a day than wearing a suit for a year' was a fine line, but then Chickenfeed had nicked it.

The verses were strings of clichés. 'We'll take the toys from the boys, they'll know what to expect, a fist in the mouth, if they don't show respect.' There was one good couplet, 'Women and queens will lead the revolution, Women and queens have got the only solution'. But it had a familiar ring to it and Chickenfeed wasn't certain whether or not he'd ripped it off from someone else.

Rock lyrics weren't works of art. A few key phrases for the fans to pick up on and the rest could be just so much garbage and it didn't matter. Chickenfeed knew his job and the words sufficed. Rock was gestural. Verbal precision didn't count for anything.

The audience was surging around the stage. Kids were jumping up and down in excitement, pushing other kids out of the way so they could see the band. This was history! They'd read in the music papers that Alienation were the future of rock and roll. That they'd been told this as a positive fact made them virtually hysterical.

Desmond Taylor, a sociologist who wrote for the **Sunday Journal**, was busy making notes. A worried expression played across his face as he caught the words to the second song:

> Smash the individual, smash this bourgeois lie,
> Don't need this bourgeois concept, don't need
> this I I I.
> Smash the individual,
> Smash the bourgeoisie,
> Can't you see identity doesn't mean anything
> to me.

We're social by nature, don't live in isolation,
The illusion of autonomy increases alienation.
Smash the individual,
Smash the bourgeoisie,
Can't you see identity doesn't mean anything
                                              to me.
I am my mother and I am my son,
I'm not an individual, I am everyone.
Smash the individual,
Smash the bourgeoisie,
Can't you see identity doesn't mean anything
                                              to me.
Replace the individual with a collective creation,
Negate oedipus and end social separation.
Smash the individual,
Smash the bourgeoisie,
Can't you see identity doesn't mean anything
                                              to me.

He frowned and made some notes on the pad in front of him. As a young man he'd fought the Nazis to defend the rights of the individual citizen. And now here, in this pub, in this country he'd been prepared to lay down his life for, a pop group were singing the praises of **identity loss** and **totalitarianism.**

Desmond smiled grimly. The music was having a dangerous effect on the crowd. They'd become a seething mass ready to explode at the slightest provocation. As their bodies were whipped into a sexual frenzy by the primitive beat, they were being brainwashed with communist propaganda. The group seemed to see themselves as Bolsheviks, as far as Taylor was concerned that was Nazism under a different brand name. Indeed Communist-style dictatorships such as that of Pol Pot in **Cambodia** were inclined to run to excesses undreamed of by self-declared fascist regimes.

Then Taylor noticed something even more disturbing. Five men were pushing their way through the crowd. The

48

one at the front was lashing out at teenagers with a heavily weighted cosh. Ten youngsters had been knocked to the ground by the time the troublemakers reached the foot of the stage. The felled teenagers were trampled underfoot as those around them danced on to the hypnotic beat of the music. The hoods were climbing onto the stage as Taylor dialled 999 on the pub's payphone.

Jim took a swing at Catfish as Mad Mick made a lunge at Alan. Steve, Tony and Big John were moving in behind them. Neither the Shadows nor their two followers had bothered to cover Christine. After all, she was only a girl! Catfish jumped to his left and the cosh glanced harmlessly down the side of his arm. The music ground to a halt. Christine lashed out with her foot. She caught Jim in the bollocks. He let out a blood-curdling scream before falling backwards off the stage.

Jim's muffled moans were lost within the general melee. When the boots of those dancing at the foot of the stage began thudding into his prostrate body he started to wish he'd never been born. The three agonising minutes before he lost consciousness seemed like an eternity to the failed rock musician.

Mad Mick got his hands around Alan's throat but didn't have a chance to tighten his grip before Christine sent a right hook cracking into his mouth. Even with the disturbance in full swing, you could hear the satisfying crunch of splintering bone as several front teeth disintegrated. Mick was gurgling on his own blood. Christine threw a haymaker which broke the bastard's nose in three places. The would-be strangler fell backwards and was pulled offstage by Alienation's teenage fans. Then the boots went in – HARD. Mad Mick's brain was flooded with the literal meaning of pain. Steel toecaps smashed into his bulk, wreaking terrible damage.

Steve, Tony and Big John turned around and attempted to flee. The closed ranks of the audience foiled their desperate bid to escape a kicking. Fists and boots thudded against their bodies. As they went down the steel toecaps rained in even harder. The kicks continued to harvest a bloody toll long after the three of them had lost consciousness.

'After this,' Christine gestured at the bodies littering the dance floor, 'there doesn't seem much point in trying to look slick, of just running through our programme set. We were going to save this number for last but it seems more appropriate to play it now. It's called **Kill, Kill, Kill For Mental Health and Inner Peace**.'

The chords were a fast-switching change between E, G and A. The whole group chanted 'Kill, Kill, Kill, fucking kill everything' over the top of them. Then the riff changed and the band were singing 'Libya, Libya, Land of the Free, Libya, Libya, Libya, Libya. All out for nuclear war and the next evolutionary stage.'

The audience went apeshit. Taking their cue from Christine they were making clenched fist salutes in time to the beat. No one seemed to notice the first verse go by, and then they were back into the chorus. Desmond Taylor caught the second verse and made a note of the words on his pad. Reading them through he shook his head sadly:

> **Kill for Libya land of the free,**
> **Assist the Kremlin assassinate capitalist scum,**
> **Blow up aeroplanes.**
> **Fucking kill everyone!**

Taylor was too busy thinking of exactly how he'd phrase the article for next Sunday's paper to catch the final verse. If he had, he might have realised there was a grim humour in Chickenfeed's lyrics:

> **Derek Hatton we salute you,**
> **We will be your faithful socialist troops,**
> **With Bernie Grant as our leader,**
> **We'll beat the capitalists with our fists and**
> **our boots.**

50

A final rendition of that dreadful chorus sent the sociologist scuttling from the pub. A **Labour Party**-supporting music hack left at the same time. He couldn't see the funny side of it either. His interest had been aroused because in their **Spins** interview the group had – on Chickenfeed's instructions – described themselves as **Bordiguists**. The hack had looked Bordiga up in a Marxist Dictionary and discovered he was head of the Italian Communist Party in the early 1920s prior to the much admired **Gramsci**. Later Bordiga had been expelled from the Communist International for **Trotskyism**. The hack wished he hadn't taken the bait. On reflection he should have realized these people were sick. Their manager had claimed in the same interview that the Michael Ryan massacre at Hungerford was the **Dictatorship of the Proletariat**.

Four

EDWARD CASE TORE A SHEET of paper from the carriage and pushed the battered typewriter away from him. He poured a generous **Hundred Pipers** and sloshed in the mix straight from the **Schweppes** bottle. At 45, Edward was a hardened professional. It didn't take him long to knock up copy. He could do it with his eyes closed.

The public thought of newsmen as boozehounds who wrote their stories at the last possible minute. This might have been the case before the War, but Edward was the leading light of a later generation. While it was true that he guzzled whisky, there was nothing slapdash about the way he worked.

Until he'd hit upon the idea of writing up news events in advance, Case had been a nothing, a nobody, a hack, hardly earning a bread and butter living.

Once Edward gained a reputation for his ability to hand in copy within minutes of a story breaking, his services went into high demand. What Case did was easy in the world of parliamentary reporting. There, the slow progress of bills as they made their way onto the statute books enabled the most dim witted reporter to write up stories in advance. It was one of the great paradoxes of democratic rule that you could predict the outcome of parliamentary business with nearly a hundred per cent accuracy.

Where Edward impressed editors was with his ability to write up crime stories before any law breaking took place. More than one reporter suspected foul play on Case's part. Fortunately for Edward, no journalist was prepared to rake up mud within their own profession. Even media scum have a natural inclination not to shit in their own nest.

Case poured another drink, lit a cigarette and tilted

back in his chair. He felt the words hit him as he read through the draft.

UNTIL TODAY, who could have imagined anyone taking objection to our national brew, the Great British Cuppa?

ONLY MINUTES AGO one of our roving reporters phoned in the news that a group of crazed ecologists are carrying out systematic attacks against anyone they discover drinking tea or coffee in public.

IT'S NOT ENOUGH for these Animal Rights extremists to tell us that we're murderers because we've saved innumerable human lives through experimentation on inferior species. These loony activists don't even stop at decrying the national diet of meat and two veg as Nazi cuisine. Now these self-styled ascetics have decided we no longer have the right to enjoy that most British of institutions, the cuppa.

IT'S TIME to teach these mindless morons a lesson. When they are caught they must learn that they can't assault innocent people who have no wish to adhere to the crackpot theories of a middle-class cult.

IN THE INTERESTS OF PRESERVING our democratic society anyone who deviates from its rules must be severely punished. Those whose antics reveal them as no better than animals should be treated as animals. Their bodies should be used for scientific experiments so their lives may in some way benefit humanity.

SUCH A POLICY would be in the best interests of ordinary tax payers who have no wish to see malcontents cocooned in centrally heated prisons at public expense.

We could also use these experiments to silence those liberals who are always bleating on about

human rights. Given the political will, it would be easy to prove that those who commit vicious and antisocial crimes are genetically defective. Once we have scientific evidence of this, let us not waste public money on the expense of putting these subhumans through judicial procedures.

We should never forget that Hitler – the most barbaric enemy the British Nation has faced – was also a vegetarian. . .

Case knew he was onto another winner. Of course the Establishment would denounce him. They always did. Edward spoke for the ordinary men and women of his country. After all, it was the dockers who marched for **Enoch** after he'd made his **Rivers of Blood** speech.

Case was feeling better. More like his usual self. That girl Tracy had done something to him. He was considering whether to dress up in his SS uniform when the doorbell rang. That would be Tracy back again. It was probably best that he hadn't geared up in his Nazi outfit. He knew instinctively that Tracy would not approve.

They had a quick kiss and cuddle on the doorstep. A minute later Tracy was inside and Edward was pressing a glass of **Hundred Pipers** into her hand. He retrieved his own glass and freshened it. Case had always considered himself a loner, but now that Tracy was back he realised he'd missed her. How could that be? She couldn't have been gone more than three hours!

'I love you,' Tracy whispered as she leaned against him, her hand on his knee.

'And I love you too,' Case replied, beginning to suspect this was true.

'Will you always love me?' Tracy demanded.

'Yes,' Case replied, somewhat at a loss because he realized he was telling the truth.

'I can't give up Paul,' she told him.

'I'd guessed as much.' Case was almost crying. 'I want you for myself, but I don't own you, so I can't stop you

54

seeing someone else. How did Paul take the news of our intimacy?'

'Oh, I tried to hint but he just didn't cotton on. I'll try again in a day or two.'

Case pulled Tracy across the sofa so that she was draped over him. He kissed her mouth. He wanted to lift her up and carry her to the bedroom, but realised she wouldn't approve of such macho posturing. She brought back memories of what it had been like before he'd been coverted to fascism.

After the original CND had collapsed in the early sixties, Case had been deeply depressed. He'd put all his youthful hopes into that movement. With the defeat of the peace marchers, the Right had seemed the only solution. But now, with Tracy, he felt as if he'd been dead for the past twenty-five years. She'd rekindled the flames of his youthful dreams. The way he was feeling now, he'd quite happily go upstairs and burn his SS uniform. Of course, he'd have to wait until Tracy had gone home. He wondered if he'd ever be able to admit his Nazi past to her.

They stayed locked in an embrace for a long time. Just holding each other and kissing. They didn't speak at all. Case had never wanted someone so much. He held his sexual urges in check. He didn't want Tracy to think of him as an animal. He wondered whether there was sin in this world. He hoped not, because if there was he had sinned more than most.

SUNDAY CAME, AND TRACY WOKE up in her own bed with Paul still asleep beside her. She'd spent all of Saturday making hints about the nature of her relationship with Edward. Her efforts had been without result. Paul seemed oblivious to everything. He appeared incapable of suspecting that Tracy could be unfaithful to him. She wouldn't say anything today since she didn't want to spoil Paul's big day. Tomorrow evening would be the opportune time for addressing the issue.

Despite his promises, Edward left a message with Chickenfeed to say he wouldn't be able to put in an appearance at **Haircuts For Peace**. He'd already written up the story, so Paul could rest assured there'd be coverage in the **Globe**. Tracy suspected an unhealthy desire on Edward's part to avoid face to face contact with Paul. Tomorrow she'd insist on making a date for the three of them to meet and talk through their tangled relationships.

Tracy got up and ran a bath. She'd not made love with Paul the previous night. She'd avoid doing so this morning. She loved Paul despite the fact that she'd gone right off the idea of having sex with him. Paul was not particularly sensitive to her moods and there'd never been any subtlety in the way he gave physical expression to his feelings.

Paul was stirring as Tracy got out of the bath. She went into the bedroom to dress. Paul tried to pull her into bed with him. He wanted a fuck.

'There isn't time,' Tracy said firmly. 'We've got to get over to Vauxhall very soon. It's your big day. The TV will be there. Chickenfeed said they rang up yesterday afternoon. Get washed and dressed. I'll make breakfast.'

'God you look beautiful,' Paul shouted after Tracy as she left the room.

He wanted her badly but knew there was no point in arguing. He liked to be teased and would enjoy sex with Tracy all the more if she made him wait. This was his day and if after breakfast she still refused to fuck, Paul wasn't going to let it get him down. His love for Tracy ran deep enough for him to accept that she was basically selfish.

'I could eat you,' Paul told Tracy as she handed him a plate of beansprouts.

'Eat that up and then get up,' Tracy instructed. 'We haven't got time to hang around.'

'I'd like to eat your snatch,' Paul told Tracy as he grabbed hold of her arm and pulled her towards him.

She pulled away and left the room. If it hadn't been Paul's big day it would have been one of those days. He could never tell how Tracy would be. He always had the hots for her, had done since the day they'd met. It didn't matter where or when, he was always ready for a fuck. Tracy's sexuality was another matter. She'd go for weeks not wanting to screw. And then *cor, not half, what a raver!*

Before he'd met Tracy, Paul had seen more than his fair share of starker antics. But nothing he'd had then could match Tracy when she put her mind to sex. It was worth not getting it as regularly as he wanted if the quality was guaranteed. There didn't seem any point in getting it together with another girl. There wasn't a woman in the world who was a match for Tracy when it came to deep sex. As long as Tracy was faithful to him, Paul was prepared to wait until she decided it was time for a fuck.

Tracy was eating her beansprouts in the kitchen. She needed some space. She loved Paul but wished he didn't need her so much. She wanted to drop the physical side of their relationship, at least for the time being. The way Paul reacted to her made Tracy wonder whether it was love or lust which formed the basis of their relationship. His antics often made her feel like one of those mindless bitches who opened their legs like a coin operated sex machine every time their boyfriend issued a command.

Of course, it was an ego-boost to be desired in that way. But still, it brought Tracy down. Sometimes she wondered whether Paul was capable of thinking about anything other than sex.

Tracy didn't want to broach the subject with him, just as she never told him not to be so randy when he wouldn't take the hint to keep his hands off her body. If he had any feeling for her moods, Paul would pick up on these things without having to be told verbally.

57

It depressed Tracy that Paul didn't seem aware of her feelings. It was so blokeish! He didn't seem capable of understanding that she needed time and space to herself. And when they were together, she wanted their relationship to be founded on something more than bedroom athletics. Perhaps this was why she'd got it together with Edward. He seemed so ready to listen, so understanding, and always had a helpful suggestion to make when she put a question to him.

But then again, perhaps the thing with Case had been chemical. No, it wasn't just that. It was definitely love! It was strange knowing you could love two different men at the same time. And difficult, trying to hold on to both of them.

These things happened. This was real life. Not a novel. Not even one of those pulp novels Chickenfeed was so fond of reading.

Paul came into the kitchen and put his bowl in the sink. Tracy was pleased to see he'd eaten all his beansprouts. She didn't let him eat cooked food in her flat. And she was well on the way to winning Chickenfeed round to her view of the body's dietary requirements. When she'd done that, Paul wouldn't eat cooked food at home either. In Swaton Road, Chickenfeed ruled the roost.

Her relationship with Chickenfeed had always been a little strange. She knew he'd been in love with her for a long time. She was very fond of him too. But in her case it was the love of a dear friend or a sibling. Chickenfeed had a pleasing face but Tracy felt no sexual attraction towards him.

She was quite impressed with the way Chickenfeed handled the situation. There'd been no sexual innuendo for at least two years. There'd been plenty before that, but now Chickenfeed had come to accept the nature of his relationship with her it was really good between them.

When she'd first met him, he'd been seeing a German girl called Kerstin. But that relationship ended shortly afterwards. These days he put most of his emotional energy into his work. But he needed a love relationship and Tracy hoped he'd find a girlfriend soon. Ambition was no substitute for sensuous psychochemical interaction with another sentient being. Tracy knew Chickenfeed had sex with a succession of pick ups. Though that might satisfy him physically, she was sure he needed something more. Hopefully one of his sex partners would develop a more deep-rooted emotional relationship with him.

Maybe Paul needed a scene with someone else. Perhaps if that happened it would give the two of them the chance to sort out their emotional relationship.

Tracy drifted along in the same train of thought until she and Paul arrived at Bonnington Square. Doug, a friend of Paul's, had acquired the necessary scissors and stools. He claimed they were stolen but wouldn't give any further details. He'd set the gear up in a derelict house.

Various TV companies were manoeuvering cameras around the house. There was an hour to go before events officially kicked off but already a small crowd had gathered in the tiny park at the centre of the square.

Tracy and Paul chatted to the TV men, then went outside to socialise with those gathered by the swings. Conversations flitted from **Greenham** to the **Convoy** to **Glastonbury** to **diet** to the fate of the **North American Grizzly Bear**. The sun was shining. Children were laughing. Their parents smiled. The world was not such a bad place to live in.

The crowd increased as the minutes ticked away and the appointed hour grew nearer. Several press cameramen arrived – as did Chickenfeed, Catfish, Christine, Wayne and Alan.

Paul announced that he was ready for people to come and get their hair cut. He added that if anyone wanted to cut hair they should come on over to the Peace Parlour too.

Scissors snipped and the hours passed quickly. People went into the Peace Parlour with long hair and left with crops which would have been the pride of an East End

59

skinhead. Doug swept up the split ends and packed them into plastic bin liners. By four o'clock nearly thirty bulging bin bags had been stacked in a back room.

The television crews concentrated on the famous who were donating their locks for peace. Of the unknowns it was only those who volunteered pubic hair who had their charitable antics filmed, the single exception being a girl one of the camera crews mistook for **Kim Wilde**.

Christine and Alan stripped off and lay side by side. A team of five peace activists worked on them until all their bodily hair had been removed. Then Christine announced that Alan and she were going to make love for peace.

The cameras followed them to an upstairs bedroom. This made room for further volunteers downstairs. Their donations were not witnessed by the newsmen. They'd left the Peace Parlour to watch Christine and Alan fuck against the bomb.

Christine stood in the centre of the room and pushed Alan onto his knees. She held his head from behind and squashed his face into her snatch.

From earliest childhood Alan had been mistreated by his parents. He'd craved their attention but the only time he received it was when they occasionally beat him. His upbringing had thus led him to confuse pleasure and pain. The pleasure of receiving his parents' attention, the pain of their beatings.

Christine knew Alan was sexually aroused by rough treatment. A mixture of tenderness and torment led to his experiencing something which he found far more pleasurable than an orgasm from a straightforward coupling.

A psychiatrist had once explained to Christine that extreme states of excitement could be brought about in Alan through interconnected acts of sex and violence. These resulted in brain-flooding. When this occurred Alan experienced loss of self and was no longer in control of his response to external stimuli. This trait could be used constructively. Christine had worked hard at finding ways to turn Alan's childhood deprivations into short cuts to exquisite pleasure. She was always very careful in her manipulations. The psychiatrist had warned her that if Alan ever saw extreme acts of brutality in a situation without any sexual connotations it might well lead to a mental breakdown.

Alan had been administering to Christine's pleasure for ten minutes when his concentration slipped for a fraction of a second and his tongue ceased to work its wonders. Christine lifted her arm, moved it back a few inches and slapped hard across Alan's face, then moved forward and squashed his mouth back into her snatch. There were three further slaps over the next fifteen minutes. Christine was no kink: she just wanted to help Alan get the best out of life. Alan didn't consider himself kinky either. The slaps were functional. They helped him get it on.

Both Christine and Alan had become more or less oblivious to the pressmen's cameras and the TV crews filming them, though the media presence did add to the general ambience. This was a rave up and a half! And one to which the **Great British Public** was playing voyeur to boot!

Christine turned around and Alan licked at her arse. There were hoots, cheers and jeers from some of the press men. A few of them broke out in a slow handclap but stopped when they noticed a TV camera had been turned on them.

Christine turned again and placed a foot on Alan's chest. She pushed until he toppled over, then ordered him to stretch flat on the floor.

'Let us not forget, ladies and gentlemen,' Chickenfeed announced as Christine mounted her man, 'that fiction has played an important role in the development of Western sexuality. Among other things, the terms **Sadism** and **Masochism** are derived from the names of men who wrote pornographic novels.'

Christine was working both herself and Alan into

a frenzy. They'd forgotten the cameras and the room, imagining instead that they'd returned to the beginning of time. Their physical response to each other was genuine enough, but any trace of individual personality had disappeared along with conscious control of their bodies. This could only be restored with the attainment of orgasm. Christine and Alan were lost in the void of non-being. They pumped up the volume and reached that peak from which two individuals can never jointly return. The descent was far from gentle. A starburst orgasm followed by a grilling from the assembled hacks.

'You gonna pull a train for peace?' one of the newsmen asked Christine. Christine beckoned the man. He was short, balding, about thirty-five. He reached out with his arms. Before he made physical contact Christine's fist thudded into his mouth. He staggered backwards, then fell to the floor spitting out gouts of blood and the occasional piece of broken tooth.

'Any other of you mothers got some bright ideas?' Christine enquired as she pulled her clothes on. 'If you think I'm some mindless bitch who opens her legs like a mechanical sex machine, you are wrong, very wrong. Such a rapist mentality sickens me and any bastard who wallows in it is a prime candidate for castration.'

'Yeah!' Alan put in. 'If you want peace you'd better prepare for war. Class war! The war to end all wars.'

'We ain't into no hippy ideology.' Christine spat. 'You'd better get that right. And it's not just a matter of smashing class oppressions. If class war is to mean anything it means smashing patriarchy, racism and homophobia at the same time.'

The pressmen were drifting out of the bedroom. They were into voyeurism not lectures, especially not lectures that shattered fantasies, that turned the hope of a fuck into yet another frustration.

Downstairs the haircuts were continuing. Volunteers were still queueing up to donate their locks to the peace movement. Some had more to give than others but this was not important. What mattered was the act of giving.

Tracy was sitting in the park at the centre of the square. She was sipping from a bottle of mineral water which Catfish had given her. She was getting impatient, it would soon be six. Time for Paul to take the hair to Whitehall and burn it: it wasn't going to be donated to the Imperial War Museum as the pre-publicity had suggested. . .

Paul was still dealing with questions from well-wishers and the press. How had he got the idea? He must have been asked that one a thousand times. He didn't really know. He'd just woken up one morning with the words **Haircuts For Peace** on his mind. They'd seemed so ridiculous that he'd had to do something with them. And with the encouragement he received from Edward he'd pushed ahead and turned the concept into hard physical reality.

Paul was pleased he'd organised the event. He liked to feel important. He liked being a celebrity. He hadn't felt this way since Tracy had forced him to give up his vocation as a performance artist. But hell, this was better than being an artist. The audience for art was so limited. Beyond them no one was interested. But this: everyone seemed concerned about politics - except, of course, for that tiny minority who swore by art.

Whenever he had a minute to pause for breath, Paul was fantasizing about the media crowning him King of the Underground. He wasn't far from officially holding such a position. Not even rock musicians received the kind of courtesy to which he'd been treated by the press. He was an important man, dealing with serious issues.

Things were running late. Paul had not expected so many people to turn up to donate their hair. But by six forty five the last locks had been cut and swept into bin liners. Paul had lost count of the number of bags which had been filled.

It was lucky that Doug had organised a couple of vans to transport the hair to Whitehall. The vans were somewhat on the small side and there was no way the entire peace offering could have been fitted into one of them. The Sunday traffic was light and it was just a four-minute glide across Vauxhall Bridge to the other side of the river, along Millbank, past the Tate, through Parliament Square, before finally pulling to a halt in **Whitehall**.

Downing Street was blocked off by traffic barriers. The vans made no attempt to break through them. Side doors were swiftly opened and hair dumped on the ground. Two bemused bobbies wandered up to find out what was going on.

'We've just abandoned our plans to start a wigmaking business,' Paul told them as Doug and several others continued to dump hair onto the street.

'Don't try and get funny with us sonny,' one of the coppers told him without putting too much authority into his voice. The scene was so ludicrous that the pig found it hard to treat very seriously. His partner, fearing some kind of protest, was about to take a harder line when the arrival of several journalists and a TV crew made him think the better of it. As long as the media were about he'd soft-pedal it. 'Come on son, what's it all about?' asked the wouldbe tough cop.

'We're from the **Derek Bainbridge Memorial Society**,' Paul explained.

The cops were feeling very uncomfortable about the media presence. That and the mention of Bainbridge, who'd burned himself alive in Downing Street as a protest against unemployment, put them wise to the fact that they were dealing with more than mere horseplay.

A huge mountain of hair had been deposited in the street. Doug unscrewed a bottle and poured petrol over the hair. Paul struck a match and tossed it onto the pyre. The cops realised there was little point in trying to douse the fire and jumped back from the flames.

The lads who'd helped unload the vans started their engines. They pulled out into the street just as the fire caught. The hair was crackling. It smelt revolting, like dead bodies burning. Paul and Doug moved over to the journalists. The coppers were radioing for a fire engine.

'Peace,' Paul was saying, 'is not simply a matter of abolishing war. To abolish war you have to abolish the economic system which supports it. That is to say the capitalist system. A system based on profit and exploitation. A system which would collapse if it wasn't propped up by a war economy.'

'But why this form of protest?' one of the reporters enquired.

'Because,' Paul explained, 'the smell of burning hair is like the smell of burning bodies. I wanted to unblock your minds and noses to the stench of the capitalist system. It's a system based on death.'

'Hair is perfect because of its symbolic qualities, traditionally it is associated with sexuality. Sexual urges are a life force which are brutally repressed in any system based on death. Particularly in a system such as ours which aestheticises death.'

'But what's that got to do with peace?' enquired a television reporter.

'Everything,' Paul replied. 'Everyone living in this society is warped from a lifetime of sexual repression. Our frustrated urges towards love and its physical expression have been twisted into hatred and anger. War is the most extreme expression of this pathological condition.'

'But surely aggression is an intrinsic part of human nature?' put in a photographer.

'That's right,' insisted a reporter, 'it's part of our universal human condition.'

'No, gentlemen,' Paul insisted. 'In my opinion. . .' Paul's monologue was cut short by a hand on his shoulder.

'I'm arresting you, and I must warn you that anything you say may be taken down and used in a court of law as evidence against you.'

'My only crime, officer,' Paul replied, 'is to protest

65

against an order which places profit above human community.'

'Save it for the judge,' the policeman told him. 'Right now you and your mates are going to take a trip down to squad headquarters.'

PAUL, DOUG, DAVE AND JOHN were in and out of the nick in just under an hour. Their activities had arosed the interest of London's many journalists. The media spotlight made the cops nervous about holding them for any longer than necessary.

There was no need for prolonged questioning. It was an open and shut case. All the cops did was take a statement from each of the lads. They all admitted dumping hair on the edge of Downing Street and then setting fire to it. There were police witnesses to cover everything. The pigs checked up on the names and addresses they'd been given, then they let the peace protesters go, saying they'd be back in contact with them once they'd decided whether or not they were going to prosecute.

'Tell me,' a female journalist asked as the four activists emerged from the police station, 'is it true you all took part in a nude orgy before leaving Vauxhall and setting fire to the hair?'

'No.' Paul replied.

'But I'm told that one of the TV companies has it on film,' the reporter insisted.

'There must be some mistake,' Doug suggested. 'But if you're willing, maybe we could all go back to your place and indulge in some bedroom athletics. Maybe you've got some friends who'd like to come too.'

'Why did you do it?' another reporter demanded.

'So that you scumbags would give a little coverage to the massive social movement which is organising against the war machine.'

'The media gives a balanced coverage.' the reporter insisted.

'If it did,' Paul replied, 'I wouldn't need to resort to hair-burning antics.'

Paul knew he was lying. He was loving every minute of this. He enjoyed making an exhibition of himself. It was Tracy who prevented him from grabbing the limelight more often.

Tracy was worth every sacrifice Paul made for her. This protest stunt was better than anything he'd done before he'd met Tracy, something which simultaneously pleased both Tracy and himself.

'Tell us about yourself Mr Johnson,' a reporter hissed. 'Do you live alone?'

'What's it to you?' Paul asked, hoping his reticence would lead the reporter on to asking further personal questions.

'Our readers want the full facts surrounding a case. Who you are, where you come from. They want a rundown on your life story so that they can understand your psychological motivations.'

'It was a political action,' Paul replied.

'Yes, but why did it take the form it did?'

'So that you'd pay some attention to the peace movement.'

'Are you a publicity seeker?' another reporter demanded.

'Have you got a steady girlfriend?' asked another.

'Are you gay?'

'What's your favourite colour?'

'When you make love do you prefer to be on top or underneath?'

The reporters singled Paul out as the ringleader. As far as they were concerned, he might as well have orchestrated the entire Haircuts For Peace event on his own. They simply weren't interested in the fact that other people had a hand in organising it. Not when they were dealing with what they perceived as a rising star. Their interest in those who'd given Paul a hand could wait. The media had to set him up before they could knock him down. Then they'd pull all his former friends out of the woodwork. People who were disgruntled that someone else had ridden to fame on their backs. These were the pawns who the media would later utilize to expose Paul as a sham.

Five

IT WAS ONE OF THOSE warm spring days which fool you into thinking summer has arrived. The sky was a brilliant blue and the sun had chased away the Victorian ghosts which haunt Soho. The aroma of coffee drifted out of Old Compton Street's cafes and bistros.

In **Enrico**'s the sun streamed through the large plateglass windows, giving the cafe a light and airy feel despite every last seat being occupied by a lunchtime customer. Enrico smiled as he served teas, coffees and sandwiches.

Few of his customers would have guessed that this smile was more than an expression of pleasure on the part of a simple man who knew his station and stuck to it. Contrary to appearances, Enrico had struck out in life and found his own direction.

Although he'd made things up with his rich Milanese family, they'd never recovered from the shock of their eldest son marrying a poor girl from Naples and then emigrating to London.

Enrico had always believed in a marriage of Italian and English culture. The Brits had the music and a Nordic stoicism, but when it came to food they were as hopeless as the French. The gastronomic efforts of both those nations were strictly gut-rot affairs. That was where Enrico and his fellow expatriates did their bit. By setting up cafes they were giving Brits the chance to eat decently.

No one had been more delighted than Enrico when Britain joined the **European Community**. The French and Germans thought they had it all stitched up to become the leaders of a New Europe. In Enrico's eyes London and Milan were the real centres of excellence.

Enrico smiled as he looked over his clientele. There were several students from the nearby St Martins College of Art. They gave him hope for the future. When he'd arrived in London anyone stylish dressed in Italian clothes, but now British fashion students had begun to turn out street gear the country could be proud of.

There were always tourists in the cafe. Enrico found the Americans too brash for his own taste but their money was good. The family of Swedes sitting in the corner were a mystery to him. He'd always found their culture antiseptic. It neither attracted nor repelled him. He was utterly indifferent to it.

Most of Enrico's regulars worked for cinematic outfits with offices on Wardour Street. Today there were also four sales girls and two rock musicians. The custom of pop personalities was particularly welcome. It was the music of **The Who, Stones** and **Small Faces** which had brought Enrico to London.

Enrico was serving coffee to a girl who sold T-shirts in a boutique across the street when seven shadows fell across the snackbar. His wife Maria, who was wiping a table let out a short gasp. The intruders wore ski masks and were armed with baseball bats.

Case led the group. He lashed out with his baseball bat and there was a sickening crunch of splintering bone as it smashed into Maria's skull. Blood spurted from the woman's cranium. Case lashed out again as she went down. Her head snapped back and she was dead before her body hit the floor.

Tracy swung her bat against a table, sending crockery flying. Christine laid into the counter. Terrified customers were showered with glass as a display case disintegrated.

Alan and Wayne stood guard at the door as Chickenfeed, Catfish and Case waded in against the tea-swilling scum. Chickenfeed let fly with his fists and an art student slumped unconscious in his seat.

70

A thirty-five year old tourist backed against a wall. His hands clawed the plaster. Case had him trapped. The bat caught the American close to the heart, breaking three ribs. He slid to the floor his face a study in agony.

Catfish pulled one of the rock musicians up by the hair and slapped him round the face. The red weals were in stark contrast to his anaemic appearance.

Christine and Tracy set to work on the kitchen, smashing machinery and throwing crockery to the ground. Case was laying into another customer, repeatedly smashing his baseball bat over the man's head. He continued with the assault for several minutes, even though his victim had died from the very first blow.

Catfish decided enough was enough and grabbed Case by the shirt collar before proceeding to drag him out of the café. He barked out an order, instructing the others to follow his lead.

Catfish had concluded that Case was a maniac. He'd pulled him out of the cafe to prevent any further deaths. As far as Catfish was concerned, the plan they'd agreed to involved roughing a few people up. Case had never even murmured anything about murder.

As they left, the raiders smashed the cafe's plateglass windows and scattered leaflets in the street:

THE PAIN you've experienced today is nothing compared to the agony foisted upon the poor and hungry of this world by the international capitalist system. You came to a public place to drink tea and coffee, cash crops that the IMF has ordered Third World countries to grow and export so they can pay off their 'debts'. These debts are the extortionate rates of interest charged on loans the Third World was seduced into making with Western Banks. Such loans benefit the ruling elites of the Third World and us in the West. They do nothing for the poor and wretched of this world. Instead of being used to grow luxury crops for the West, every available acre of land should be used to grow food for the hungry. Drinking tea and coffee makes you responsible for the deaths of millions.

However, the issues which concern us go beyond the question of cash crops. It's also a matter of the meat and dairy products you consume. All form a part of the same exploitative system. Tea and coffee represent the exploitation of the poor of your own species, meat and dairy the exploitation of other species. When will you act upon the fact that a sane and peaceful world depends upon the abandonment of such naked self-interest and greed? We came here today to teach you a lesson. We will return again and again until that lesson is learnt.

Morrissey & Marr Commando.

THE VEGAN VIGILANTES MADE THEIR getaway in a couple of VWs they'd parked in Soho Square. Alan, Wayne and Christine headed for **Richmond Park**. Tracy, Catfish, Chickenfeed and Case drove East to **Epping Forest**.

'I thought you went a bit over the top with the violence,' Tracy chided Case as they drove along Euston Road.

'It was necessary,' Case replied. 'If you want decent publicity you've got to kill a few people.'

'I don't know if I can go along with that,' was Tracy's rebuke.

'I did it for you,' Case protested. 'I didn't have the slightest interest in veganism or ecology until we got it together. I'm prepared to risk a murder rap to help you achieve your political aims and all you can do is moan.'

'Oh, forget it,' Tracy snarled, wishing she hadn't brought up the subject.

Edward's remarks were a giveaway. If Catfish and Chickenfeed hadn't sussed that Case was Tracy's bit on the side then they were plain thick. Either one of them might tell Paul of her infidelity before she got the chance to explain it herself. She'd have to get to him first. This time there was no question of subtle hints. She'd just come straight to the point and tell him what was going on.

Having reached Epping Forest they headed straight for a pub. With the exception of Case, they were all in need of a stiff drink. His was the only hand which didn't shake as it lifted a **Hundred Pipers** to his lips.

Tracy and Case took a walk in the woods. Catfish and Chickenfeed stayed in the pub.

Tracy and Edward walked into a clearing and un- dressed. They both knew exactly what they were going to do. It was Tracy who seemed in greater need of the physical relief. Case was outwardly calm. From looking at him, no one would have guessed he'd just committed two murders and was about to have sex with a beautiful woman. His face was as blank as a television screen during a power cut. Only his penis revealed he was excited by the prospect of sex.

Neither of them had spoken since they'd left the pub. Tracy put her lips against Edward's mouth and pulled him down onto the grass.

Edward pumped his leg between her thighs. He held her tightly, marvelling at the way her tongue worked wonders in his mouth. In a few minutes he'd give vent to the second of the two great passions in his life.

Tracy's sex juice trickled onto his calf. He slipped his other leg between her thighs. He was trying his best to be cool and calculated. To take his time. He wasn't doing too well.

'Fuck me, fuck me,' Tracey hissed.

73

Case smiled grimly. He was rushing it, but that was what she wanted. He thrust forward, penetrated the moist mystery of her sex and began to pound out the primitive rhythm of the swamps.

IN RICHMOND PARK, ALAN WAS crying. Christine and Wayne were doing their best to comfort him. They were pretty churned up themselves. The picnic they'd brought with them sat uneaten. They didn't feel in the least bit hungry. Christine and Wayne would have gone for a drink in a pub, but Alan was too hysterical. They didn't want to push their luck.

Every time Alan screamed 'He didn't have to kill them!' Christine would French kiss him to keep him quiet. She'd continue snogging until he calmed down. Then she'd wait for the next bout of hysteria to come on.

Neither she nor Wayne were particularly happy about what had happened. But they both understood that the only thing they could do was to keep their mouths shut. Neither of them wanted to get done as accessories to murder.

Chickenfeed had persuaded them to take part in the raid. He'd said it was for a good cause. That however it went, they couldn't lose. If they got away with it, great! If they didn't, it would be good publicity for the group. Even if they got caught, the penalty for a first offence was unlikely to be more than a fine. They could start a defence fund which would raise money and get them publicity at the same time. Chickenfeed was some manager!

Both Christine and Wayne understood that Chickenfeed hadn't counted on Case being a psychopath. 'Edward' was a friend of Tracy's and no doubt she'd persuaded Chickenfeed to go along with the scheme. Everyone knew he was crazy about her.

Christine led Alan further into the park. They left Wayne behind with the picnic. When they'd climbed over the crest of a hill and ambled into a clump of trees, Christine halted. She pulled Alan to the ground, reached for his mouth and kissed him passionately.

Alan responded immediately. Christine's hand was resting on his flies and she could feel his stiffy. She cupped her palm under his groin, brought it up and then cupped it under again.

Christine reached for the top of Alan's flies and tugged on the zip. It took a second pull before they opened. She unfastened his belt. Alan's hand had slipped underneath Christine's T-shirt and as it moved up her back the garment rode towards her breasts.

Christine pushed Alan's pants down his athletically built legs. Her mouth broke from his and she caught sight of his swollen manhood. She stroked the love stick.

Alan's hand brushed over Christine's nipples and her whole body shook. He reached down and began working on her **Levi's**. Having unbuttoned them he pushed the jeans down her thighs. Christine kicked free of the 501s.

Alan reached down and pulled his trousers over his ankles. His arms went around Christine's waist and he pulled himself up her body so that his love muscle could penetrate her mystery.

The pair of them beat out the primitive rhythm of the swamps. As they did so they lost all consciousness of the present along with any conceptual understanding of time. The universe was reduced to the pounding of pure sensation. Their bodies functioned smoothly, efficiently, without any conscious control. They were closer to dissolution than unity. Their twin bulks worked down to the zero point of the real. More natural than the natural. So natural it becomes unnatural. Eldritch; sinister.

Memory is not necessarily located in the brain. Some scientists speculate that it is diffused throughout the body. The brain may function in a similar fashion to a

TV monitor. Memories are played back in the brain, but stored elsewhere.

If the brain becomes damaged, memories can no longer be activated. This in itself does not mean that the memories are lost. They remain encoded in the DNA, awaiting recall by those future generations destined to inherit them. The act of sex is a cipher, temporarily scrambling the DNA records that are dispersed across the body, so they may be passed on for future use if the sex act should result in conception.

The body becomes pure surface, a screen on which the genetic history of the world can be re-enacted. The relation between this and the so called death instinct is of relatively minor importance.

Loss of self is not necessarily connected to death, although it is inextricably linked to sexual pleasure in a culture based on the aestheticizisation of death. It is a pleasure of limited duration, to be shattered by the apocalypse of orgasm. Christine and Alan experienced this apocalypse as a DNA encoded memory of the first star exploding. They had reached that place in cyber-space from which man and woman can never jointly return.

Alan wondered whether loss of control during sex could be linked to the loss of self an individual experiences when subjugated to an outside authority. Like a boss, or the state, or the cops. He repressed the thought. He didn't want to spoil his pleasure.

BACK IN THE EPPING FOREST pub, Chickenfeed and Catfish were being eyed up by a couple of typists who'd taken the day off work.

'What do you think?' Sharon asked Meg.

'I dunno,' she replied, her gaze switching between Chickenfeed and Catfish. She didn't like the gear Catfish was wearing. Bikers' jackets weren't her scene. On the other hand, he was better looking than his mate, whose nose was too big.

'Well, you can't be too choosy,' Sharon was mouthing as she looked straight at the two lads. 'There's nothing else in here but pensioners.'

'Yeah, I know!' Meg shot back. 'I'll have the short one in the leather jacket. You can have big nose.'

'Thanks a lot!' Sharon hissed.

'Jesus!' Meg spat. 'He ain't that bad. And I prefer his gear to what short-arse has on.'

'You never did like leather jackets did you!' Sharon was frowning. Then after a pause she said, 'OK, it's a deal.'

The two girls got up from their seats, leaving their empty glasses on the table. They walked over to the bar and sat on the stools next to Catfish and Chickenfeed. Sharon was the first to speak.

'Mine's a Pernod and black.'

Chickenfeed nodded as he appraised the situation.

'I want a Grant's with soda.' Meg put in.

'Two Hundred Pipers with a tonic mix, a Grant's with soda and a Pernod and black,' Chickenfeed shouted to the barmaid as he removed a crisp tenner from his wallet.

Sharon was pressing her leg against Chickenfeed's thigh and smiling grimly. They were all smiling grimly. No one needed to speak, they knew the score. All were experienced enough to be uninterested in their prospective partners' names. Even the barmaid was smiling as she came back from the till. She caught hold of Chickenfeed's hand as she gave him his change.

Seconds later she was ringing a bell and shouting: 'Last orders!'

As the foursome finished their drinks Sharon uttered the word 'Walk?' It was more a command than a question.

Their minds focused on orgy and indulgence, they headed straight for the woods. No one needed a consultation about which direction they should take! They stopped

77

in a clearing, not knowing that Tracy and Case had vacated this space just twenty minutes before their arrival.

There was grim laughter as they stripped off, but no words were spoken. Sharon pulled Chickenfeed on top of her. Soon both couples were pounding out the primitive rhythm of the swamps. The British countryside shimmered around them and then melted in the heat of pure sensation.

Catfish was only vaguely aware of Meg's hot breath as she panted beneath him. Her body was warm but he was several million years away in seas which had supported an emerging eco-system.

Meg had returned to the absolute blankness of a world without time, the cool certainty which existed aeons before light shot through this universe.

Chickenfeed's body was moving, but his mind was in a state of suspension. Time and the void lost their meaning. Pleasure could no longer be differentiated from pain. For what seemed an eternity he was drained of all ambition.

Sharon writhed in the grass, ecstatic. Time had converged for her. All of history existed as physical sensation. The encoded memories of her genes were unblocked in an endorphine-soaked brain-flooding.

All four of them heard the internal thunder that marks the point of satiation, a simultaneous orgasm exploding through their four separate bulks. An experience from which man and woman, man and man, woman and woman, can never jointly return.

Both Meg and Sharon wondered whether the pre-orgasm sensations of oneness were bound up with their social conditioning. They pondered the possibility that this drive for loss of self had a social function and that the associated desires might be the root cause of their compliance with the capitalist system. But such self-questioning is painful. Ultimately the typists found it was easier to push the thoughts aside than to deal with them.

Chickenfeed and Catfish rolled off their partners and onto the grass.

'Fancy some more?' Sharon asked Meg.

'Yeah!' Meg grinned back.

Meg climbed on top of Chickenfeed and Sharon took Catfish.

'I prefer being on top.' Sharon was saying to no one in particular. 'It gives me a greater sense of control.'

'Me too.' Meg confirmed.

The two girls worked the lads into a frenzy, their sweat adding body to the heady spring air. Few smells are as pleasant as the pungent aroma of human nature. Few thrills are as satisfying as indulgence of the flesh.

Tracy and Case were making their way back to the car when they stumbled across this heaving tableau playing tribute to the power of genetics. The ramblers became voyeurs as they sat down to watch the sexual athletics. They'd have joined in had they not satiated themselves earlier that afternoon.

The girls moved mechanically. They were jerking back and forth on their mounts with their mouths open and their heads thrown back. The boys writhed beneath them, moaning. Their cries were inhuman. They approximated the wailings of amphibians who had taken their first tentative steps onto land and were experiencing the sweet sensation of sunlight playing over their skin.

The volume and frequency of these cries increased as consciousness was all but eclipsed. The two boys' bodies reacted, but their brains exercised no control over these muscular spasms. The brain's function was simply to act as a screen for scenes from a primeval past. Movement was dictated by the codes strung throughout each protagonist's bulk.

There was a low rumble as a genetically stored memory of the first star exploding was flashed through four separate skulls. The pleasure seekers had reached that point in the game from which group sex participants can

79

never jointly return. As the swingers regained consciousness of their surroundings they took in Tracy and Case. They gasped, not yet in any condition to speak. They wanted to shout out greetings and questions, but had to wait a minute and a half before normal speech could be resumed.

'You looked like you were enjoying yourselves!' Case said, slapping a thigh and smiling grimly.

'I feel exhausted from having watched,' Tracy put in.

Chickenfeed and Catfish managed to grin. They weren't quite ready for speech. Sharon and Meg were wondering who the hell these newcomers were. They were beginning to suspect they were friends of the two lads they'd picked up.

'We were thinking of going back to the car and getting the picnic,' Tracy said. 'We could bring it back here if you like. That would give you a chance to recover.'

Chickenfeed and Catfish nodded their approval. Sharon and Meg grinned in assent. It was pleasant lying naked in the grass with the sun warming flesh which only rarely saw daylight. If someone brought food and drink, that would make it all the nicer.

Tracy and Case disappeared in the direction of the pub. First Catfish, and then Chickenfeed stood up. They eyed each other up and decided to do something about the sex juice glistening on their pricks.

'Got any **Kleenex**?' Chickenfeed asked the girls.

'In my handbag,' Sharon replied. 'You get them, and throw some over for me and Meg.'

Chickenfeed fished out an unopened pocket pack. He tore off the cellophane wrapper. There were ten extra strength paper tissues inside. More than enough to go round. He handed a couple to Catfish, then threw a few down at the girls. He kept two for himself and put the one that remained back in Sharon's handbag.

'Christ, I'm hungry!' Catfish swore.

'Then get on your belly and eat my snatch,' Meg retorted.

Catfish obeyed. It was warm and moist down there. Very pleasant indeed. Meg liked men to lap at her pubic mound. Catfish reminded her of a contented cat.

Chickenfeed wiped himself down and got dressed. Sharon was pulling on her clothes when Tracy and Case returned. Between them they carried a huge picnic hamper.

'You can stop now,' Chickenfeed quipped at Catfish. 'Something else has arrived with which you can indulge your oral cravings.'

Catfish took Chickenfeed up on this advice. He and Meg wiped themselves while the others spread food across a table cloth. As Catfish and Meg dressed, Case put a hip-flask to his lips and knocked back three shots of **Hundred Pipers**. Tracy was tucking into a **beansprout salad**.

'Got anything with some protein in?' Meg demanded.

'There's plenty of energy in the beansprouts.' Tracy assured her.

'But haven't you got any cheese or meat?' Meg persisted.

'We're vegans,' Tracy explained, 'We don't eat meat or dairy products.

'I've heard about your type,' Sharon put in. 'You're extremist vegetarians. There was a newsflash at lunchtime about some of your lot doing over a cafe in **Soho**.'

'Really?' Case was interested. 'What did it say?'

'Oh, not much,' Sharon told him. 'The news had just come in and it was a bit sketchy. But they did say that these Vegans had killed a couple of people to protest about them drinking tea.'

'I couldn't understand it,' Meg was saying. 'I don't see what drinking tea has to do with being cruel to animals.'

'Oh, you know what these nutters are like,' Sharon explained. 'They just want an excuse to cause trouble. If it wasn't tea it would be anything with wheat in it. I don't

81

imagine tea means anything to them. They probably picked on it because everyone drinks it. After all, who could have any serious objections to people drinking tea?'

Tracy bit her lip. Meg laughed. The others smiled politely.

IN RICHMOND PARK CHRISTINE AND Alan had returned to Wayne and their picnic. The sex had calmed Alan's nerves. Wayne was hungry and Christine thought she might as well eat.

Wayne broke open a four pack of **Stella**. He handed a can of lager to Christine, another to Alan. Wayne and Christine gulped down the golden fluid and soon finished their measures. Alan sipped sulkily at his brew.

'Have a sandwich Alan,' Christine suggested.

'No,' he snapped back.

'It's peanut butter, your favourite,' Christine coaxed.

'I don't give a fuck,' Alan swore. 'How can you eat after taking part in those murders?'

'Look Alan,' Wayne put in, 'it isn't our fault. We weren't to know that Case character was a nut. Chickenfeed didn't know, or else he wouldn't have got involved in the raid. Not even Tracy would have brought him along if she'd known what he was gonna do.'

'But two people were killed.'

'We didn't kill them!' Wayne protested.

'You can't shirk responsibility just like that,' Alan was shaking with anger as he said it.

'What can I do?' Wayne shrugged. 'I can't bring them back from the dead.'

'I'd never seen a corpse before today,' Alan was sobbing.

Christine put an arm around him and picked up a peanut butter sandwich. 'Come on love,' she coaxed waving the snack in front of his mouth, 'eat some of this.'

Alan let out another series of sobs. Christine kissed his cheek, still holding the sandwich in front of his mouth.

'Come on love,' she repeated.

Eventually Alan's lips parted. Christine kissed his cheek again and pushed a corner of the sandwich into his gob. Alan bit it off and chewed very slowly.

Christine pulled Alan's body closer to hers. His trembling was not visible to Wayne, but she could feel it. He opened his mouth again. Christine put a bit more of the sandwich into it. He bit it off and chewed faster this time, then puked up.

'Come on Wayne,' Christine commanded, 'let's pack up and go home.'

Wayne gave a snort of protest. Christine's cutting glance halted the verbal argument with which he'd intended to follow it. He packed away plates and food while Christine wiped Alan's mouth. Wayne shook out the tablecloth and packed it into the hamper.

'Come on love,' Christine said as she got up and pulled Alan to his feet, 'we'll get you home and to bed. You'll feel better after a good night's sleep.'

Six

AFTER HEARING THE FIRST NEWS report, Paul made his way to Tracy's flat. He had his own set of keys and, when his knocks failed to elicit a response, let himself in. He waited impatiently for Tracy to come home, only popping out to buy an evening paper. Splashed over the front page of **The Chronicle** was the headline:

VEGAN TERROR

Paul preferred **The Recorder**'s snappier summation:

EXPRESSO MASSACRE

ran the headline. The subheadings of **Nutty** and **Bananas** revealed just how sick the subeditors' sense of humour was. The 'facts' were pretty much the same as those given on the radio. As far as Paul could tell, the cops didn't have any leads.

Paul leafed through the paper and found **The Recorder** managed to be bang up to date. An inside feature related to their cover story.

VEGANS STEP UP ECO-WAR IN BRITAINS INNER CITIES

ran the headline. Jake Phibbs was credited in the byline.

JUST BEFORE 1 pm TODAY five men and two women entered an Italian cafe in Soho. They were armed with baseball bats and using these they worked over customers and staff. They also smashed up the premises. In just five minutes, their brand of eco-mayhem left two people dead and seventeen requiring hospital treatment. Leaflets scattered at the scene were signed by the Morrissey and Marr Commando. Scotland Yard say they have never heard of this group but speculate that it is connected to the Animal Liberation Front.

ALF'S ACTIVISTS are drawn mainly from the ranks of young militant vegans. Detectives are receiving reports that vegans have been involved in an increasing number of attacks on butchers, fur traders and retail outlets for animal products. Police round the country have been instructed to keep a close eye on their activities.

OUR INQUIRIES HAVE SHOWN that vegans are becoming increasingly involved in attacks such as one by two youths who threw a concrete block through the front window of Harry Mathews' home in West London. Mathews is the actor who plays the leading role in a series of adverts for British meats.

IN RECENT MONTHS:

• Vegans BEAT UP Brian Jeffries, leader of Hackney Council's trading committee after he refused to use his powers to crack down on the traditional slaughter methods used by muslims. Activists claim Halal abbatoir rituals are unnecessarily cruel.

• STARS of various TV cookery shows were ATTACKED when the Class Justice group accused them of being meat-chomping show business sell outs.

• Prominent meat traders' homes and cars were DESTROYED after vegan publications gave their home addresses.

• Dozens of butchers' windows in inner-city areas have been SMASHED or DAUBED with paint or acid. Vegan groups are planning a campaign to remove 'meat-chomping scum' from such areas.

• Hundreds of cafes serving traditional English and continental foods have had their locks glued. Until today this was thought to be in protest against the use of meat in the dishes served. It is now apparent that it is also linked to protests against the cash crops of tea and coffee which certain extremists believe are the cause of Third World famine. They say that the Third World should use all available land for growing essential foods instead of producing luxury crops at cheap prices for the West.

IN THE LAST 10 YEARS veganism, an ideology which advocates that all animal products should be eliminated from human dietary programmes, has increased its support from a few hundred to a point where tens of thousands of young people describe themselves as vegans.

THIS GENERATION'S POLITICALLY ACTIVE YOUTH have rejected such left-wing groups as the Anarchist Workers' League or the International Communist Current, whose policies they denounce as being based on human greed and ecological destruction. These young activists claim that the old style revolutionary groups ignore the key issues of animal rights and environmental concerns.

OUR SURVEY FOUND 16 vegan groups in universities and polytechnics where there were none 10 years ago. The vegan society at Portsmouth Polytechnic has 87 members and another collective in the town has 30 members.

GEOFFREY BROWNE, an organiser of the pressure group Animal Aid, said: 'Vegans are young, mostly bright working class kids who have dropped out from college or who are unemployed. They have gone for the reality of direct action on environmental and moral issues.'

VEGANS ARE CLOSELY ASSOCIATED with the nature magazine *Green Valley*. Little love is lost between them and trade unionists, who feel that vegans attack traditional working class values and create splits within the movement.

PETER GRAY, LEADER OF THE SYNDICALIST UNION CNT, which has an estimated 2,000 vegan members, said: 'Vegans have moved into the movement and

are trying to convert our members. Veganism is a luxury that the working class cannot afford.'

IT IS MISLEADING to judge the influence of the new vegan groups by membership. Unlike traditional political groups where membership is everything, vegans are more interested in the effects of their actions than the numbers of people carrying them out. As a result there are more supporters of the vegan cause than members of its groups.

ACCORDING TO A SPECIAL BRANCH source, Scotland Yard has assigned six officers full time to monitoring vegans in the capital.

Paul read through the article twice, laughing at its appalling inaccuracies. He was about to put the radio on to listen for further reports about the attack when Tracy arrived home.

They hugged. Their mouths met. Paul had to stoop to kiss Tracy – even though she was standing on tiptoes. He thought the result was well worth the crick in his neck!

'I was so worried about you,' Paul said as they broke the embrace and sat down.

'I'm okay,' Tracy reassured him. 'Edward was a bit zealous and killed a couple of people. Catfish hauled him out of the cafe to stop him killing a third. He seemed to think the deaths would ensure better publicity.'

'He was right!' Paul sighed pointing at the opened newspaper. 'But I wish I'd never introduced you to him.'

'There's more reasons you'll wish that than you can imagine at present,' Tracy replied, grim-faced.

'The petrol bombings were bad enough,' Paul croaked. 'I had nightmares of us both being sent down for a long time. But this, an accessory to murder, if you get done I might never see you again.'

'Don't talk like that Paul.' Tracy's breathing was laboured. 'I'm not going to get caught. Anyway, there's something else I've been trying to tell you. I've tried hinting but you just don't seem to catch on.'

'Look, all I know is I don't want you mixed up with Case anymore. I can't live without you, and I don't want to see you sent down on a murder rap.'

'I've been trying to tell you about Case,' Tracy sobbed.

'I know all about him,' Paul replied irritably. 'He's a nutter, there's nothing more you need to tell me.'

'Yes there is!' Tracy protested. 'I've been having sex with him.'

Paul's jaw dropped. He was stunned. He looked as if all the meaning had just been drained out of his life. Tracy went over to him and put her arms around him. She licked his ear and kissed him on the cheek. She pulled him through to the lounge where they sat down on the sofa. 'I still love you Paul,' Tracy whispered. 'I can't explain what happened, but I still love you.'

'You won't see him again?' Paul sounded very tentative.

'I love you both,' Tracy whispered.

'If you love me you won't see him again,' Paul's voice was no longer tentative.

Tracy kissed him on the mouth. 'I want to go on seeing both of you,' she whispered.

'He's evil,' Paul hissed. 'He steals people's girlfriends!'

'Please Paul,' Tracy was almost crying. 'I'm not your property. You don't own me, no one can steal me from you.'

'Bitch!' Paul screamed as he rose and hauled Tracy up from the sofa. 'We're going to the tattooists and I'm going to get the words 'This is the property of Paul Johnson' inscribed on your forehead. That should make things clear to bastards like Case.'

Paul was pulling Tracy toward the door and she was pulling as hard as she could in the opposite direction. Suddenly, Paul pushed Tracy back in the direction she was pulling. She went careering towards the sofa but tripped before she reached it and sprawled over the floor. Tracy began to sob. It was the fact that Paul had been violent, rather than the few bruises she'd received, that hurt her.

'I'm sorry! I didn't mean it!' Paul was bending over her, helping her to her feet. 'Are you okay?'

'I guess so,' Tracy replied.

She sat back down on the sofa and Paul sat down next to her. He put an arm around her.

'I don't know what came over me,' Paul sounded as if he was choking. 'I love you more than anything. I've got no future without you. Forgive me.'

'It's okay,' Tracy reassured him.

Paul snuggled up to her. His hands roamed her body and his lips found her mouth. Tracy's mouth was firmly set but Paul eventually forced it open and got his tongue inside.

After five minutes probing had brought no response, he withdrew his tongue and moved his head round. He began to lick Tracy's ear.

'Paul,' Tracy pleaded as his hands began to hitch up her skirt, 'just hug me. I've had too much for one day and I just don't want sex.'

Paul must have heard the words, but he behaved as if he hadn't, or, if he had, that they simply didn't make sense. Tracy resigned herself to what was happening. He wanted reassuring. He wanted something physical. She'd let him have sex, although her heart wasn't in it. Tracy presumed the way Paul's hands were moving over her body was meant to excite her. It just seemed mechanical. Boring. He pulled down her knickers.

Tracy knew what was coming next. Paul was so predictable. He lapped at her pubic mound. A little sex juice began to flow. Emotionally, the last thing Tracy wanted was a fuck. She forced herself to make a few grunts. These only served to encourage Paul in his misapprehension. Tracy was not enjoying this thing at all.

Paul pulled off Tracy's T-shirt. She didn't resist. She didn't help any more than was necessary. She just lifted her arms and shifted her body weight as required. She didn't pull at Paul's clothes. She gave no sign that she wanted him to take them off, but he took them off anyway.

Paul was on top of her. Kissing her. He was passionate and her response was mechanical. He was beating out the primitive rhythm of the swamps. He kept pumping and pumping and pumping. Tracy's breathing was heavy but other than this she was not responding. She was nowhere near orgasm.

Paul came once. But he wouldn't be satisfied until Tracy came too. 'What's the matter?' he demanded as he kept pumping away. 'Don't I turn you on any more? Are you too busy thinking of your new boyfriend?'

He'd put the thought into Tracy's mind. She thought of Edward. Imagined that Paul was Edward. She was thrashing about now. Enjoying it; screaming.

'Fuck me, for christ's sake put some effort into it,' she hissed.

Paul was excited too. He'd almost come to believe she was bored with him, but he only had to look at her now to see this wasn't true.

Tracy's arms were bent up around her head. Beads of sweat were glistening in her armpits. Paul put his head down and began to lick the salty fluid. His hands went up and caught hers and pinned her arms above her head.

Tracy was thinking of Case, of how it had been when she'd made love with him in the woods earlier that afternoon. She was imagining it was Edward making love to her again. That Paul was Edward. She knew that if Edward had turned up and ordered her to have sex with him in front of Paul she could not have refused.

These thoughts of Edward set off a DNA encoded chain reaction. Tracy's orgasm set off Paul's. Paul was imagining they'd reached a peak from which lover and loved one can never jointly return. 'I bet Case can't make you come like that!' Paul was smirking.

90

'It's not a competition.' Tracy was gentle with him.

Paul ignored the remark. It was the sort of thing Tracy would say. It wasn't really a putdown. Even if it had been, he felt nothing could cheat him of his moment of glory. He'd been making it with Tracy for a long time, and by his own estimation had just given her the best fuck she'd had in years.

Tracy went downstairs and ran a bath. Naked, Paul descended the staircase and joined her. They'd not made it in the bath for a long time. Paul slipped into the water with his back to the taps. The way Tracy thrashed beneath him in the living room had convinced Paul that what she needed was a bit more of his brand of genetic ecstacy. Then there'd be no question about the fact that he was the only man for her.

Tracy soaped herself. When she started soaping Paul, he kissed her and put a hand on her breasts. The hand glanced over her pubic mound.

Tracy pulled back.

'Paul, as it is I don't think I'll be able to sit down for a week!' She smiled at him coyly.

Tracy hoped this sentence would be enough to mollify his male pride. If she hadn't felt so guilty about her affair with Case she'd have spat at him rather than say such a thing. She didn't understand why she felt guilty about Case. There was no reason why she shouldn't have a scene with him. She supposed it was the responsibility she felt towards Paul which caused her to feel this way. Paul was such a baby and now part of this responsibility was to make him grow up.

'Admit that I'm a better fuck than Case,' Paul insisted.

'It's not a competition Paul,' Tracy was being extremely patient.

'Okay,' Paul replied, 'it's not a competition, but I'm still the best.'

Tracy realized it would be futile to contradict him so she kissed him on the mouth instead. She wondered how

91

she could love someone who was so childish. Perhaps that was part of his appeal.

Tracy got out of the water before Paul had the chance to make a further play for libidinal gratification. She towelled herself down and went into the bedroom to find clean clothes. Fortunately Paul didn't follow her. 'I'll make some food,' she shouted through to Paul as she dressed.

As Tracy chopped up salad she reflected on the state of her relationships. She hadn't expected Paul to react well to the news that she was making it with Edward. She wanted to see both of them, but knew she couldn't take many more scenes like the one she'd just been through.

It would be days, maybe weeks, before she really knew how Paul was going to take the situation. Only time would tell whether he would settle down and accept the fact that she intended to see two men. It was unfair to judge him on tonight's behaviour. Perhaps it was just the unexpectedness of the revelation which had caused him to act in such an irrational manner.

Tracy was worried about Case too. Her relationship with him had begun so suddenly, so unexpectedly. Until today she'd never even dreamed that a man would kill for her. She'd have to sort that out with him. Make it clear that death was too high a price to pay for publicity.

PAUL WAS UNABLE TO SLEEP. He kept thinking about that bastard Case. About the fact that Tracy had refused to swear an oath of loyalty and fidelity. She'd gone as far as insisting that she'd go on seeing Case!

When they'd got into bed he'd been very tender with her. He'd been kind, loving and understanding for at least twenty minutes before asking her to promise that she'd not see Case again. When she'd refused he'd pulled away from her. He'd been tossing restlessly on the far edge of the bed for three hours. He kept wondering

92

whether Tracy was asleep or if she was just pretending.

If she'd promised to be faithful, Paul reflected, they'd both be sleeping well. She didn't understand how good he was to her. She was just selfish. That was her problem. If she'd been a little nicer to him he'd have fucked the arse off her and she'd have enjoyed it even more than she had earlier in the evening when they'd made it on the sofa.

Paul thought of all the things he'd like to do to Case if he got hold of him. There were wide variations in the preludes, but they all concluded with Case dying a slow and painful death.

Paul decided not to masturbate. He got up and dressed instead. In the kitchen he rooted out a bottle, a box of matches, a hammer, a screwdriver and a piece of rubber tubing. He left the flat, slamming the front door as he went. He hoped the noise disturbed Tracy's dreams. This thought gave him a grim satisfaction. He didn't see why she should slumber when it was her fault that he couldn't sleep.

The estate was quiet and there were plenty of cars parked in front of the flats. Paul filled his bottle by siphoning petrol out of a tank. Then he scraped the words USE PUBLIC TRANSPORT YOU BLOATED SCUM into the paintwork of several vehicles.

He went up to a **Capri** and placed his screwdriver against the windscreen. He banged the end with his hammer and knocked a hole through the glass. If didn't make much noise. Not like a brick being put through a window.

Paul repeated the operation on a further five cars. He poured petrol through the holes in the windscreens. He had to siphon off more fuel in order to carry out this operation. Then he had a change of plan. He walked back to David House and took the lift to the eighth floor. He opened Tracy's front door and left the tools and bottle on her kitchen table. He also left a note to say there'd been petrol in the bottle.

Paul left the flat. The lift was waiting for him and he took it to the ground floor. He walked out of the block and along to one of the cars he'd prepared. He leaned over the motor and dropped a lighted match through the hole he'd knocked in its windscreen. There was a whoosh of flame which scorched his hands, face, hair and jacket. The box of matches caught fire and Paul dropped them on the bonnet of the **Cortina**.

There was another change of plan. Paul ran in the direction of the canal and clambered over the brick wall which separated it from the estate. As he pounded along the towpath he heard the Cortina exploding. He hadn't thought things through very well. There hadn't been time to set six cars on fire and make good his escape.

Lights went on all over the Teviot. Faces peered from windows, and several citizens simultaneously reached for their phones and dialled the cops. No one had seen Paul, and it wasn't until later that people realized more than one car had been attacked.

When Paul reached Violet Road he left the tow-path and clambered up to the street. He walked briskly to Devons Road and then onto Campbell Road. It only took him a few minutes to get home. He shut the front door and, breathing heavily, leaned back against it. He hadn't seen anyone, and, as far as he was aware, no one had seen him.

When his breathing had slowed, Paul went upstairs. He could see the light was on in Chickenfeed's room. He went in without knocking. Chickenfeed was working at his word processor. Paul read the words on the computer screen:

"Fancy a spliff?" Kevin enquired as he put his hand on the girl's knee.

"Drugs is for hippies!" Tina shouted in protest.

"Glass of Hundred Pipers," Kevin tried.

94

"That's more like it!" The girl was enthusiastic.

Kevin got up and walked over to the drinks cabinet. He pulled out a bottle and poured the amber liquid into two tumblers. He returned to the girl, smiling grimly and holding out a glass for her.

"Now you've given me the drink," she instructed, "just put your hand up my skirt like you want to. I can't stand all this fucking about. If you wanna be a top flight casual. . ."

Chickenfeed completed the sentence:

"you'll have to drop these middle class inhibitions."

Then he turned round and faced Paul. 'Christ, you look rough!'

'I'm not badly burnt,' Paul grinned. 'Any chance of a drink?'

'Sure!' Chickenfeed replied. He grabbed hold of his half-finished bottle of Hundred Pipers and reached for a glass.

'Forget the glass,' Paul commanded. 'I need a real drink!'

Chickenfeed handed him the bottle. Paul unscrewed the cap and took a long slug. Chickenfeed turned back to his computer. He pressed the keys ALT and K simultaneously. Then he pressed the key D and the computer saved his document. He removed the disk from the disk drive and put it away. He pressed the power button to the off position and the screen went blank.

Paul was still standing, taking a long slug of Hundred Pipers. Chickenfeed made a mental note to buy another bottle in the morning. He could see his supply wasn't going to last the night. Like most writers, he liked to imbibe steadily while creating and if for some reason he couldn't, it was odds on that his inspiration would dry up.

'Take a seat,' Chickenfeed said, making a sweeping gesture at the bed with his right arm, 'and tell me about it.'

Paul shuffled over to the bed and sat down. Chickenfeed picked up his glass and drained it. He held out the glass and Paul refilled it. Chickenfeed sloshed in a soda mix before settling down in a battered easy chair.

'She's fucking Case.' Paul said bitterly.

'Tracy?' Chickenfeed queried.

Paul nodded and took another long slug from the bottle of Hundred Pipers.

'I suspected as much,' Chickenfeed told him. 'The pair of them made a few remarks today which gave the game away.'

'I asked her to promise not to see him and she refused.' Paul gulped down another slug of whisky.

Chickenfeed nodded.

'I can't believe how fucking selfish she is!' Spit accompanied the words as they poured out of Paul's mouth. 'I'd do anything for her. I just don't understand it. What's he got that I haven't? He's over the hill. I should know, I introduced him to her. She admitted I'm a much better fuck. Maybe she's just winding me up. Maybe she wants to make me jealous.'

Paul took another slug from the bottle of Hundred Pipers. 'I'll kill the bastard when I see him. If he thinks he can pull better eco stunts than me, he's got another thing coming. He's just an old Nazi.' Paul lapsed into silence.

'How'd you get burnt?' Chickenfeed asked.

'Setting fire to a car.' Paul took another slug of whisky. There was silence for several minutes.

'You know this novel I'm working on,' Chickenfeed jerked a thumb at his computer. 'I need some help with it.'

'What sort of help?' Paul enquired.

'You're hetero, right?'

'Of course I am!' Paul shouted before taking another slug of Hundred Pipers.

'You've,' Chickenfeed hesitated for a few seconds, 'you've never done it with a guy?'

96

'Fuck you!' Paul wasn't going to take that kind of insult lying down.

'You know I'm bisexual?'

'No!' Paul was genuinely surprised.

'Well, in this new book I want to recreate my first sexual encounter. It was with my next-door neighbour. He was a respectable businessman. Married with a couple of kids. He offered me money if I'd do things with him. He kept pestering me. I was only twelve and I needed the dosh, so in the end I agreed. He'd take me into his garage. The first time he just sucked my cock.'

'Fucking queers!' Paul swore. 'They're all perverts!'

'No, they're not!' Chickenfeed protested. 'Scene guys are fine, guys who've come out are fine. I've had good sexual and emotional relationships with guys like that. It's the people who won't come out of the closet who cause problems. They're usually middle class, married and hold respectable positions in the community. In fact, on the surface they're usually the worst homophobics.'

'But what's this got to do with your book?' Paul enquired.

'I want to recreate my first sexual experience in one scene,' Chickenfeed explained. 'The trouble is, it's so long ago that I can hardly remember it. I thought if you'd let me blow you, then you could tell me what it's like getting it from a man for the first time.'

Paul took another slug from the bottle of Hundred Pipers, almost draining it. He was lost for words.

'Well, think about it for a few minutes,' Chickenfeed suggested, hoping the whisky would weave its magic spell. After all, Paul had drunk enough of the fucking stuff!

Paul's head was spinning. He wasn't going to tell Chickenfeed he'd had sex with Case. He was heterosexual. The way Tracy reacted to him proved that.

Paul tried to force his thoughts into something resembling a logical structure. While he certainly wasn't queer, he did want to help Chickenfeed and his encounter with

Case had left him with a much more objective view of gay sex than that held by your average straight.

It was unlikely Chickenfeed would find anybody else as suitable for the blowjob. It was in the cause of art, or at least that lesser art of literature. And that first time he'd made it with Case had been so extraordinarily pleasant. Chickenfeed wasn't bad looking. In fact Paul decided he fancied him. 'Okay,' Paul slurred.

Chickenfeed didn't need a second invitation. Within seconds he was on his knees. Paul felt Chickenfeed's hands on his flies. His excitement increased as the zip came down and Chickenfeed's fingers massaged his length. The member stiffened. Chickenfeed put his mouth around it.

Chickenfeed sucked, chewed and swallowed. At first he could think of nothing beyond the fact that Paul's cock had recently been inside Tracy. There were probably still traces of her sex juice on it. But these thoughts were abandoned as his genetic programming took control.

The two men were no longer in Bow but out on the mudflats. It was hot, dark and humid. The earth was a body and they were a part of that body. Lava hissed in the distance. Then an even older genetic memory seized control of their heaving (un)consciousness. They experienced Paul's orgasm as a digital recording of the first star exploding. The movie that played across their skulls was in 3D sensorama.

Chickenfeed eased Paul's cock out of his mouth and swallowed hard on the liquid genetics which were left behind. His breathing was deep and even. Paul's was somewhat more erratic. 'How was it for you, darling?' Chickenfeed enquired.

This failed to elicit a response, so Chickenfeed slapped Paul and asked again.

'How was it?' Chickenfeed demanded. 'I need to know for the book.'

'Pleasant,' Paul slurred, 'very pleasant.'

Paul swayed and then slumped on the bed. He was unconscious. Chickenfeed picked him up and carried him through to his own room. He undressed him and put him into bed.

Chickenfeed sat down at his desk. He was surprised at how quickly he'd lost hold of the thought that he'd been sucking something which had recently been inside Tracy. He wrote up the encounter, even though he had doubts as to whether he'd need this record for future reference. Despite months of fantasizing, it had turned out to be a non-event. An average encounter, nothing to write home about.

Seven

CHICKENFEED WOKE AT NINE. INSTEAD of making breakfast he went straight to **Chrisp Street Market** where he bought two bottles of **Hundred Pipers**. He'd more or less completed his novel. It was simply a question of making a few revisions. He hoped to have a final draft at the publishers within a week. The booze would fuel him through to the end.

Chickenfeed was thinking about **Alienation**. If the group hit the charts his fifty per cent management fee would be big money. And if he could use Alienation to promote war between rival **youth cults**, then sales of his book were likely to skyrocket.

Alan would have to go. He was cracking up, couldn't take the pace. He'd do for another month or two. Chickenfeed would time the sacking to gain maximum publicity. Perhaps Alan could be persuaded to commit suicide. Such a stunt would pay dividends in terms of publicity. Chickenfeed wondered who he could get in as a replacement. If the worst came to the worst, he could fill in himself. He knew the rudiments of the bassist's craft, Catfish could teach him anything else he needed to know. After all, he only had to pick a chord, go twang and he had music!

The phone was ringing as he let himself back into his squat. He pounded down the hall, his two bottles of Hundred Pipers clanking against each other in a plastic carrier. 'Hello,' Chickenfeed hissed breathlessly.

'Hello Chickenfeed.' It was Tracy. 'Can I speak to Paul?'

'He's not up and he got pretty drunk last night, so he'll probably take a bit of waking.'

'He's in a bad way.' Tracy was making a statement rather than asking a question.

'Yeah,' Chickenfeed replied, 'he says you've been sleeping with that nutter Case.'

'I have.' Tracy didn't need to confirm this fact but it gave Chickenfeed a grim satisfaction to hear an admission from her own lips.

'He's pretty cut up about it.' The words came out in a flat neutral tone, which screamed I'm-not-gonna-give-you-a-hard-time-about-it. 'But I reckon he'll get over it.'

'I've run out of money,' Tracy said.

'If you need someone to talk to you know where I am.' Chickenfeed's words were urgent.

'Thanks, I'll. . .' the sentence was cut off as the phone went dead.

Chickenfeed jogged upstairs and deposited the bottles of whisky on his desk. He looked through some typescripts. **Casual** had turned out well. Everything was marked up with the required changes annotated in red ink. Chickenfeed thumbed through the pages. The final touches would require very little mental effort. He'd already marked out what was to be done. Finishing something off was always easier than sitting down in front of a blank computer screen and working from scratch.

Hunger cut through Chickenfeed's dreams of success. The mental picture he had of himself walking through **Notting Hill** with a dolly bird on either arm faded from his mind.

The radio blared as Chickenfeed grilled toast. It was only a matter of time until he pulled himself out of the **poverty trap**. He'd be able to buy himself a toaster. Perhaps he wouldn't need one. The daily allowance from his royalties would pay for a cafe breakfast, a pub lunch and an evening meal in a West End restaurant.

'News every hour on the hour,' the radio announced. There was a jingle which repeated the name of the radio station and the word 'news' several times.

101

'Militant ecologists have wreaked further havoc in the capital,' a newcaster announced. 'They struck at cars parked on the Teviot Estate, Poplar, East London at 3am this morning. One car was completely destroyed after being set on fire and more than a dozen others damaged. Police have not ruled out a connection with Monday's 'cuppa protest' murders. . .'

EDWARD CASE PUSHED THE BATTERED typewriter away from him and poured a generous shot from the **Hundred Pipers** bottle he kept on his desk. He smelled the blend. His face, which had been wrinkled in concentration, relaxed into a broad smile as the familiar aroma filled his nostrils.

Edward knew that more than one journalistic career had been built on the inspirational qualities of this fine scotch. He put the glass to his lips and tossed down a mouthful of the elixir. The warm sensation in his chest lifted him above the workaday world. He knew instinctively that as long as the country maintained its ability to produce products of this quality then **Britain** would always be Great.

Edward took another slug of Hundred Pipers. His smile spread as far as his ears. He pulled a sheet of paper from the carriage and felt the words hit him as he read through the draft.

The attack on **Enrico**'s had been more successful than even he'd anticipated. The coverage had been phenomenal, and as an experienced journalist he understood the necessity to strike again while the iron was hot.

He'd selected **Harry's Diner**, a lorry driver's stop-off, as the next target. It was on the edge of **Silvertown**, an appallingly blighted part of **Newham**. And that was saying something because Newham was the least attractive

102

borough in **London**. The Thames barrier stretched from Woolwich on the south side of the river to Silvertown on the north. If there was any justice in this world, the barrier would be used soon. All it took was one particularly high tide. The barrier would go up and, rather than sweeping down the river and flooding central London, millions of gallons of water would spill over the Newham section of the Thames embankment and wipe Silvertown from the face of the earth.

Case's train of thought was interrupted by a ring on his doorbell. He wondered who the hell it could be at 11am in the morning. Perhaps it was the gasman come to read the meter. The bell rang again. No, it wasn't somebody to read a meter, the gasman wouldn't ring twice.

Case heaved himself out of his chair and padded down the hall to his front door. Somehow he wasn't surprised to find Tracy standing on his doorstep.

She threw her arms around Case and smothered him in kisses. Eventually she released his neck from the vice-like grip of her arms. Case took her hand and led her into the house. He was pleased to see her. She'd promised to ring last night but hadn't. Nevertheless he was worried. He couldn't quite fathom her mood. He'd expected her to be a little cooler. He knew she'd been upset by the deaths at Enrico's. He'd assumed she hadn't phoned because she was angry. Perhaps this display of affection meant she'd come to understand the political necessity of murder.

'Herb tea? Fruit juice? Mineral water?' Case enquired, not wanting to offer alcohol or admit he drank so early in the day.

'I could do with a bit of what you've been drinking!' Tracy replied.

Case looked somewhat taken aback.

'I can smell it on your breath,' Tracy persisted. 'I'd like a Hundred Pipers too!'

103

Case took the bottle from his desk and poured them each a dram. He carried the glasses to the coffee table and placed one gracefully in front of Tracy.

Tracy picked up her glass and swallowed the drink in a single gulp. Case sipped his, savouring the warmth of the whisky. It complemented the warmth of Tracy's body as she nestled against him. Case knew there was something wrong, but he didn't want to broach the subject. 'Another?' he enquired tentatively.

'No,' Tracy replied, 'I just wanted one to relax me a little.'

'What's the matter?' Case enquired, accepting that Tracy wanted him to lead her into whatever it was she wished to talk about.

'It's Paul,' Tracy whispered. 'I've told him about us.'

Case drew in his breath. His back straightened. Very shortly he would either get the big E or be in line for sole rights. He feared the former just as much as he desired the latter.

'How did he take it?' Case enquired, still holding in most of his breath.

'Very badly,' Tracy replied, 'particularly when I told him I wasn't prepared to give you up.'

Case let out his breath and slumped back against the settee. He drained his glass of whisky, put it down on the table, then placed his hand on Tracy's knee.

'I'm afraid that if I hold onto you I'll lose Paul,' Tracy sobbed.

'It's alright,' Case said putting his arms around her, 'there's no reason why you shouldn't have both of us.'

Tracy sniffed. She'd only shed a few tears, and with the last of them rolling down her cheek she looked devastatingly beautiful. Case had to admit he'd been wrong in his first estimation of her. Her features might not bear any resemblance to those of top salary models, but there was something about her. Whereas models tended to

104

look bland without makeup, Tracy was striking even before she used a little paint to enhance what nature had given her.

Tracy turned her head. Her lips rushed forward to meet Edward's. His breath was hot and fiery. Tracy knew Case wasn't much to look at. She'd never judged men, and in particular her boyfriends, on beefcake criteria. Beneath Edward's cynical persona she sensed the brutal repression of an extremely sensitive personality. Tracy saw it as her personal mission to bring his tender side to the fore.

Edward had not yet admitted to her that he was a fanatical Nazi. He'd given Paul strict instructions to keep Tracy in the dark about his fascist beliefs. Unfortunately for Edward, Paul's loyalties lay with Tracy and so she'd been informed of the jounalist's fanatical views from the time of her earliest dealings with the man.

Tracy was convinced the love of a good woman would cure even the most recalcitrant fascist of their Nazi cultism. With her help, Paul had overcome his socially regressive artistic tendencies. Now Tracy would do the same for Edward. The men she loved would be comrades in the Green vanguard.

Tracy pulled free of Edward's embrace and stood up. She held out her hand and Edward took it. Tracy pulled him up from the settee, led him upstairs and into his own bedroom. Case fell back onto his satin sheets, pulling Tracy down with him. Edward's heart was beating out the primitive rhythm of the swamps. He wanted to rip Tracy's knickers off and crush her body against his. However, he understood that on this occasion it was important to do things the way Tracy wanted.

Something told him she enjoyed variations in the rhythm of their sexual encounters. If he always took her hard and fast, she'd soon grow bored of his lovemaking. This was a mistake Case had made as a young man.

105

He'd memorise the moves made the first time he bedded someone and then try to recreate that first occasion at every subsequent encounter.

Case didn't need to prove himself with Tracy. She was already convinced of his sexual abilities – just as he was of hers. He was mature enough to have overcome most of his male insecurities relating to bedroom athletics.

Tracy had an arm around Edward's neck and a hand inside his shirt. With this she massaged his chest. Her fingers moved in circular motions over Edward's skin.

Tracy's movements were very delicate and this excited Case all the more. He concentrated on her body, on caressing it with the lightest possible touch. He didn't want to give in to his impulse to rush. To pound. To beat out the primitive rhythm of the swamps without any regard for subtlety.

Tracy's breathing was still light. Case was straining to keep his that way. Although he didn't give in to the urgent throbbing in his groin, his physical response was not quite as cool as he'd have liked.

Tracy had not prevented him from pulling off her clothes, but there'd been a gap of half an hour between Edward throwing Tracy's underwear to the floor and Tracy getting around to removing his. What Case could congratulate himself on was resisting the urge to pull off his own clothes. If he'd done that, it would have shown he had no feeling for the way Tracy liked to do things. No subtlety. No class. Somehow he'd managed to hold back despite being driven half-mad.

Case entered Tracy very slowly, hardly moving at all. It was Tracy tightening and then relaxing her vaginal muscles that seemed to draw him in. Once Tracy's love hole had clasped his penis to its very hilt, Case instinctively knew that he was expected to lie still. Tracy's hot breath was burning into his ear and the tightening and relaxation of her snatch was driving him crazier than their interminable undressing.

The speed of Edward's breathing increased to match the rising tempo of the muscle contractions within Tracy's cunt. Love juice was boiling through Edward's prick and Tracy was in the full throes of orgasm. The DNA kept flowing from Edward's dick. It wasn't just a squirt, this was heaven. The supply of liquid genetics only dried up when Tracy slowed and then stopped the contraction of her muscles. Edward's prick slid out of Tracy's fuck hole. He shifted his bulk so that he could press his lips against hers. Tracy's tongue darted into his mouth.

After that they lay next to each other, holding hands beneath the satin sheets. There was no need for either of them to speak. Theirs was the total understanding of two people who care very much for each other. They both knew that sex was not necessarily a peak from which each partner returns individually. Tracy had just shown Case that orgasm can also be the means of increasing empathy between two lovers.

Case flipped onto his side and kissed Tracy. 'Are you hungry?' he asked.

'Mmm, a little,' she replied, and kissed him on the nose.

'Shall I make something to eat?'

'Have you got any beansprouts?' Tracy asked.

'No,' Case said, 'but I can nip out to **Asda**'s and buy some.'

'It's okay,' Tracy replied, 'I'm not that hungry.'

'It's no trouble,' Case said getting out of bed.

'Well,' Tracy replied while simultaneously grabbing hold of Edward's arm, 'I'll let you go if you'll give me a kiss first.'

Case bent over her and kissed her on the lips, then stood up and turned to move away.

'I want another before you go,' Tracy insisted pulling him back towards her.'

'My pleasure!' Case replied, bending over her once more and kissing her.

'Is it okay if I have a bath?' Tracy asked as Case pulled his clothes on.

'Sure,' he replied.

TRACY WAS PREPARING A BEANSPROUT salad. She heard Paul's key in the lock. That irritated her. He might have a key but it was her flat. She wished he'd have the decency to knock instead of just letting himself in.

Tracy kept chopping at the salad. She knew Paul was drunk even before he made it into the kitchen. He'd bumped into the bicycle she kept in the hallway and knocked it over. He seemed to have considerable difficulty getting it to lean upright against the wall.

Tracy remained bent over the salad as Paul came up behind her. He plonked a bottle of **Hundred Pipers** on the table and put his arms around her waist. Tracy noticed the cap was missing from the bottle. Paul kissed the back of her neck. 'I love you,' he slurred.

Tracy dropped the knife she was holding and turned round. She kissed Paul on the mouth. 'I love you too,' she whispered.

'I don't believe you,' Paul replied.

'You know I do,' Tracy insisted.

'Then why have you been screwing that nutter Case?' Paul demanded.

'I love both of you.' Tracy kissed him again.

'You can't love two people,' Paul insisted. 'If you love someone then you're theirs, and you don't fuck them around by being unfaithful. You don't love me, you're just playing with my feelings.'

'Paul!' Tracy screamed, breaking free of his embrace. Then recovering she asked, 'Would you like some food?'

'No, I just wanna drink whisky.'

108

Tracy took two plates from the dish rack and placed one in front of Paul anyway. Then she got the cutlery and put a fork to the side of Paul's plate. Tracy served herself a helping of the beansprout salad.

Paul took a slug from the bottle of whisky. Tracy got up and took two glasses from the cupboard. She poured herself an apple juice and put the empty glass in front of Paul. Paul took another slug from the bottle of whisky.

'For Christ's sake Paul,' Tracy hissed, 'use the glass.'

Paul poured whisky into the glass. He reached over for Tracy's glass of fruit juice, picked it up and gulped it down. Then he poured whisky into Tracy's glass.

'Listen Paul,' Tracy said, 'I'll drink the whisky if you'll eat some salad.'

Paul served himself some salad. He picked up his fork and dug into the beansprouts. Tracy picked up her glass of Hundred Pipers and drank half of it in a gulp. Paul drained his own glass. Then he picked up the whisky bottle and refilled both glasses. 'I've got no future without you Trace,' Paul said dolefuly.

'Then it's lucky I love you. Lucky I like us having a scene.'

'I can't share you with anybody else.' Paul put his glass to his mouth and drained it.

'I'm not a piece of cake. We have a relationship. I'm not something that you own and can keep for your private use.' Tracy was indignant.

Paul poured himself another scotch and drank it in one gulp. 'I don't care if I die.' Paul put on his most pathetic look as he said this.

'Why did you set fire to that car?' Tracy asked, trying to change the subject.

'I did it for you.'

'Is that how you burnt yourself?'

'Yes, I've already told you I don't care if I die.'

Tracy munched her salad. Paul ate a little of his, then poured himself another whisky and drank it. Tracy gulped down her Hundred Pipers. She kept the glass in her hand as she got up and went over to the fridge. She poured herself another apple juice.

'Will you give him up?' Paul asked.

'I've told you, I love you both. There's no reason why I can't see you and Edward.'

Tracy felt confused. She couldn't let Paul just gulp down whisky. Couldn't allow him to disregard his personal safety. If he pulled any more stunts like the previous night's car burning, then he might end up killing himself. She felt she had to help him and yet she didn't see why she should give up Case. After all, she was sincere about wanting to see both of them. If only Paul had been a little more understanding then maybe she wouldn't have started the relationship with Case.

'You're selfish. You don't consider anyone else's feelings. If you've got any decency you'll promise not to see that nutter again. Apart from anything, I wonder if you're safe with him. He's a murderous bastard. What would you do if he turned on you?' Paul lapsed into silence when he realised Tracy wasn't going to reply.

Tracy was thinking she needed a little more space. She wished Paul was less dependent upon her. If only she'd been a little firmer earlier on in their relationship. If she'd been insistent about Paul not seeing her every day perhaps things would have turned out better.

'I'm going to bed,' she announced.

'I'll follow you, once I've finished the Hundred Pipers.' Paul said holding up the scotch.

It didn't take Paul long to empty the bottle. He didn't bother cleaning his teeth. He just walked into Tracy's room and stripped off. When he got into bed, Tracy turned her back to him and moved against the wall. Paul snuggled up against her. He pumped his knees into the space where her arse and legs met.

'Can't you stay still!' Tracy snapped.

110

Paul ignored her comment. His legs kept moving and he began to kiss the back of her neck.

'Look,' Tracy pleaded, 'I just want to go to sleep.'

Paul ignored her. His left hand snaked over her thighs and darted towards her pubic mound. Tracy tightened her muscles as Paul tried to prise her legs open.

'Leave me alone,' Tracy pleaded.

'Don't you love me?' Paul demanded.

'Of course I love you.'

'Then why don't you want me?' There was anger in Paul's voice. 'You never used to complain about my love making.'

Tracy decided it was best not to reply. Paul persisted in kissing her, rubbing his legs against the back of her thighs, rubbing her pubic mound with his hand. Tracy was tired. She wanted to sleep. She'd have liked to have had her bed to herself.

'I need you,' Paul whispered in her ear. 'I love you so much, and that love demands physical expression.'

It seemed as if Paul had been kissing her, stroking her, rubbing her. poking her, for an eternity. Tracy knew she couldn't take much more. It was easier to turn around and have sex. She didn't want sex, she just wanted to go to sleep. She turned over because she knew once she'd let Paul screw her, she'd be able to get some sleep.

Paul put a hand on her shoulder and his lips against her mouth. He was kissing her and applying quite a hard pressure with his hand. A few seconds later Tracy was on her back and Paul was on top of her.

Paul shoved his prick against her cunt. Tracy winced and let out a strangled scream. 'That's not very nice,' she said with a slight tremble in her voice.

Paul rolled off her. Tracy got out of bed and went into the bathroom. Paul stayed where he was. He wondered what she was up to. Tracy was thinking of Edward. She was thinking of the way they'd made love that morning.

111

Sex didn't have to be rough. With Edward it had been very gentle.

In her mind's eye she could see Edward lying on top of her. He remained very still and she was bringing him to orgasm by contraction and relaxation of her vaginal muscles. Tracy's fingers were rubbing her clitoris. She could feel Edward's hot breath against her cheek. She could feel his breath burning into her ear.

Tracy was enjoying the fantasy but she stopped short of orgasm. She cut it dead. She understood how much Paul wanted her and how insecure he felt. She wanted to help him. It would take some time but hopefully the two of them could sort everything out. Tracy hadn't wanted sex with Paul tonight. She was going back into the bedroom to make love with him because she understood his insecurities and wanted to help him overcome them.

A relationship is a partnership. Each party has to make sacrifices for it to work. That was the way Tracy felt. Paul wasn't being very considerate, but she'd excuse him on this occasion because he was so upset. If the sex calmed him down enough they could talk things through afterwards.

Tracy climbed between the sheets. She put a finger in her mouth and then made a circle on Paul's chest with her spit. She moistened the finger again and made a circle on his cheek. Then one on his stomach.

Paul was excited by what Tracy was doing. She took his erection into her mouth. Paul was hoping she'd swing a leg over his head so that he could get his tongue into her cunt. Tracy kept her knees at Paul's side as she bent over him, sucking and chewing at his prick. She knew Paul would like it better if she let him lap at her snatch. She knew but couldn't bring herself to make this ultimate sacrifice.

Paul was close to orgasm. Tracy removed the member from her mouth. She crawled over Paul. She wanted to be on top of him but he pushed her onto her back. Paul had no trouble entering her, as she was still wet from her fantasy about Edward.

112

Tracy tried not to think about Edward, to fantasise that it was Edward on top of her instead of Paul. With a great deal of effort she pushed such thoughts from her mind. She concentrated on Paul. He was on top of her and he was coming. Tracy felt the sperm boil through his penis and shoot out. She was concentrating on the fact that it was Paul's penis inside her. She didn't find this fact very exciting. She lay limply beneath him, nowhere near an orgasm.

'You didn't come!' Paul was virtually hysterical. His penis was limp but he kept pumping away. It took a few minutes but eventually he got it hard again. He was pumping like crazy. 'For fuck's sake come.' Paul was screaming. 'If you love me you'll come. I bet you come for that bastard Case.'

Tracy knew what would make her come, but pushed the thought from her mind. If she thought of Case and immediately reached a climax then Paul might suspect what had been going on in her head.

Paul kept thrashing, kept Tracy pinned down. It was really unpleasant having to concentrate on the fact that it was Paul on top of her. But Tracy kept it up. She felt empty and abused. She wished Paul would stop but knew that he wouldn't.

She wondered if she'd given it long enough. She knew she couldn't take much more. It would have to do. She closed her eyes and imagined it was Case on top of her. She imagined that her partner was being gentle and considerate. She pushed Paul and his macho egotism completely from her mind.

At last, Paul thought, she's beginning to respond. I knew she wanted it. I knew she meant yes although she'd said no. If she really hadn't wanted it, she wouldn't be moaning the way she is now.

Tracy was thinking of Case. His image was fixed in her mind. They came together, Edward and she. It was Edward's spunk shooting through the penis inside her. It was Edward's penis, not Paul's.

113

As Paul came he imagined that the sensation he felt was a genetically encoded memory of the first star exploding. Tracy experienced similar thoughts until she opened her eyes and saw Paul staring back at her. The memory hadn't been genetically encoded after all. It was recent. She'd had sex with Edward less than twelve hours before.

Paul kissed her on the mouth, then rolled off her.

'You really enjoyed that, didn't you.' Paul was making a statement rather than asking a question.

'Yes,' Tracy said, thinking it would make him happy if she confirmed his opinion.

'It's not often you come like that,' Paul said.

'I know,' Tracy replied.

'Admit that I'm a better fuck than Case,' Paul demanded.

'Its not a competition,' Tracy insisted.

'I know,' Paul replied, 'but you've got to admit that I'm a million times better than that old has been. He must be forty-five. There's no way he could compete with me. I might be twenty-four, but I've still got more energy than an eighteen-year old.'

'Stop boasting,' Tracy said softly.

'I'm not boasting,' Paul insisted. 'It's objectively true.'

'Paul,' Tracy's voice was very soft, 'let's talk about us. How long is it going to be before you accept the fact that I can love someone else and still love you?'

'All I want,' Paul said it very slowly as though he was talking to a rather stupid child, 'is for you to promise me that you won't see Case again.'

'Be reasonable,' Tracy pleaded. 'There's no point in me making you a promise that I'm not going to keep.'

'I want you to promise me not to see Case.' Paul repeated. 'Promise me, and if you love me you'll keep the promise.'

Paul turned over so that his back was to Tracy. He closed his eyes. Tracy went on talking for a long time.

114

Paul remained silent. He'd decided he wouldn't speak to her again that night unless she promised to be faithful. Tracy didn't make the promise. Eventually she realised Paul wasn't prepared to talk through the changes in their relationship and so she too fell silent. She closed her eyes and hoped Paul would be more reasonable in the morning.

Eight

CHICKENFEED AND THE FOUR MEMBERS of **Alienation** huddled together in a corner of the **Hustler,** a gay pub just off
Soho Square. Chickenfeed and Catfish had **Hundred Pipers**
in their hands. The rest of the group were drinking lager.

'When will he be here?' Wayne was demanding.

Chickenfeed glanced at his watch. They'd been early
and J.J. Moore, the top writer with **Spins,** was a little late.
Music journalists could afford to keep unsigned bands
hanging around. There was no shortage of groups wanting coverage. Alienation, however, were a little different.
Although they didn't have a record contract, they were
firmly established as an act to watch in the future. The
night they'd taken the stage in a battle royal with the
Stockbrokers had paid dividends in terms of publicity.
The efficient way they'd dealt with the **Blood Shadows**
had kept their name in the headlines.

Alienation were the leading band and main force
behind a new cult. In the course of a few weeks a dozen
groups had jumped on the bandwagon. **Contradiction**
had been the first but now there was also **Sex Kick,
Defiant Pose, Amadeo Bordiga and the Ultra Leftists
From Hell, Death Squad, Teenage Pricks, KU 422, Fifth
International, Red Guards, Insurrection, Subversion** and
Noir et Rouge.

New bands were forming every day and existing
groups were changing their image to grab some of the
media attention being heaped upon **déjà vu.** The ideology
behind this movement was something completely new to
the rock scene. The groups were not revivalists but neither
did they seek to create a 'new' sound. **Punk** was the most
obvious influence. But by spurning the notion of formal

116

innovation, déjà vu came as a breath of fresh air. There was an energy in these copyist bands which wasn't to be found in those seventeenth generation punk groups who still paid lip service to the idea of change.

Déjà vu not only inspired an exciting musical scene, it had its own camp followers. They were known as **sorts**. This was short for 'all sorts', since the **rainbow alliance** to which they subscribed was made up of many different peoples and groups.

Moore appeared at last. Chickenfeed recognised him and waved frantically. The journalist strolled over. 'Hi,' he said and then followed up with: 'Drinks everybody?'

'Lager.'

'Lager.'

'Hundred Pipers with soda mix.'

'Lager.'

'Hundred Pipers with soda mix.'

All five of them beamed as they replied. Everyone has heard about the fringe benefits which accompany a career in journalism, but too few of us come into direct contact with this category of expense account. No wonder most media types are booze hounds!

Moore returned carrying the drinks on a tray. Taking a triple **Grants** in his hand, he squeezed in between Chickenfeed and Christine. Moore was a small man. His long hair was tied back in a pony tail. His leather jacket looked shabby five years ago. His weathered features told a tale of drug addiction.

'I'm Chickenfeed, the manager,' Chickenfeed said taking charge of the situation. 'This is Christine, vocals. Alan, bass. Wayne, drums. Catfish, guitar.'

'Well,' Moore took a long pause, 'I saw you at the Moulders Arms and I was most impressed. You've really got something.'

There were smiles all round.

'Now, tell me,' Moore continued, 'how did you arrive at your sound?'

117

'We don't try to sound like a '77 punk band,' Catfish explained, 'it just comes out that way when we play.'

'You see,' Christine continued, 'Catfish has never had an original thought in his life. When he decides to write a new song he just goes through his collection of old punk records. He'll take riffs from various songs and put them together in a fresh combination. So what might have been the main riff of a forgotten punk classic becomes the middle eight in one of our songs.'

'Yeah,' Catfish continued, 'but I'm careful with what I nick. I never steal a whole song. The tunes I write are always put together from at least three different sources.'

'Why did you pick on old punk records to steal riffs from?' Moore enquired.

'Well,' Catfish replied, 'for one thing I've got a lot of them. I inherited them from my older brother who OD-ed on smack a few years back. And another reason is I don't have much talent. Punk is pretty simple to play. I'd happily rip off something a bit more complex but I just don't have the musical skill.'

'So who writes the words?' Moore enquired. 'And why do you go in for such controversial subject matter?'

'I write the lyrics,' Chickenfeed put in. 'Well, I put them together anyway. Most of the lines are ripped off from various places. Terrorist communiqués and things like that. That's why they're so controversial. I only find extremist stuff interesting.'

'Isn't it a little unusual for the manager to write the group's lyrics?' Moore enquired.

'We're all just Chickenfeed's puppets,' Wayne explained. 'He totally manipulates us. All the ideas are his. We're just the hacks who help carry out his plans.'

'And what are your plans?' Moore raised his eyebrows and stared at the manager.

'World domination,' Chickenfeed explained. 'Sex,

drugs and money. A place in Mayfair. Holiday homes in the sun. And of course, worldwide proletarian revolution with unlicensed pleasure as its only aim.'

'Are you **situationists**?' Moore wanted to know.

'You're joking!' Christine exclaimed. 'None of us has been to university and we're certainly not from upper-class backgrounds!'

'So explain to me just what it is you're trying to do,' Moore demanded.

'It's like this,' Chickenfeed replied. 'Until now most rock bands have been trying to do something new. That's boring, its old hat. Déjà vu is a complete break from that. We're the only honest band to hit this planet in about two million years because we're not trying to pull off the **modernist** con. We hate **post-modernism** too! We're not trying to be original and that makes us incredibly original. We'll rip anything off and that's why we're so subversive. We're **plagiarists** and we're proud of it. There's never been anything like déjà vu before. Everything was completely different the first time around.'

'So what do you think of the other déjà vu bands?' Moore wanted to know.

'They're all heroes of ours ain't they,' Christine drawled.

'They're not as good as us,' Chickenfeed insisted. 'They're not as unoriginal. Some of them aren't bad but there's too much expression in most of the music. We're the only band that are completely anti-expressive. All our songs, the gear we wear, how we move, it's all copied from other people. When you see and hear us, its absolute déjà vu. You can't say that about any of those other groups. You'll find that hardly any of their songs are consciously ripped off. You ask them, see if they can name the numbers from which their riffs were stolen. We're the only band that can do that. Those other bands try hard to copy us but they fail. They always put too much of themselves into

119

it. They're too original. They're too expressive. They're too individual. They just aren't as good as us.'

CHRISTINE HAD TAKEN ALAN BACK to her place on Hackney Road. Alan lived in Whitechapel and she'd suggested they head there but he'd not wanted to go home. She hadn't been thrilled at the prospect of taking him back to her pad. It was easier walking out of his flat if she got fed up with him, much easier than getting him out of her shared house. He'd been pretty weird since the attack on the café, withdrawn and not speaking much.

Christine had already talked to Chickenfeed about sacking Alan. She couldn't pack him in until he'd been thrown out of the band. He could be replaced easily enough. Good bass players were two a penny and Alan wasn't even a good musician. He'd only got into the group because he was her boyfriend. He had plenty of gigging experience, but before joining Alienation he'd always been in no-hope outfits.

Catfish had originally wanted to get Chickenfeed in as bass player. Chickenfeed's playing was rudimentary but Catfish said it wouldn't be a problem if he had his bass lines written for him and someone to show him how to play them. Christine had insisted she wanted Alan in the band after he'd hassled her about it. At that time, Chickenfeed hadn't been bothered about whether or not he was in the group.

'What did you think of the interview?' Christine asked to get some kind of conversation going.

Alan had exchanged no more than a few token words with J.J. Moore and the only conversation he'd made since leaving the pub was when he insisted on going back to Christine's place and not to his flat.

'It was okay.'

120

'I thought Chickenfeed was really good.'

'Most managers stay out of the way when their groups are being interviewed.'

'Yeah, but we're not one of those run of the mill groups. And anyway, Chickenfeed writes all the lyrics and has worked hard on developing our image.'

'I could write lyrics for you.'

'I know but we've got a brash image and your lyrics are too literary, too thought out. Our stuff's all flash. It's not reflective and thoughtful the way you write songs.'

Christine was being diplomatic. She actually thought Alan was completely lacking in song writing ability. Every lyric she'd ever seen of his had been horrendously sentimental, and a crock of shit to boot. A bit like the letters he'd sent her when she'd packed him in a few months back.

It had been a mistake on her part to get back together with Alan. Vanity was to blame. It'd been a real ego trip when he'd told her he couldn't live without her.

Their relationship was fatally flawed. At first there'd been a genuine attraction. But now Christine kept going with Alan because he boosted her ego. But not to the extent that their affair would last more than a few more months. The daily hassles Alan put her through had already begun to outweigh the benefits of having a scene with him.

'Fancy something to eat?' Christine asked.

She was in the kitchen, chopping an onion, before she noticed Alan hadn't bothered to reply. He didn't need to reply. He always ate if he was offered food.

The water was boiling and Christine added pasta shells. She looked at the clock, taking a mental note of the time. She'd already added the garlic and spices to the pan in which she'd lightly fried the onion. The spices had burnt in. She added half a tin of tomatoes and turned the heat up to reduce the sauce.

Christine stirred the pasta. Then she stirred the sauce. She looked at the clock. The pasta had been on seven minutes. She spooned out a shell and tasted it. Perfect. She liked her pasta *al dente*. She called Alan down from her room and they ate in the kitchen.

'Haven't you got anything stronger to drink?' Alan complained, eyeing the glass of water at the side of his plate.

'You know alcohol doesn't last in this house. It doesn't matter whether I leave it in the kitchen or hide it in my room, Jill always finds it and drinks it before I get the chance.'

'You should put a lock on your door.' Alan didn't know how many times he'd made the suggestion.

'It's not like that,' Christine protested. 'Whatever food and drink is in this house is here to be shared.'

'Well, I'm bleedin' thirsty,' Alan complained. 'I'll nip round to the offie when we've finished eating and buy some cans.'

'Don't bother. I'll make a herb tea.'

'I want a lager.'

'You must have had six pints already today.'

'Nag, nag, nag.'

Alan pushed his plate across the table and got up. At least, Christine reflected, he didn't slam the door as he went out. She began the washing up while she waited for the kettle to boil. She was drinking camomile tea in her bedroom when Alan knocked at the front door. It was inconvenient having to go and open it for him but she was glad she'd never given him a key. Christine never gave her boyfriends keys. She liked to maintain her sense of independence.

They sat on the bed, Christine drinking camomile tea and Alan drinking lager. What the fuck did Alan think he was playing at, she wondered. She didn't like the fact that two people had died but it was hardly her fault. As for Alan, he'd always tried to put himself across as the strong and silent type. What a joke! She'd never yet met a man who was both strong and silent.

122

Christine had met plenty who were silent and weak, who'd bottle up their feelings until they came pouring out in an emotional explosion. The best thing she could say about Alan was he cried. He'd often try and bottle his feelings up but he could never do it for long. The worst men were the ones who wouldn't cry. When they got upset they just let loose with a torrent of verbals.

Christine finished her herb tea. Alan was on his second can of lager. His hand was on Christine's thigh and she was predicting that once he'd finished his can he'd manouvre her backwards onto the bed.

Alan didn't even put the can on the floor. He simply dropped it. He put his lips against Christine's and his left hand against her right shoulder. His right arm was around her waist. He pushed Christine and she fell back onto the bed. Alan went down with her.

Christine let Alan undress her. She sprawled across the bed as he undressed himself. There was no indication that she wanted him to get naked. Alan didn't take the hint. Didn't notice she was finding the whole thing mechanical and boring.

Alan reached down with his hand and found her clitoris. He massaged it and Christine juiced up. His lips were against hers, his tongue in her mouth. Normally Christine's tongue would have found its way into his mouth at some point. Alan was too wrapped up in his misery to wonder why Christine made no response whatsoever.

Alan shifted his bulk and Christine's legs spread beneath him. They'd done this a million times before. To Christine's mind it had become all form and no content. Alan didn't notice.

Alan beat out the primitive rhythm of sex. Christine could feel the rhythm and knew that it had lost its magic. If only Alan could work in some changes, some variation which would excite. It wouldn't take much, he need only shift his position.

123

Alan came quickly. He rolled off Christine and fell into a doze. Christine went through to the bathroom and washed herself. She was back in her room and dressing when Alan woke up.

'Did you enjoy it?' she asked.

'Enjoy what?' Alan mumbled, still groggy.

'Fucking,' the word was spoken in a flat, even, tone.

'I always enjoy fucking you! You know that.'

'I didn't enjoy it,' Christine informed him.

'What do you mean? I didn't rape you! I didn't make you do it!' there was anger in Alan's voice.

'I didn't encourage you either. I wanted to see whether you'd respond to my feelings. Whether you'd pick up my mood.'

'Look,' Alan's voice was strained, 'if you want to play funny games that's your problem. If you didn't want sex you only had to say. I wouldn't have raped you, I'd have understood.'

'I shouldn't have to tell you whether I want sex or not. You should be able to judge from my response to your initial approach.'

'I'm not a mindreader!'

'You don't have to be one. If you looked upon me as a human being with human feelings, instead of a mindless bitch who opens her legs every time you want sex, then you'd be able to tell when I did and when I didn't want to fuck.'

'I don't know why you're trying to get at me.'

'I'm not trying to get at you. I just want you to understand, that's all.'

'You are trying to get at me!'

'Oh, forget it.'

'No, I won't forget it. Are you trying to insinuate I'm a lousy screw? You've never complained before. Nobody's ever complained about my performance.'

'Why don't you just go home?'

'No, I won't go home. I wanna have this out with you.

124

You can't just treat me like shit for no reason. What's your problem? Got pre-menstrual tension or something?'

'Alan, have you ever stopped to consider that it takes two people to make a relationship?'

'Of course I have. But it only takes one to wreck it.'

'Forget it.'

'No, I won't forget it. What're you trying to tell me?!'

EDWARD CASE HAD BEEN BURIED in research. It wasn't just his love for Tracy – he was a genuine convert to deep ecology. It might have been possible to square certain brands of eco-activism with his former Nazi cultism but he'd gone beyond that. He'd abandoned Hitlerism, and very soon he'd abandon his career in the media.

The trouble with Tracy's ideology, Case reflected, was that it didn't go far enough. Although Edward had plenty of schemes for further reprisals against tea-swilling scum, he was planning actions which went much further. There would be assaults on bookshops, libraries, museums and art galleries.

Edward figured one more cafe raid would be enough to inspire copy-cat protesters to take up the anti-cash crop campaign. Cars were going up in flames all over the capital. No action was needed there. What was truly insidious was the written and spoken word. No one had even made a start on human language, it had to be destroyed everywhere.

Case had been turned against the print industry by a report he'd just read. According to this learned paper, if current trends in world publishing continued, then within a hundred years there'd be more than enough printed matter to cover the entire surface of the earth. Of course, such a situation would never arise, but something had to be done now before things started to reach danger proportions.

Case was working on a five-year plan. To start with, what needed to be hit were symbolic targets: cafes, bookshops, publisher's offices, museums. These attacks wouldn't have much practical effect, they were propaganda actions.

Later, when the masses had been won over to the cause, Case would organise a truly disruptive campaign of direct action. Communication lines would be hit, bridges and sections of railway track blown up, power plants attacked. The country could be brought to its knees very easily, all it took was a small but determined group of activists.

The doorbell rang. Case had been so busy working on his political programme that he'd not noticed Tracy was late.

It had been raining and Tracy was a little wet. Case hung up her coat, she went to the bathroom and dried her hair with a towel. Having joined Edward in the living room, Tracy stripped and laid her clothes out in front of the fire.

'Another Hundred Pipers?' Case suggested.

'Why not?' Tracy grinned.

Case took the glass from her hand and padded to the drinks cabinet. He poured Tracy a straight, sloshed soda in with his whisky. Edward handed Tracy her triple. He sat down beside her, his bottom sinking into the deep pile shag of the carpet. 'I've a confession to make,' he told her.

'Really?' Tracy kept her eyes on the fire.

'It's the only thing standing in the way of our love. Once I've told you this I think everything will work out.'

'Oh.' Tracy wondered if Edward was going to tell her he was a Nazi. It wasn't such a big deal since she knew anyway.

'The first night I met Paul,' Case was saying, 'I had sex with him. Can you forgive me?'

'It would be a bit hypocritical if I didn't.' Somehow Tracy wasn't suprised. 'After all, I'm still bedding him.'

'There's something else too,' Case was amazed at how

126

casually she was taking it, 'until very recently I was a fanatical Nazi.'

'My informant told me you were still a rabid Hitlerite.' Tracy's eyes remained on the fire.

'How could you love me if you thought I was a racist bigot?' Case wanted to know.

'I don't know,' Tracy replied softly. 'I didn't understand your Nazi fanaticism, but I figured it couldn't have a permanent hold on you if I loved you. I thought maybe I could help you see the error of your ways.'

'You have!' Case said clasping her hand. 'I've burnt my SS uniform!'

'Good,' Tracy replied.

Case could see she didn't understand the significance of this act. For him it had taken on the proportions of heroism. He had loved the uniform as he'd loved no human being until he'd met Tracy. He'd polished its leather accessories with obsessive devotion. But then Tracy didn't know this and thus couldn't be brought to understand what an important thing it had been for him to destroy it. 'I've been laying plans.' Case told her.

'What sort of plans?' Tracy asked.

'Another attack on a cafe. . .'

'No!' Tracy screamed. 'I don't want anybody else to be killed!'

'This will be different,' Case assured her. 'No one will die. I'll be careful. I thought the deaths were necessary but now I realise I was wrong. This time, we'll just rough up the customers. That's all.'

'I can't go along with it,' Tracy told him. 'I won't take part in it.'

'You don't need to take part in it,' Case reassured her. 'But I must see this thing through. It may be symbolic but at least it makes people aware that there are challenges and threats to the existing order.'

'I hope you know what you're doing.' Tracy gazed directly into Edward's eyes as she said it.

'So do I!' Case put his arms around Tracy. 'I've been wrong about so much in the past. I don't think I could live with myself if what I'm doing now comes to no good.'

Edward's lips met Tracy's, his tongue darted into her mouth. Tracy pushed Case backwards and fell with him. She crawled on top of him, worked her hand underneath his shirt and gently massaged his chest.

Tracy undid the buttons on Edward's **Ben Sherman**. He held his arms above his head so she could remove it. Case felt young again. Tracy made him feel that way. As she undressed him, it was as if all the years of evil, of Nazi fanaticism, were being stripped away, revealing the real Case underneath, a virile eighteen-year old with a humanistic love of the world.

If only CND hadn't gone into such a spiral of decline! If only Edward's youthful hopes had not been so mercilessly dashed! Race hatred and rabid lust for power had never been a natural feature of Edward's character. It was the defeat of those movements he'd placed his youthful optimism in – and his subsequent depression and disillusionment – which sent him into the waiting arms of Hitlerite fanatics.

Edward's character had been twisted from years of involvement with race-hate creeds. But now **the love of a good woman** was putting him back on the straight and narrow.

Edward's cock was in Tracy's mouth. The way she sucked and chewed at it did more for his moral reform than anything the **Pope**, or even **Christ** himself, could have done. The way her teeth, lips and tongue moved over Edward's erect love muscle brought out humanistic qualities which had been repressed for years.

Tracy's lips moved up Edward's body. Kissing his stomach. His chest. His mouth. Edward entered her and began to beat out the **primitive rhythm** of a life affirming force. The years of fanatical hatred disappeared. Case no longer dreamed the Powellite fantasy of **Rivers of Blood**.

He no longer wished for a government headed by Enoch, no longer imagined that he, himself, might become an English **Le Pen**. His European nationalism, his adherence to centuries old traditions of racial bigotry, were cast aside. Edward's immediate surroundings were the swamps, but in his mind's eye he maintained a **global perspective**.

Tracy was moaning, screaming, offering obscene encouragements as they pumped up towards orgasm. The DNA inside them shrieked out in ecstatic acknowledgement of their common origin. It screamed of the equality of all sexes, races, species, evolutionary experiences. Social conditioning might influence how the gene was percieved but modern (wo)man could never conquer the almighty DNA. It was the life force, the origin and the end.

Edward was gasping as Tracy worked him up and down the scales of ecstacy. Her whole body demanded, screamed, shrieked for MORE. Edward gave as he had never given before. The tension inside him. The desire. The Will. This truly was the Dictatorship of the DNA.

At last they came in a great shuddering of flesh, blood and bone. It was a genetic memory of the flood. It was the pleasure of the first amphibians as they crawled from the sea and experienced the delightful warmth of the sun's rays playing over their skin. It was like scoring the winning goal in a football match which put your team in line for the league title. Like seeing your face on that morning's front page next to a headline proclaiming you to be the greatest thing since sliced bread.

'ARE YOU AWAKE?' TRACY ASKED sleepily.

There was no reply. She wondered how long she'd been lying on the floor. Her back was burning from the heat of the fire. Her mouth felt swollen and dry.

She got up, staggered to the drinks cabinet and poured herself a **Hundred Pipers**. Once she'd gulped it down she felt a little better. She climbed the stairs to the bathroom, sat in the bath as she ran the water.

Tracy fell asleep in the tub and was only woken when Edward got in beside her. They grinned at each other, Edward picked up the soap and began to sud Tracy.

'Oh, be careful!' Tracy winced as he lifted one of her legs. 'It's going to be painful every time I sit down.'

'I'm not that rough!' Edward protested.

'No,' Tracy confirmed. 'But you've come on top of Paul and he's being very rough at the moment. The way he fucks makes me feel like a punchball.'

'You could pack him in.'

'You don't understand,' Tracy admonished. 'I love him.'

Case frowned.

'I love you too,' Tracy said softly.

'Are you sure?' Case demanded.

'It's hard, Paul needs me. He hardly gives me any time to myself. He just comes around and won't go away, if I go out he follows me.'

'I don't know why you put up with it.'

'I'm hoping he'll get over it.'

'What if he doesn't?' Case wanted to know.

'I don't know. He keeps trying to make me promise not to see you. I tell him there's no point me making a promise just to keep him quiet, a promise we both know I won't keep. It's as if he's trying to wear me down.'

Tracy got out of the bath. Case followed suit and they towelled each other down. They dressed in the lounge. Tracy sat on the settee while Case went into the kitchen and prepared a beansprout salad.

It was funny, Case reflected as he cut up vegetables, how he was changing. His initial reason for becoming a vegetarian had been because a former hero of his believed that a healthy diet should not include meat. It was only recently he'd acquired an idealistic belief in Animal Rights. But now his diet had changed again, this

130

time because the woman he loved believed raw food was an essential for bodily health. At first Case considered this mere crankiness on her part, but time had convinced him of the idea's validity.

She'd certainly won him over to her way of thinking. He hoped there were now some topics he'd considered more seriously than Tracy. It wasn't that he was competitive, just that he wanted her by his side whenever he launched an attack on a bookshop or museum.

Nine

CASE WAS LESS THAN HAPPY with the way things were going. The gang refused point blank to take part in his new caper. And he wasn't seeing much of Tracy. She was spending all her time with that creep Johnson. She kept making excuses about Paul 'needing her'.

'Like fuck!' Case swore. 'What the bastard actually needs is a sudden death.'

The **Silvertown** truck drivers' stop was a smart choice as a target. The gang's refusal to participate was no problem because Edward had everything sussed for carrying out the raid on his own.

Case gunned his VW down Manchester Road, turned right into East India Dock Road and headed for **Canning Town**. God what a dump, he thought as he reached the place. Then he turned right again and was speeding along Silvertown Way.

Case parked the car at the **Royal Victoria Dock**. Yuppies were windsurfing on water which had once served as a bay for cargo ships. With containerisation all the work had been moved up river to **Tilbury** and **Gravesend**. The resulting wasteland had been turned into a pleasure park for the rich bastards whose ranks Case had recently deserted.

Case locked his car and slipped on a pair of leather gloves. In his hand was a carrier filled with copies of the leaflet which had been dumped on the pavement outside Enrico's.

Case walked until he saw a likely car. He bent over and pretended to tie his shoelace. He'd learnt the trick from a detective novel. His car stealing technique was based almost exclusively on what he'd read in pulps written by the likes of **James Moffatt**.

132

The door was open, the steering lock broken. The owner probably wanted the BMW nicked as part of some insurance scam. Case slipped into the drivers seat and tried an assortment of skeleton keys.

He was on his fifth key before the engine caught. The car was a pleasure to drive. The motor did no more than give off a soothing hum.

It took three minutes to reach **Harry's Diner**. The place was easy to spot because articulated lorries were parked all around it. The cafe itself was a brick building. The front had been stripped away and replaced by plate glass windows. They were supported by wood surrounds with a door in between them. There was a car park immediately in front of the diner. But, since it was lunchtime, trucks were also strung out down either side of the street.

The BMW skidded as it careered into the car park at 40mph. The sudden swerve reduced its speed, but it was still travelling at a dangerously fast rate. Edward's foot slammed hard on the accelerator. The noise attracted the attention of truckers enjoying their midday meal, those not facing the window jerked around, all were horrified by what they saw. The BMW was coming straight for them. In split seconds it would smash through the plate glass windows, posing a serious threat to their safety.

The truckers stared in disbelief at the leather clad madman hunched over the wheel of the car. They sat rooted to their seats, confronted by the fact that there was something terribly wrong with the world. Until a second or two ago their lives had seemed so orderly. Days came and went in a very repetitive fashion. Long distance lorry driving is a tedious occupation. It was only now that the full violence of this world smashed into their collective (un)consciousness. They were looking death in the face and he was an evil eco-vegan who was telling them that they, personally, were responsible for the fucked-up state of the world.

The BMW smashed through the plate glass windows. Tables were overturned, men were thrown to the floor, shards of glass flew everywhere. Hundreds of leaflets were scattered across the cafe. Case flung them through the front windscreen of the BMW, which had been shattered in the head on collision.

Edward had been protected from the flying glass by the leather clothing he was geared up in. Reversing at high speed through the car park and onto the street, he made his escape.

There were several minutes of shocked silence, then a dozen truckers rushed to their cabs. The gesture was futile, by the time they'd revved up their engines they had no hope of catching the BMW.

Case was already back at the Royal Victoria Docks. He'd dumped the BMW near his own car, removed his leather gear and was about to make his way home.

ELIZABETH CRANSHAW EYED HER FIND. He wasn't bad looking, at least as far as writers go. As a successful critic in her middle thirties, Elizabeth was an expert on this subject. Most writers were wimps, nobodies whose work she praised because she felt sorry for them.

Elizabeth had this thing about creative men. She liked to seduce them. And bedding writers was the easiest task in the world for someone in her position. Still, it was only rarely she found one who merited a rating at sexual athletics. Elizabeth had high hopes in this area with her new find.

Kelvin was five nine tall and couldn't have weighed more than a hundred and forty pounds. Not quite as skinny as she liked them but he'd pass. Where he really scored was with his cropped hair, fierce blue eyes, and the fact that he was geared up like an early seventies skin. Doctor Marten boots, **sta-prest** and **Ben Sherman**. When he'd arrived at her pad he'd been wearing a **Harrington** jacket, but that was now tucked away in a cupboard.

Elizabeth liked the way Kelvin wrote too, hard and aggressive with a strong driving edge. There was plenty of sex in his stories. And none of that wimpish shit about how alienated he felt when screwing. Elizabeth could tell from his writing that Kelvin was a man who enjoyed a good fuck, particularly if a few variations were thrown in to spice it up.

Of course, Kelvin Callahan was a pen name. His publishers had told her his legal name was Hubert Hoxton-Moore and that most people addressed him by the nickname Chickenfeed. Elizabeth preferred to think of him as 'her' Kelvin. She hadn't made it with him yet, but she figured on it happening within the next hour. If it didn't, she wouldn't bother to complete the rave review that lay half-finished on the desk in her study.

Elizabeth adored Kelvin's blue eyes and baby face. He looked liked a teenager, although he was actually in his mid twenties. She decided it would be amusing to be seen around town with him. People who didn't know better would think she was his mother. Elizabeth enjoyed shocking people. She could imagine the looks they'd get when those around them sussed out the actual nature of their relationship.

'Another **Hundred Pipers**?' Elizabeth enquired in silken tones.

'That would be wonderful!' Chickenfeed confirmed, holding out his glass as Liz advanced on him with the bottle.

Chickenfeed found it amusing to come on with the upper class bit. Didn't they just love it! His roots were actually suburban and lower middle class. He'd made it to Chelmsford Grammar School and by exaggerating the 'manners' of those failures who taught him, he was able to pass himself off as a blue blood.

His legal name sounded pretty posh, but it was pure affectation on the part of his parents. His father, Henry, had scraped to make the grade in middle management – and

135

he'd only reached those heights since Chickenfeed left home.

His mother taught in a primary school. She was a bitter woman who claimed she'd married beneath herself. That was a joke! When Chickenfeed was sixteen, his dad warned him of the many mistakes a man could make in life. He'd confessed to his son that marrying Susan was the most foolish thing he'd ever done. He'd loved her at the time. If he'd only been a little more mercenary he could have hitched up with an heiress.

The last words of advice 'Henry' gave his son before the boy left home were: 'And remember, when you get married do it for money not love. The love is bound to turn sour, but I can assure you that money will see you happily through life.'

'So tell me Kelvin,' Elizabeth enquired as she seated herself again, 'what is it that makes you write? Is it some uncontrollable expressive urge?'

'You're joking!' Chickenfeed laughed.

'Come now,' Elizabeth smiled as she said it, 'there must be some reason.'

'There is,' Chickenfeed confided, 'but its not because I believe in literature as an art or any of that bollocks.'

'I'm glad you're being so frank with me.' Elizabeth gave him a wink as she said it. 'Some women might find your language crude, but I'm a connoisseur. I appreciate your earthy qualities.'

'The way I see it,' Chickenfeed continued, 'is that birds like a bloke with a creative edge to his personality. That's why I started writing, to give me a boost and help me get bedmates.'

'Oh!' Elizabeth laughed. 'I'd have thought you could have managed that with your looks.'

'Well,' Chickenfeed reflected, 'every bit you've got going for you helps.'

'But you must have other reasons for writing too!' Elizabeth insisted.

'Sure,' Chickenfeed continued. 'It always seemed a good medium for winding people up. Affront the moralists and all that. And when I got my stuff published in the underground press, people started treating me as if I was important. I liked that! Then, I figured if the stories became popular I could make a bob or two from it. I've always fancied a pad in the West End. But that's not the main thing. Like all writers, I'm just extremely vain and self-obsessed.'

'What about the sex in your books?' Elizabeth wanted to know. 'It reads like it's all written from experience.'

'You're joking!' Chickenfeed laughed. 'I haven't been in an aeroplane since I was twelve. All the stuff about being an elite member of the Eight Mile High Club and making it with stewardesses on the way to international games is pure fantasy. It's what I'd like to get up to, rather than an accurate reflection of my sex life.'

'Really?' as she said it, Elizabeth got up from her chair and moved over to the leather sofa on which Chickenfeed was sitting. She put her hand on his knee and pressed her mouth against his lips.

Elizabeth's tongue probed Chickenfeed's mouth and she pushed him onto his back. She was strong. She needed to dominate men and liked to be on top. Chickenfeed didn't mind, he'd always enjoyed variations.

Elizabeth pinned Chickenfeed's arms above his head with her right hand. He lay there in a position of total submission while her left hand worked at his clothes, undoing buttons, pushing and pulling at cloth.

Elizabeth wasn't wearing any underwear. She hitched her skirt around her thighs. Chickenfeed's mind was a blank screen as he entered the site of her mystery. There was no conscious decision to beat out the primitive rhythm of sex. There was no choice, it was inevitable.

There was pounding, and it might have been the rushing of blood through veins. It might have been the crashing of waves on a volcanic beach. It was the primal

137

rhythm. It was a heterosexual couple fucking. The swamps all around them, warm and lush.

Chickenfeed was there on the beach, the first amphibian to crawl out of the sea and feel the chill of the wind on his skin. Elizabeth had descended to the depths of the ocean. They'd turned over during their lovemaking, Chickenfeed was now on top. Elizabeth's arms were above her head, but no hand was restraining them. It was social convention which held them in place.

Chickenfeed was licking Elizabeth's armpits as he pumped his partner up towards orgasm. His face, buried in the depths of her underarm hair, remained a blank mask of ecstacy, of loss, all personality dissolved, or so he imagined. As though one could shed social conditioning in the course of such a socially conditioned act.

Sex inscribed the whole of their lives. The taboos against it. The belief that an uncontrollable urge animates our bodily rhythms. At one and the same time, the penultimate expression of the self and the ultimate dissolution of the personality. Sex, the final frontier. More natural than the natural. It has become the most ritualised aspect of human behaviour, where the triumph of authority is perceived as absolute freedom in some unfathomable loss of control.

Loss of self is the triumph of authority. Power always flows in two directions. At the moment of sex as death, the flow of power has reached a peak in its uneven distribution. Until the moment of resolution, orgasm, the self can offer no further resistance to power. Of course, the self is socially constructed, but paradoxically it is still the most resistive force we can mobilise against the corrosive effects of authority.

Elizabeth and Chickenfeed came together. They imagined the orgasm flooding their twin bulks to be a powerful echo of the force with which the first star exploded. They imagined this primal act as a genetically-encoded memory being played back across time. In actual fact they were experiencing the ultimate flowering of social control. They

138

were not perverts, they were an ordinary man and woman whose personalities had been warped from living in a repressive capitalist society.

They lay exhausted upon the settee. Chickenfeed's hot breath was burning into Elizabeth's ear. Neither awake nor asleep, they were the zombie playthings of an authoritarian system which had broken free of all human control.

'Will you turn our fuck into a scene in your next book?' Elizabeth asked as she stirred.

'You dirty bit.' Chickenfeed caught himself as he remembered who he was with. 'Of course I will, darling!'

'How do you know when to put in a sex scene?' Elizabeth enquired.

'Oh, it's easy,' Chickenfeed replied. 'I have this system where I write four thousand words at each session. It doesn't take long before I get stuck about what to write next, so I just put in a bit of sex to fill up the space.'

'Oh, you're such a genius!' Elizabeth exclaimed. 'Most writers experience agonies over the careful plotting of their books. You don't seem to care.'

'That's the way I am,' Chickenfeed replied. 'You see I hate that literary shit. Of course, I read **Joyce**, **Beckett**, **Robbe-Grillet, Proust** and all that other crap when I was young. But while still a teenager I came to the conclusion that experimentation was a waste of time. You won't even find **Chandler** or **Hammett** on my bookshelves. That stuff is for dopes. And as for people who read existentialist or post modernist texts, they're not even alive. **André Breton** fans make me puke. None of that stuff's writing – it's just snobbery! You'll only find the pulp masters on my book-shelves – **James Moffatt, Donald Franklin, Mick Norman, Hugh Miller** and their ilk!'

'So you're totally in favour of exploitation novels.'

'Of course!' Chickenfeed replied. 'Anything else is dishonest, pretentious and worst of all boring. Anyone who reads that literary stuff has given themselves away as a fake, a no-hoper, a social climber without talent or taste. My ambition is to see every book in the British Library pulped and the resulting paper used for reprints of my work.'

'You're so cool!' Elizabeth exclaimed.

'I can't help being a trendsetter,' Chickenfeed said modestly. 'I've got a head start on everybody because I make absolutely no effort to be fashionable.'

'You should see the review I'm working on,' Elizabeth told him. 'I'm hailing you as the greatest writer since **de Sade**.'

'I'm better than that schmuck!' Chickenfeed pouted.

'I know!' Elizabeth reassured him. 'But the public don't like being told the truth.'

'Wait till they see the book. It'll be out in less than a month!'

'I've seen the finished draft already and I'm astounded!'

Elizabeth put her arms around Chickenfeed and pulled him down on top of her. Their mouths met and Chickenfeed's tongue snaked over her teeth and gums. They gasped ánd clasped. In their minds, foreplay was just a stepping stone to higher states of immoralism.

Chickenfeed was inside Elizabeth. They were beating out the primitve rhythm of the swamps. Pumping up and pumping out. Their orgasms felt like the mythical first star exploding. But it didn't stop there. They kissed and caressed. Fucked again. Rested. Started up. It carried on all afternoon.

Chickenfeed was pleased with his publishers. He'd only given them a copy of the completed manuscript three days ago. After they'd read it, they rushed copies to Elizabeth and several other critics. The typesetting was to be done from Chickenfeed's computer disk and the book would be at the printers within a week.

The property was so hot that the publishers couldn't get it out quick enough. Like most businessmen engaged in porno publishing, they wanted to clean up before a Private Members Bill outlawing erotica had a chance of getting through Parliament. This particular piece of anti-porn legislation had somehow managed to get the backing of all party leaders. Consequently the porn merchants were rushing out as much dodgy material as they could. If the Bill became law they were assured of massive sales immediately before its implementation.

TRACY HAD NEVER FELT SO trapped. Paul had not left her alone for a week. The only break had been when he'd gone to sign on. He'd not even gone home to pick up the social security giro which should have arrived two days later. Tracy was fully aware of what Paul was doing. He was trying to wear down her resistance.

She'd tried going out. Paul had followed her. At first she'd shouted at him to leave her alone. After that he'd let a fifty yard distance develop between them. To Tracy this was worse than having him at her side. After half an hour she gave in and allowed him to walk next to her.

When they went to bed Paul insisted on having sex with her. That was the worst part. It was a nightmare every time. Tracy would try to resist thinking of Edward. Paul would be going crazy because he couldn't bring her to orgasm. Then she'd think of Edward and things would go wild. The word ecstasy didn't do justice to the sensations she'd experience.

'Can't you do anything but stare?' Tracy snapped as she looked up from the beansprout salad she was preparing.

'I could move mountains if you'd promise not to see Case again.'

'We've been though this so many times I've lost count. If I'm blackmailed into making a promise, I'm not very likely to keep it.'

'I'm not blackmailing you.'

'You're trying to make me promise something I don't want to promise.'

'If you loved me you'd make the promise!' Paul insisted. 'I can't imagine a future without you.'

141

'Did I say I wanted to split up with you?' Tracy asked.

'No, but your actions speak louder than your words.'

'For Christ's sake!' Tracy swore.

Then Paul started sobbing. His face went into his hands. Tracy could see the tears running down his forearms. They ran off his elbows and came to rest in little pools on the kitchen table. Tracy put down the knife she was holding, went over to Paul and took him in her arms.

She stood motionless, holding Paul tightly against her body while uncontrollable sobbing wracked his frame. Tears were streaming down his face. His eyes were red. Snot was hanging from his nose.

'You'll be alright,' Tracy tried to reassure him.

'Promise me you won't see Case again.'

'I love you,' Tracy whispered in his ear.

'Promise me,' Paul pleaded.

Tracy tightened her grip on him, and kissed his head.

'It's him or me. Either you promise me now that you'll never see him again or else I'm going and you'll never see me again.'

'I've told you Paul.' Tracy's voice was faltering. She had trouble getting the words out. 'I love you both. I'm not going to make you a promise I can't keep.'

Paul slapped Tracy hard across the cheek, his fingers left dark red marks on her white skin. She released her grip on his body and her hands went to her face. Paul shoved Tracy away, she staggered backwards. Her legs buckled beneath her and she fell to the floor. She was still lying on the floor ten minutes after she'd heard the door slam as Paul left the flat.

THE MOULDERS ARMS WAS AS hot and steamy as a sauna. Sweat dripped from the walls and ceiling. T-shirts and leather jackets stuck to bodies which were jammed so close together that it was almost impossible to move. If you could

142

fight your way to the bar and were lucky enough to get served, you soon discovered that nothing money could buy offered respite from the suffocating atmosphere.

On stage, Christine's voice was becoming hoarse. Still, the band were magic by anyone's standards. Rock and roll had long been recognised as the pounding rhythm of the swamps. Sex was inseparable from rock music. Alienation combined sex and rebellion in a heady mix. Theirs was the kind of glamour that with it London teenagers just couldn't resist!

Come to me and make me come,
Come to me and make me come,
Lick me, suck me, make me sweat,
Lick me, suck me, make me sweat.

It was a new number and the tempo was ultra fast. The words were just right for the night since the pub reeked of teenage bodies, the sweet perfume of sex. But you didn't have to be a teenage nympho to identify with the lyrics Christine was screaming.

Run your tongue along my arse.

Christine shouted, and there were a couple of hundred lads in the audience who given half a chance would have been prepared to get on stage and do just that.

I lose my personality

Christine screamed. Then Alan and Catfish shouted out their response:

In the slaughterhouse of love.

Christine came back with:

I supercede morality.

Then it was Catfish and Alan's turn again:

In the slaughterhouse of love.

Terry Nolan, a soaraway tabloid journalist, was making notes on those lyrics he could catch. What a story this would make. Whoever wrote the songs was nearly as dirty-minded as his editor. And that was saying something! Terry felt like masturbating as he stared at the girl screaming these perverse requests. He was prepared to put his tongue anywhere she asked. Unfortunately there was a story to be written. There'd be time for a wank once he got home to his lonely bed. Terry held on to his note pad with his left hand while the right worked a pen across its pages:

Polymorphous perversity,
In the slaughterhouse of love,
Butcher individuality,
In the slaughterhouse of love,
Dissolve sexual polarity,
In the slaughterhouse of love,
Communist society,
In the slaughterhouse of love.

Terry's brain was working double time. He'd try and get an interview with the group after they'd finished playing. Perhaps he could even pull the bird singer with the promise of a plug for her band in one of the nationals.

Terry was not the only middle-aged man impressed by Alienation's performance. At 45, Derek Jacobs had reached an executive position at the **International Music Corporation** through sheer hard graft and a total lack of feeling for anyone who got in the way of his meteoric rise to success. He'd left school at fifteen and started off as a tea boy to music industry moguls. He'd come a long way from his parents' council house in Plaistow. A mansion in Essex and more modest flats in Chelsea and the Canaries were among the most visible signs of his wealth.

Derek had kept an eye on Alienation since they'd hit headline status in the music papers. Their attack on the Stockbrokers had been a deft move indeed. It marked the collapse of the yuppie rock scene. But more importantly, it meant the music industry needed a new cult to manipulate. And déjà vu with its sort followers was undoubtably the

144

trend best suited to fit the bill. Alienation's music did nothing for Derek. But then Derek didn't like music per se. What he could empathise with was how the group were clawing their way to the top. Here was a band who would make some lucky record company a fortune. Their sexy rebelliousness made them a certainty with the teenage market. Then give it a few years and the act could be toned down enough to induce with it mums and dads to buy their records.

Derek had not seen a group get such a reaction since the halcyon days of punk. What he'd witnessed tonight convinced him that he had to sign the group on the lowest percentage deal he could persuade them to take. And knowing himself as well as he did, it was certain to be very low!

TRACY HADN'T SEEN PAUL FOR three days. She wished it hadn't ended the way it had. There'd been no communication between them at all, except for the five brief notes which Paul had pushed through her letter box. All of them had said more or less the same thing – that he never wanted to see her, or hear from her, again.

Tracy was preparing a beansprout salad when she heard the knock at the door. She wondered who it could be. She wasn't expecting anyone. She thought it might be the gasman. There was a second knock and she knew it wasn't the gasman because he never knocked twice.

Tracy was surprised when she opened the door and saw Paul standing in front of her.

'Can I come in?' The words were slurred and his breath smelt of whisky.

Tracy led Paul through to the kitchen and served him a beansprout salad. She boiled the kettle and put camomile into her tea pot.

'How've you been?' she asked Paul.

'I just wanna die,' he slurred. 'I can't live without you. I've no future without you.'

Then he started crying into his beansprout salad. Tracy put a hand on his shoulder. Before either of them knew what was happening, they were hugging and kissing.

'Will you promise not to see Case again?' Paul asked.

'I dunno,' Tracy replied.

They held each other close. Then Paul started crying again. Gently at first, but the sobbing became increasingly violent. His body was shaking spasmodically. Tracy wondered if he'd slither through her arms as she held him tightly against her chest.

'Promise me, promise me,' Paul was panting between his tears.

'I've been so worried about you,' Tracy said kissing him.

'I should think so too!' Paul managed to pant out as tears still streamed from his eyes. 'You're responsible for the condition I'm in. If you don't promise to stop seeing Case, then you'll be responsible for my death.'

'Paul,' Tracy pleaded, 'don't blackmail me with suicide.'

'I'm not,' he sobbed. 'Suicide will be a lot more humane than the slow death I'm going through. I can't take any more of it.'

Tracy held Paul against her, his tears and snot falling onto her shoulder. Thoughts were flashing through her mind. She loved Paul and she loved Case. But Paul was saying she could only have one of them. She felt trapped with Paul, but, on the other hand, found it flattering that he was so dependent upon her. He needed her and she could not refuse him. 'Paul, I won't see Edward again,' Tracy whispered.

'Do you promise?' the flood of Paul's tears eased off.

'I promise, Paul.'

It was like the lull before a storm. Paul's tears were flowing ten times harder than Tracy had ever seen anybody cry. She held him against her body and told him that she loved him. She stroked his hair and kissed his cheek. She kissed the eyes from which his tears were streaming.

It seemed like a long time but eventually the sobbing subsided. Tracy handed Paul her handkerchief and he blew his nose. The two of them sat down at the table and ate the beansprout salad. They ate in silence and devoured each other with their eyes.

Ten

CASE WAS DISAPPOINTED BY TRACY'S call – but not surprised. He was well aware of the hold Johnson had on her. Somehow he'd known Paul would force Tracy into making an oath of fidelity. On the phone she'd said she'd not be able to contact him for a while. She hoped once things cooled down with Paul they'd be able to see each other as friends.

Edward had been very reasonable about the whole thing. There wasn't much else he could do. He could have abused Tracy, cried, told her she'd been playing with his feelings. These were Johnson's tactics and Case couldn't see any point in adopting them. He'd lost the battle, but not necessarily the war. For the time being, his association with Tracy had been suspended. Giving her a hard time about the fact would only make it more difficult for them to get back together once she realised that Johnson was actually a repulsive little creep.

In any case, Edward felt indebted to the girl. She'd shown him the error of his ways, rescued him from the quagmire into which he'd sunk. Edward knew that in his heart he'd never been a fascist. Nazi cultism had simply provided a cover for all the disappointments he'd suffered in life. Thanks to Tracy he now knew that in his 'soul' he was an eco-revolutionary. His burning ambition was the desire to save (wo)mankind from ecocide.

Case poured himself a generous **Hundred Pipers** and mixed in soda straight from the **Schweppes** bottle. He pulled his battered typewriter to the edge of the desk and began tapping out words. Edward worked at a leisurely pace, pushing the typewriter away as his inspiration ebbed. Then, when he'd poured another whisky and tasted the mix, he'd pull the typewriter back to the edge of his desk and inspiration would flow again.

Edward was adapting himself to natural rhythms. The work he was engaged in was not being 'executed' to pay the bills. His pace was not frantic. For the first time in years he was actually enjoying the act of writing. For too long it had been an exercise in knocking out the required number of words at maximum speed. A case of keeping up the quantity and not worrying about the content.

Edward smiled as he removed a sheet of paper from the carriage. He pushed the typewriter away and poured a Hundred Pipers. Lent back in his chair and 'felt' the words hit him as he read through the draft. He knew he'd hit the nail on the head. It was not a question of creating another 'winner' which the general public would pay to read. All Edward wanted to do was write the truth about the capitalist culture in which he lived.

Edward was not a Marxist. He considered it myopic to foreground a single aspect of social organisation (such as its economic dimension) and then through action within that sphere attempt a revolutionary transformation of society. Edward saw things in their totality and was thus convinced that there is a dynamic interaction between culture (in its normative everyday sense), politics and economics.

As far as Edward was concerned, everything had to be changed. Marxists and anarchists alike tend to ignore the role of high culture in the maintenance of class oppression. Indeed, many Marxists talk about proletarian art as though such an idea is not a contradiction in terms. Art has always been the culture of the ruling elite. For the past two hundred years ruling class culture has been marked by aesthetic distancing which privileges formal innovation over meaning and content.

Ruling class culture is in conflict with the norms of popular taste. Among 'lowbrow' cultural consumers there is a sense of identification with 'their own' culture. So-called plebs harbour a deep seated hatred of formal

149

innovation for its own sake. In pop culture there is generally a sense of going forward, newness, the latest thing, which requires minor changes in the means of formal depiction, but any product which is too much at variance with previous models is doomed to failure.

These different cultural models – and the oppressive role of high culture which is massively subsidised by big business and the state – need to be brought into focus. Case had a plan which would draw attention to the issues involved. He'd been making regular trips to the National Gallery. The draft he was working on represented an attempt at a theoretical explanation of what would soon be decried as a terrorist attack.

PAUL EASED OFF ON TRACY. He couldn't understand why she kept asking him to give her some space. He'd decided to allow her another week before he started hassling again. They'd been together four years so he didn't see why he shouldn't move into her flat. He felt it was his right to do so. After all, Tracy had given him a set of keys so he could get in and out when he wanted.

Paul was hung over. He'd had a heavy session last night. It'd got late and he'd ended up staying in Acton. He caught the headline as he was making his way into the tube station:

COPS ROUND UP VEGAN NUTTERS

it screamed in letters two inches high. Paul stopped and bought a copy of the paper. He got onto an eastbound train and decided he wouldn't read the report until he'd bought himself something to drink.

Paul considered himself lucky. After the hair-burning incident, he'd been ordered to go and see Inspector Paul Stevens at Westminster Police Station. Stevens told him he didn't like to see well-qualified young men getting into trouble. Particularly when they had the same name as him!

Paul got off with a warning and was told he wasn't being prosecuted because he was just a mindless publicity seeker. But if he tried pulling any further stunts the Mets would come down on him like a ton of bricks.

Paul got off at Tottenham Court Road. The newspaper tucked under his arm was still unread. He'd take a look at it once he'd bought some booze. Sweat dripped from his armpits. He was hoping like hell that Tracy had got away. The headline said nutters. That was plural. He hoped they'd got Case, but obviously some of the others had been nicked as well. Paul supposed it was the end of the band. That was a shame because Alienation were doing really well.

Paul bought a bottle of **Hundred Pipers**. He doubled back on his tracks. Soho Square was green and inviting. He hardly noticed the sun as he sat down on a bench drenched in its heat. He placed the newspaper on his lap, opened the whisky bottle and took a swig. Then he looked down at the headline:

COPS ROUND UP VEGAN NUTTERS

He scanned the story beneath:

> **Three youths were arrested in Dalston, East London, in the early hours of this morning as police staged 2am raids on the homes of vegan extremists.**
>
> **The youths, Nigel Berrick (17), Peter Hicks (20), and Michael Jenner (19), have been charged with a series of attacks on cafés in the London area.**

Paul went through the rest of the story. He'd didn't know any of the youths who'd been arrested. Apparently their fingerprints had been found on the car used in the attack on Harry's Diner in Silvertown. They'd also been seen loitering near where the BMW was parked in Hampstead, just before it was stolen.

Paul had been told by Tracy that Case was involved in the Silvertown raid. Tracy had speculated that most, if not all, of the growing number of attacks on cafes were copy-cat actions inspired by the earlier raids but carried out by individuals who had no direct links with Case. Paul couldn't work out where the arrested boys fitted in. He wasn't going to worry about it either! He took another slug of Hundred Pipers, relieved that Tracy was still a free citizen.

CHICKENFEED WAS GRINNING. THE SONG sounded good, not only was he hitting all the right notes in all the right places, he was managing to move around as he did it. Christine's voice was getting stronger every day. Catfish and Wayne would never be great musicians, but they could handle what was required. The sound was gutsy, rock 'n' roll had never been about finesse. Live **Alienation**'s shortcomings didn't matter, in the studio any weaknesses could be cleaned up by the producer, and if necessary session musicians would be brought in to play what the group couldn't do themselves.

Elizabeth Cranshaw was sitting on a plastic chair. She smiled at Chickenfeed. She felt indulgent towards her protégé. She liked to see him enjoying himself. His first book had been published the previous week. She'd hailed him as a poet of the proletarian experience. Most of the other reviews he'd got were extremely snide. Chickenfeed had been criticised for being a pornographer, for failing to distance himself from his writing, for poor plot construction, atrocious dialogue, wooden characterisation. Still, the reports from the shops said **Casual** was selling like hot cakes. And that was what counted!

'Kelvin' wasn't worried by the critical hostility he'd aroused. As he'd said to Elizabeth, **de Sade** had often been criticised for the poor quality of his writing but his work had survived for 200 years whereas that by most of his contemporaries hadn't. 'Kelvin' believed that like de Sade and the great **Richard Allen**, it

152

was his anti-humanism that really got up reviewers' noses. If you didn't believe in all that literary bullshit then they didn't know how to cope with your work.

'Kelvin' had almost completed his follow up – **Yo Boy**. He was now writing an average of ten thousand words a day, and hitting peaks of fifteen thousand. Somehow he still found time to manage the band. He was also learning the bass runs to all the group's songs. Alan didn't know it, but when the opportune time arose Alienation intended to give him the boot. Chickenfeed was preparing to step into his shoes.

As far as Elizabeth understood it, the bass player had been having an affair with the singer but they'd fallen out. She wasn't really interested. Alienation's cacophonous sound was not to her taste. **Bach** or **Mozart** was much more her scene.

'Okay,' Chickenfeed was saying, 'we'll run through **"Victory To The Death Squads"** one more time then we'll knock off for today.'

'It's okay for you!' Wayne complained. 'But we've got to have a rehearsal with Alan this evening.'

'Don't knock it!' Chickenfeed reproached him. 'We're all gonna be stars. If you can just hang on until after we've finalised this contract with IMC, then we'll sack Alan at a time when the move will get us maximum publicity.'

'But why do we have to do the support tour for the **Judas Freaks** with him still in the band?' Christine was demanding.

'Because,' Chickenfeed persisted, 'we've got plenty to keep our names in the papers. We're gonna save sacking Alan until there's a lull in the publicity.'

'I get sick of all your plotting.' Catfish was complaining.

'Look,' Chickenfeed's voice was hard as steel, 'let's just do the song. One. Two. Three. Four!'

Chickenfeed's count-in ended the argument. Christine

was chanting the names of various terrorists and terrorist organisations over a taut backing. Catfish and Chickenfeed came in on the chorus:

**Victory to the death squads
Bringing fear onto the streets,
Victory to the death squads
Its fear of death that makes life sweet!**

Then Christine was chanting the names of more terrorists and more terrorist organisations. Elizabeth was smiling. The words passed right over her head. She was lost in her own train of thought. She'd heard all the stories about sexpots. But 'Kelvin' was the first person she'd met who lived up to them. The pair of them had gone bonking bonkers. Eight times a night just wasn't enough as far as they were concerned. It wasn't surprising either. Kelvin's body had bulges in all the right places and his prick was a pretty nice size too!

Elizabeth was pleased when the song ended. Not because she found the music tiresome – she'd put up with it if it meant her Kelvin was enjoying himself. She was glad because it meant they could go home and bonk. When she said eight times a night wasn't enough for them, she meant they had to do it several times during the day as well. It was the only way they could keep each other satisfied.

Elizabeth had wanted to drive to the rehearsal studio, but Kelvin insisted they take the tube. Since he'd moved into her pad on **Elgin Avenue** they'd taken public transport wherever they went. Kelvin claimed to love the architecture of **Maida Vale** tube station. He'd only been living with Elizabeth for ten days and she'd decided to indulge this particular fetish for a month, before putting her foot down about it. In her book, the **private motor car** would always be superior to public transport because you didn't have to share it with thousands of people you didn't know and didn't want to know.

Getting off the tube, Chickenfeed decided he was sick of Maida Vale. He was sick of West London. Mayfair had lost its attraction. For a week it had been great living in a flat situated at the smart end of Elgin Avenue. But now, having looked at London from both East and West, he realised there was something terribly wrong with the city.

There was no centre, no focal point to London. It was just one vast sprawling suburb. Hundreds of little villages with nothing in common but geographical location. Bloomsbury, Knightsbridge, Hampstead and St John's Wood predominated in terms of prestige. But their boasts were hollow and empty. The ancient London had been obliterated by the dreams of Victorian and Edwardian architects. They'd seen the city as the hub of an empire, but thankfully the empire had been lost. Now the British capital was a sprawling nothingness. Grey, cold and damp. Not even the Blitz had put it out of its misery.

Chickenfeed saw London as a city haunted by its own past, by spectres which will not be exorcised until its inhabitants find the Will to demolish, erase and destroy every last trace of the Victorian era.

Chickenfeed was in Elizabeth's flat. He was making love to his girl. Her pad was better than the squat he'd left behind in Bow. The plumbing amd electrics were brand new. It was kitted out with fitted carpets and plush furniture. But it seemed less of a home than Swaton Road. Here he felt as if he was just another appendage to Elizabeth's fashionable lifestyle. He suspected Liz viewed him more as a sex object than a human being, a toy boy to show off to her friends.

'Kelvin, Kelvin,' she moaned as they beat out the primitive rhythm of sex.

Chickenfeed wished she wouldn't call him Kelvin.

Elizabeth liked variations. Slow and gentle, then hard and fast. Many of the positions they tried weren't even in the Karma Sutra! Chickenfeed performed. He knew he'd

155

go on performing for Elizabeth until a better proposition came along. Someone richer and more powerful. Someone who could do more for his career.

'I love you,' he was panting as his hot breath burnt into Elizabeth's ear.

Elizabeth pretended she was out on the mudflats. Chickenfeed knew very well they were both still in her pad. They came together and Elizabeth imagined the orgasm was a DNA encoded memory of the first star exploding. Chickenfeed was responsible for this particular fantasy. He used the image several times in **Casual**.

To Chickenfeed, an orgasm was an orgasm was an orgasm. People thought he was dirty-minded because of the things he wrote. Actually he was just a normal guy. He liked sex and liked it often! But there were times when he didn't feel like indulging in bedroom athletics and Elizabeth was completely insensitive to these moods.

Elizabeth was grinding her hips against Chickenfeed. His penis was hardening again. He began to pump up the volume.

'You dirty bastard!' Elizabeth screamed. 'Don't you ever want to stop?'

Chickenfeed would have liked to stop, but he wouldn't. Elizabeth was part of his meal ticket to the top, what she wanted he would give. He had become cynical and success was the only thing that seemed to offer any relief from the effects of his condition.

THE TORQUEE CLUB WAS SITUATED in Rupert Street, just off Shaftesbury Avenue. It had started out on Tottenham Court Road in the late fifties. Back then it had been a place where jazz musicians came to play blues on nights off from paid work. As the British blues boom took off, the management realised they could make far more money on the door than from the bar. Through the sixties and seventies the club had been an essential step up the ladder for every rock group hoping to make the big time. For a place that only held four hundred punters it was incredibly prestigous.

The **Judas Freaks** were a tenth generation punk band. Somehow they'd managed to get a deal with the International Music Corporation. Rumour had it one of the Freaks was related to a director of the company. IMC had told them to take Alienation as the support act on their British tour. The Freaks were less than happy about this situation. They knew if the tour went well for the support band, then the success of the déjà vu cult would be guaranteed and not just a faint hope on the part of a few die-hard fanatics. And if déjà vu took off, old punk groups such as the Freaks would be forced out of business!

Alvin Peters, lead guitar and voice with the Freaks, watched Alienation run through their sound check. He was impressed. They were tight, fresh, had a lot of energy. If he'd been a disinterested observer, he'd have become a fan. But since he saw himself as a rival he was worried, bloody worried. This mob would blow his band off stage. They were a new breed of rocker bringing a much needed breath of fresh air to a stale and jaded music scene. A phenomenon likely to dash his own musical ambitions.

The trade papers had associated the Judas Freaks with the déjà vu scene and this had boosted their publicity rating. But soon it would become obvious to everyone that the Freaks were left-overs from an older generation. There were a lot of similarities with '76. Back then, pub bands like **Doctor Feelgood** and **Eddie and the Hot Rods** had been mistaken for punk acts and reaped an initial benefit. But there'd been a backlash once it was recognised that the brand of boogie blasted out by the Feelgoods and Rods lacked the piledriving energy and critical edge of punk rock.

The Judas Freaks had been invited to take part in the **First European Festival of Déjà Vu** at Arras in France. Peters knew that Alienation had been invited to take part too. This did not please him. Nevertheless, the Freaks had accepted their manager's advice and decided to appear at the event.

Alienation's sound was good – too good. Peters walked over to Fred, the PA man they'd hired to do the sound on this tour. Fred nodded to Peters and held out the joint he'd been smoking. Peters took it and sucked hard – drawing the smoke down into his lungs. The 'toke' helped relax him. This tour was important. It could make or break not just the Freaks' career, but the entire déjà vu cult.

'Fred,' Peters said softly. 'You're a great soundman. The mix you've organised for Alienation is just a little too good. Do you understand my meaning?'

Fred understood, it was standard practice to give support groups a terrible sound, to fix it with the PA man for them to have a rough time with 'faulty' equipment which will be miraculously patched up by the time the headliners come on. Normally Fred wouldn't have worked so hard on the sound for a support act, but for this tour he'd received special instructions.

'I'd like to help you Alvin,' Fred's voice was shaky. 'Honestly I would. But I've had orders.'

'I'm giving you orders,' Peters said coldly.

'I'd like to obey them but I can't.' Worry lines creased Fred's forehead.

'I'm your employer,' Peters said as he took the other man's T-shirt in his hand and screwed it into a ball. 'You'll do as I say.'

'I'd like to, honestly I'd like to!' Fred was visibly shaking. 'But I've had orders. Derek Jacobs told me to give this group a good mix. He said if he had any complaints from the band or their management he'd personally ensure that I never work for an IMC act again.'

'Fuck Jacobs! You'll do as I say!' Peters screamed.

'I'm afraid I've got to obey Derek. I'm sorry Alvin, but you're just one band. Derek could force me out of business

158

if he felt like it. He's a mean bastard, I wouldn't like to cross him.'

Peters screwed his face into a mask of rage. He lashed out with his fist and heard the satisfying crunch of splintering bone as the blow connected with his victim's jaw. Fred staggered backwards spitting out gouts of blood and the occasional piece of broken tooth. The PA man hit a wall and slid to the floor. Then Peters' boots went in – HARD. The agony as the steel toe-capped DM's rained in against ribs and skull was almost unbearable, for Fred unconsciousness came as a much needed relief.

THE TORQUEE FILLED QUICKLY. MUSIC industry types crowded the bar. Street kids whose curiosity had been aroused by déjà vu packed the area immediately in front of the stage. They'd read about the cult in the music papers and wanted to find out more.

The Judas Freaks had a following of sorts, but they'd never managed to attract a loyal army of supporters in the South-East. Although the lads were all Londoners, the group had actually formed in Newcastle. Alvin had been a student at the University while bassist Gary Green and drummer Darren Volk were studying at Newcastle Polytechnic. Their following in the North-East was loyal and a few Geordies had made the trip down to London to support the group on the first date of their tour. They needed that support because the success of this London date was crucial if they were going to up their media rating this time around.

Provincial kids would take a while to catch on to déjà vu, but in the capital word was already out. Teenagers had come from as far as Ealing, Brent Cross, Ilford and Wimbledon to see Alienation at the Torquee. It was the first time the group had played in one of the city's more reputable venues. The club was was accessible to kids from every area of Greater London.

There were, of course, many loyal followers from Hackney and Tower Hamlets. But the most vocal supporters were from a North London suburb. The **Finchley Philistines** outnumbered their nearest rivals for Alienation's affection by nearly two to one. This rivalry had been approaching explosive proportions at recent gigs. It was not helped by the fact that the two factions came from different sides of the river.

The **Merton Malcontents** were some of South London's finest. They felt their claim to **Alienation** equalled that of any Cockney or North Londoner. The group members might live in the East End but that was not where they were from. Catfish was born in Lewisham and brought up in Orpington. Christine was born in Merton and lived in Wimbledon until she was ten, before spending eight years in Raynes Park. Alan and Wayne were from Hounslow and Twickenham respectively.

There has always been a rivalry between the various parts of London. South Londoners are rightly proud of their origins. After all, they've given the world **Charlie Chaplin**, **Ken Livingston** and **Michael Caine**, among many others. And theirs is the part of London which has best resisted take-over by yuppie scum. North Poplar might be forever cockney, but that's only because the place is a complete fucking dump. Hackney, the Isle of Dogs and the cockney heartland of Bow were long ago overrun by young businessmen searching for homes near the City.

North Londoners, too, considered their culture quite distinct from that of East, West or South. Islington and Camden might have been lost to the trendies, but in Finchley you could still feel proud of your roots. The Cockneys had Roman Road, South London Lavender Hill and Lambeth Walk, but North London could flatten all comers with the M1!

160

Jed, the unchallenged leader of The Philistines, had lived in North London all his life. As a teenager he'd gone in for squatting abandoned properties located in Stoke Newington and Stamford Hill. He'd lived out of Finchley for five long years but eventually felt the need to return.

Chickenfeed had named the Philistines. He'd been talking to Jed about the need to possess a cultivated philistinism. To know all about art and literature and yet still prefer **Spillane** to **Beckett**, **Moffatt** to **Joyce**. Chickenfeed had emphasised the necessity of having a class analysis of culture and Jed had agreed with every word. When the others had been given this explanation of why they were to be called the Finchley Philistines they'd not understood it. But they'd gone along with the idea because they figured Chickenfeed and Jed would know what was what.

The Malcontents were led by Claire Dickson, a nineteen-year-old nutter who craved all the excitement she could get. Whereas Jed made derogatory references to places north of Watford, Claire hated anything to be found north of the Thames. Her reputation stretched to Waterloo and that was as far north as she deemed desirable. In her manor people did what she said.

Both the Malcontents and the Philistines had considered it uncool to turn up early for the gig. As a result they found themselves battling through the seven hundred who'd been turned away after being told the event was a sellout. Claire and Jed arrived at the door within seconds of each other. Claire managed to get there just before her rival.

'What do ya mean I can't go in?' she shouted. 'I'm on the guest list, and so are my friends.'

'Name?' The bouncer demanded.

'Claire Dickson.'

The bouncer looked down the list and found the name. He jerked his thumb up the club's corridor and Claire walked in. Jed got in too. They both made straight for the dressing room.

'You've got to get John, Susie, Geoff and Alastair in,' Claire screamed at Chickenfeed as Jed pushed his way in behind her.

'Fuck them!' Jed spat. 'You've got to get my pals onto the guest list. There's nine Philistines out there who are loyal fans. Don't muck about. Get them in quick!'

'We're on in five minutes,' Wayne chipped in.

'Well hurry up man!' Jed was screaming. 'There's no time to lose.'

'Fuck his mob!' Claire shouted. 'Just make sure you get the Malcontents in.'

'Go and open the back door,' Chickenfeed commanded. 'I'll lead them round to it.'

Chickenfeed was as good as his word. He got the two rival gangs in. He steered them away from the dressing rooms, directed them into the main part of the club. Claire and Jed led their respective crews as they pushed their way to the front of the stage.

Seconds later, **Alienation** launched into **Fuck Off**, the first song in their set. Chickenfeed was straining to hear the words. The mix was all wrong. You couldn't hear the vocals at all, only a lip reader would have known that Christine was screaming 'Turn my mike up,' instead of singing the lyric.

The drums were drowning out the guitar and the bass was barely audible. Onstage the group were wondering why they weren't getting any sound on the foldback.

Chickenfeed fought his way to the mixing desk. He knew Derek Jacobs had given the PA man, Fred, strict instructions that they were to have a decent mix. Fred wasn't at the desk. Toad, one of the Freaks' personal roadies was controlling the sound. Chickenfeed shoved his way through the crowd. He caught Claire's attention, then Jed's.

The noise was deafening but Chickenfeed was able to make himself understood with gesticulations. He hardly had to do more than point at the mixing desk. The two gang leaders fought their way through the crowd. Claire reached Toad first. She slammed a right hook into his mouth. The roadie staggered backwards and slid to the floor spitting out gouts of blood and the occasional piece of broken tooth.

Claire had done all she could. She'd been determined to get to the mixing desk first and do over the roadie. She didn't have a clue about how the equipment worked, that was Jed's speciality. The Philistine came up behind her and pushed her out of the way. The band had stopped playing.

'There's nothing coming through on the monitors!' Christine shouted.

Jed didn't catch the first part of what she was saying. But he got the word monitors because he'd turned her mike up before she screamed it. Jed adjusted the foldback, turned up the bass, took down the drums.

The band went into **Leave Me Alone**. It sounded a bit muddy but at least you could hear everything. Jed made further adjustments to the instrument levels. The band was tight. Their confidence increased as the wonders Jed was working at the mixing desk came back through the monitors. The group were scorching by the time they finished the song.

Toad twitched and so Claire laid into him with her steel-toe-capped boots. She could see him screaming but the sound was drowned out by Alienation's sweet music. Claire lashed out again and again. First with her right foot, then with her left.

Jed grinned at Claire, he was enjoying himself. He knew he made a good soundman and was sure Alienation would make use of his services in the future. He had more to offer them than Claire. She knew this too, and so left him on his own at the mixing desk. It didn't take her long to make her way to the front of the stage.

After the band finished – and they'd run way over schedule because the audience demanded three encores – a

163

bouncer came up to Jed and grabbed hold of the scruff of his neck.

'Did you operate the PA after the soundman got a kicking?' the bouncer demanded.

'Sure,' Jed replied. 'But only so the group could finish their set. I don't know anything about how he got beat up. Seems to me whoever did it wanted to fuck up Alienation's act.'

'He was the second mixing desk operater to get beat up tonight,' the bouncer said gruffly. 'I can't blame the first one on you because I saw you come in after it happened. However, since you've obviously got an ear for music, you can do the mix for the Judas Freaks. If you've got any objections I'll hand you over to the cops as prime candidate for a GBH charge.'

'I'll do the mix for the headliners.' Jed smiled sweetly as he said it.

Jed knew just what to do. He was more subtle than the Freaks had been. The mix they got wasn't atrocious, just poor. And when he got complaints, he had the perfect excuse. He was doing what sounded right to him. It was the best he could do in view of the fact that he wasn't familiar with the Judas Freaks' sound.

Eleven

IT WAS FIVE O'CLOCK AND Alienation had been in the historic town of Guildford for thirty-five minutes. Catfish didn't like the place. Surrey University was one of those red brick developments nestled on a hillside well away from the main shopping areas. It was a product of that post-war affluence and optimism which no longer played a role in the daily life of the benighted British Isles.

Technically Guildford was a city. It had a cathedral and the remains of a castle. But the atmosphere on its cobbled High Street was closer to that of a village. Living in one of the most exclusive parts of London's stockbroker belt, Guildford's inhabitants enjoyed the benefits of county - if not country - life; while even British Rail was capable of speeding them to their high-powered jobs in the capital in less than forty minutes.

Traditionally Guildford's youth got to see the mid-range rock acts at either the beginning or end of their tours. These were the bands who'd play thirty dates across the country in as many days. The town was far enough away from the capital to have a distinctive' local scene. Lots of teenagers attended local rock concerts to be seen as much as to see the bands who performed.

The Judas Freaks and Alienation had been booked to play at the University. It was less prestigious than the Civic Hall, which could hold two thousand. Still, a good act at the University would attract a thousand paying customers. While the Civic offered plush seating, the Student Ents committee thought standing only was just fine for the sheep they herded into the college gym. There, students and non-students alike let their hair down to live rock music.

Alienation were seated in a student bar. Unfortunately

they couldn't get anything to drink because there were a couple of hours to go before opening time – and the booze had been carefully locked away. An air of gloom hung over the group. They'd played out of London for the first time a few weeks before. A one-off gig in Stoke, and then another the following night in Burton-on-Trent. To be told they weren't going to play tonight was a blow. The fact that the Judas Freaks had told them they wouldn't have them on the tour was a real piss off. Especially when they'd gone to the trouble of driving out of London to play.

'They're just jealous because we blew them off stage last night,' Catfish reflected.

'Fucking wankers!' Wayne swore.

'What do we do?' Christine wanted to know.

'I'll phone Derek Jacobs and see what he says.' As manager, Chickenfeed felt he had to take some sort of initiative.

Alan was the only one who remained silent throughout everything. He was becoming more and more withdrawn. He knew something had gone wrong in his relationship with Christine. They still slept together but she didn't seem to enjoy the sex. He had recurrent nightmares about the expresso murders and that psychopath Case. But he didn't have the guts to go into a police station and admit to the part he'd played in that brutal crime. He was just letting things slide while three Dalston lads were being prosecuted for his sins.

'Jacobs says he'll throw the Freaks off IMC if they don't let us play,' Chickenfeed announced as he strode back into the room. 'And the Freaks and their manager say they don't care. They say they'll get another contract, because they've no intention of letting us play.'

'Shit!' Wayne screamed. 'What the fuck can we do?'

'I've spoken to the Entertainments Secretary and he says there's nothing he can do.'

'Well, lets piss off home then,' Catfish suggested.

'No,' Chickenfeed's voice was hard, 'there'll be friends

and fans down from London to see us. We've got to be here to chat to them even if we don't play. I'm still hoping to sort something out. I phoned Paul, he knows this neck of the woods, knows people round here from way back. He's given me a few phone numbers with which I should be able to arrange an impromptu gig. I think we're still in business.'

CHICKENFEED WAS AS GOOD AS his word. The back room of the Star Hotel was not a particularly glamorous venue but the band had played in worse. They'd managed to hire a 200 watt PA with three mikes for forty quid. A bit on the steep side considering the condition it was in. The place they'd got it from offered to send a guy to operate it for an extra thirty quid. Chickenfeed had vetoed that. The people at the shop were crazy if they thought he'd pay for someone to operate a vocal PA. Perhaps they just tried it on with everyone.

Christine and Chickenfeed hung around at the University, waiting for fans to appear so that they could direct them to the Star. The rest of the band were in the back room of the pub doing a sound check. There was no support act and the entrance fee was a measly quid.

All in all, about thirty-five kids made the trip from London to see Alienation. Warned about the situation at the university, they headed straight to the Star. Tracy and Paul appeared with a couple of their mates from the Vegan Movement. Derek Jacobs arrived in a Mercedes to tell the Judas Freaks that he, personally, would make sure they never worked again. Then he too made his way to the Star.

A hundred locals turned up. They were indecisive about what to do. The hipper ones had read about Alienation in the music press and realised this was the band to see. But they had to persuade uncool mates that **Alienation** were, indeed, a clenched fist rammed hard into the flabby belly of what rock had become. The lower entrance fee at the Star was an important factor for some kids. It would mean they could afford a couple of extra pints from their pocket money.

The University Ents committee opened their doors and a gaggle of teenagers paid to get in. All ten of them were students. They didn't feel safe if they wandered too far from the campus. A group of twenty kids decided to go to the Wooden Bridge where three local acts were playing. Neither of the out-of-town bands had much of a name and a gig without a support act just wasn't value for money. Another group of ten decided they weren't interested in any of the music going on that night. They headed to the Britannia to chat up the local talent.

After much arguing fifty teenagers decided to go to the Star with Christine and Chickenfeed. They left twenty kids behind them who couldn't make up their minds about what they wanted to do. They were still bickering when local reporter David Henry chanced upon them. Once he realised what was going on his eyes lit up. He was struck by one of those flashes of inspiration common to men of genius. The headline **Battle Of The Bands** flashed through his mind. His own paper would pay him to cover this, then he could resell the story to one of the music weeklies at a handsome profit and without needing to do any extra work.

Dale Griffin, the Star's landlord, smiled when he saw the 90 plus teenagers crammed into the back room of his pub. He'd only charged the group a tenner to hire it out because he'd counted on making a packet from the sale of booze. As a young man he'd taken part in the uprisings of '68. He'd been at Hornsey when the art school was occupied. But seeing his teenage rebellion turned into profits for pop groups and other counter cultural entrepreneurs, he'd decided that diligent pursuit of the almighty quid paid better than chanting revolutionary slogans.

Griffin quit art school and moved to a bedsit in Notting

168

Hill Gate. From here he'd studied the local bohemians and churned out sensational paperbacks under a series of pen names. The hipsters he based his books upon thought Griffin bought them drinks because he was lonely. But while they lazed about failing to complete threatened literary classics, Griffin knocked out eight novels a year. In Griffin's eyes, it was a sick joke that those intransigents who shouted loudest about the necessity of revolutionising everyday life, never got off their arses to do anything more than spray quotes from **Coleridge** on local walls.

He'd never been able to fathom the punk thing and by that time was sick of writing anyway. With the royalties he'd amassed from his novels, Griffin had bought the pub in Guildford. Of course, he'd never been able to admit his previous occupation to the locals. The older ones tended to read **Penguin Classics**, the youngsters anything put out by **Picador**. Guildford was a pretentious town and if anyone ever unearthed Griffin's past, he'd be looked upon as crude. Not that any of them would ever match his sixty-plus book output. They were all too busy making fortunes with their stocks and shares to write anything more than their signatures on documents which would make them yet more dosh. Literature was just a prop to their lifestyle, a signifier of their upper middle class status.

Griffin retreated to the main bar when Alienation launched their set with a raucous rendition of their terrace anthem **Aggro Addict**. In the sixties Griffin had grooved to the likes of **Jimi Hendrix** and **The Cream**. For the past decade he'd bored himself stiff listening to **Mozart** and **Bach** so his neighbours would think of him as cultured. These days it was only when he was making a long distance trip in his MG that he allowed himself the luxury of blasting out **Electric Ladyland** on his in-car stereo.

Chickenfeed had ripped off the chorus and title for **Aggro Addict** from a **Richard Allen** pulp classic called **Glam**. Unfortunately he wasn't able to rip off an entire lyric because Allen had included no more than the chorus in the

169

book. The guitar was hard and driving. Catfish had nicked the main riff from an old **Vibrators** song. The chorus chords came from an obscure number by the **Art Attacks**. The middle eight was stolen from **Slaughter and the Dogs**.

Arsehole came next and it was an established stage favourite. Normally the whole band sang the chorus. But tonight Christine held out her mike so that the London kids who knew the words could sing the song. Alan and Catfish helped out with the backing:

**Arsehole, Wanker, Shitbag, Scum,
Plonker, Dickhead, Extension, Length!**

There was a piercing lead break in the first half of each verse, then Catfish strummed a few fast chord changes before it was back into the chorus.

The London kids went ape. The locals stood behind them and gaped, they'd never seen anything like it. Most of them got it together to applaud between songs – a handful were too stunned to manage even that.

David Henry caught the beginning of the Judas Freaks set but soon left in disgust. The fact there'd only been thirty kids dotted about the massive hall hadn't helped. He'd gone to the Wooden Bridge next. There he'd found forty teenagers downing lagers as a very dodgy local act failed to get them out of their seats. A lone groover, who Henry clocked as the singer's girlfriend, was getting down on her 'thang' as the band murdered **Solomon Burke's** soul classic **Everybody Needs Somebody To Love**.

He'd missed the first few numbers of Alienation's set and deeply regretted it. Their gutsy sound made him realise how stale most music had become. He'd not seen anything as exciting since **The Clash** played at the Guildford club **Bunters** back in '76. That was the gig which converted Henry into a punk aficionado. Now Alienation had won him over to déjà vu. Theirs was a rock *de luxe*. A revolt into style. A sound that summed up the anger and frustration of an entire generation. His editor wasn't going to like the

170

lyrical content, but he could gloss over the verbals in his write-up for the local press. If challenged later he'd claim he'd been unable to make out the words.

Alienation played five encores and could have taken several more. The landlord tried telling them they'd run over time but to no avail. He'd never been much of an authoritarian and felt it was mean to actually pull the plugs on them. His second trick worked, however. He grabbed hold of a mike and announced that anyone who was heading back to London had better leave immediately because the last train would be pulling out of the station in ten minutes. It was a blatant lie, but the hardcore following fell for it. There wouldn't be room to take very many of them back in the van.

Derek Jacobs told Chickenfeed to come to his office at 11am the next morning so they could discuss a contract. Wayne was in the ladies' toilet with the sixteen year old daughter of a top city financier. She'd told him her name was Miranda. Wayne had forgotten it by the time he got her knickers down.

There they were, in a tiny cubicle pounding out the primitive rhythm of the swamps. Their body odour boogie overpowering the smell of bleach and disinfectant. They pumped up the volume and set the controls for the heart of the sun. When they came both of them imagined the sensation to be a genetically encoded recording of Alienation's scorching set.

Miranda wrote her name, address and telephone number on a piece of paper and gave it to Wayne. Wayne shoved it into his pocket, promising he'd stay in touch. He had no intention of doing so and wondered whether Miranda really expected to see him again. There were plenty more dolly birds where she came from.

IT TOOK UNTIL MIDNIGHT TO get everything packed up. Then the PA had to be dropped off at the house where the

171

music shop's manager lived. His pad on the London Road wasn't difficult to find. From there it was onto the A3 and back home. Chickenfeed was glad it was Wayne's turn to drive the van. He was tired and would have to get up early tomorrow if he was going to get to Jacobs' office on time.

Chickenfeed was dropped off in Elgin Avenue at 1.40am. He ate a bowl of cornflakes before creeping up to bed. He'd hoped Elizabeth would be asleep. She wasn't.

When he got into bed she put her arms around him. Their mouths met. Chickenfeed's tongue darted into Elizabeth's open gob. He ran his hands down her back and brought his thigh up against her crotch. She was sticky and getting wetter every second.

Chickenfeed had found a way of dealing with her almost insatiable sexual demands. If he was in the mood when she wanted sex then he just grooved. If he'd had more than he could take then he imagined she was someone else. This trick certainly kept his interest up. Most often he'd pretend she was Tracy, but the pop singer **Kim Wilde** was also a firm favourite in his fantasy stakes. Tonight he was pretending Elizabeth was Kim.

Elizabeth rolled and forced him onto his back. Chickenfeed was not quite ready to plumb the sticky depths of her desire. She was trying to get him inside her, but he kept shifting his weight. 'Fuck me you bastard!' she screamed hoarsely.

'No,' Chickenfeed replied, 'I'm just a tease.'

He kept it up for a few minutes, then conceded defeat and plunged his plonker into the depths of her genetic mystery. They beat out the primitive rhythm of sex. Elizabeth grabbed Chickenfeed's arms and pinned them behind his head. She fixed her mouth on his, her tongue dripping with saliva. Her body slithered. She was no longer conscious of Chickenfeed's bulk, it was the mudflats that called her.

Chickenfeed was still concentrating on his fantasy. Imagining that it was Kim who was demanding he fuck her. Imagining that he'd agreed after she'd treated him to a private rendition of **Chequered Love** accompanied by a strip *de luxe*. His eyes were closed and in his imagination he was inside Kim's cunt. It was her mouth against his. Her hair falling across his face.

Eventually Chickenfeed let the most deep-rooted aspects of his social conditioning take control of his body. Now he too could smell salty air blowing across the mudflats.

Elizabeth and Chickenfeed's body odour boogie had advanced way past the middle eight. They'd sung the final verse and were pumping up the volume on the chorus, running through it twice. The orgasm swept through their twin bulks in an explosion of fluid. They imagined the sensation to be a mark of their break with consensus reality. They'd reached that point at which atomised individuals no longer recognise the root cause of their immiseration.

Elizabeth pulled on Chickenfeed's shoulder and rolled so they were lying on their sides, facing each other. She moved gently and Chickenfeed got the idea. This time Elizabeth wasn't in a hurry to reach a climax. A long and very slow screw was great after deep sex, but Elizabeth couldn't fathom the kinks of those who regularly used this position. She'd never understand people who didn't go in for more energetic kicks, who didn't indulge their desire for variations because they were afraid of being labelled perverts or sexists. In Elizabeth's book, trendies who mouth off about egalitarian sex are actually practising some peculiar brand of masochism.

EDWARD CASE WAS WELL PLEASED with the way things were going. Since the cops had nicked the so called 'Dalston Three', there'd been a lot of sympathy attacks on cafés in their support. Suddenly thousands of anonymous kids up and down the country were clashing head on with the immorality of the cash crop economy. And the plethora of copycat actions carried out against cafes left Case free to concentrate on other targets.

London, like all 'ancient' cities, has certain areas in which specific types of sales and service outlets have congregated. If you're rich, you go to Harley Street to find a doctor, Hatton Garden for jewels, Savile Row for tailors, Cork Street for paintings – and, of course, the Charing Cross Road for books.

The road runs south from Oxford Street to within a couple of hundred yards of Trafalgar Square. It marks the Eastern boundary of Soho and functions as a major tourist route. It's possible to visit every bookshop in the street over a period of a few hours and remain anonymous, because thousands of shoppers are doing exactly the same thing. Case exploited this fact when he launched his assault on the printed word.

Edward was carrying several bags filled with books. This was not unusual, there were customers from all over the world using a series of specialist shops to make hard-to-find purchases. But instead of buying books, Case left one in each retail outlet.

Edward was an experienced shoplifter. He knew that to avoid drawing attention to his actions it was best to go early in the morning when there were few 'customers' about. That way he could place his books in obscure parts of each shop when no one was looking. Later on, when the street became crowded, you could never tell whether the person next to you was an innocent shopper or a malicious store detective.

The amount of explosive you can pack into a slim paperback is limited. When you add wiring and a timing device you reduce the potential power of your bomb still further. But even a small amount of explosive material can be deadly. Particularly when detonated in a confined area where there's plenty of paper to catch fire.

The explosions began just after 9pm. By five past the whole of Charing Cross Road was in flames. Everywhere firemen were battling to prevent the gutting of buildings. The cops were fighting a losing battle to keep journalists out of the street. The police tried to be polite. They didn't want to blacken the media image of their profession still further. The newshounds exploited this fact. They ran rings around the custodians of law and order, getting their stories and simultaneously lowering police morale.

Several newspapers received anonymous phone calls telling them to check out the slogans daubed around the area. The graffiti had appeared over the previous week. The bombings made its meaning horrifyingly clear:

STUMPS SUCK
  NO TO DEFORESTATION
SAVE OUR ENVIRONMENT
  SAVE THE BOG LEMMING
READING MAKES YOU GO BLIND
  RONNIE LEE'S VEGAN ARMY RULES O.K.!
McDONALD'S IS NEXT
  WILDERNESS PRESERVATION BEGINS IN THE CITY

There could be no doubt about the fact that the fires were started deliberately. The next day not a single bookshop was open on the Charing Cross Road. Newpapers headlined their stories with references to evil vegans. No longer was this new breed of agitator being jokingly referred to as 'nutty' or 'bananas'. The reportage was sombre and deadly serious. The environmental war was heating up. No one had died this time but vegans had demonstrated once again that they could be as much of a menace to Western-style democracy as the Angry Brigade or the IRA.

THE PARTY WAS TO CELEBRATE the fact that **Alienation** had been offered a recording contract by IMC. And, in particular, the fact that they'd turned the company down! Other labels were interested, IMC were the most prestigious but there was no way Chickenfeed was going to accept a measly 3 per cent royalty rate. After all, he took 50 per cent of Alienation's earnings as a management fee before the band even saw a penny. So he was going to make damn sure they got a fair whack when they put their names on the dotted line.

The party was in Swaton Road. Catfish had locked his room. Books, records and clothes were disappearing from Paul's room at an alarming rate. But no one would have to worry about it until Monday. Paul had stuck to a long standing arrangement to go and stay with some friends in Norfolk over the weekend.

Elizabeth and Chickenfeed arrived early. Elizabeth left after an hour, declaring that it was not really her scene. She decided to race off and meet some friends at **Stringfellows** instead of staying until things started to swing.

The **Finchley Philistines** also arrived early. They were well liked by the band but it was a pain in the arse when they began to square off against the **Merton Malcontents**. Jed's mob had planned on arriving before the Malcontents, and were rather pissed off to discover they hadn't.

'We could 'ave you any day!' Jed spat as he jabbed a finger at Claire.

'Listen,' Claire spat back, 'you might 'ave the numbers but we'll still slaughter you if it comes to an aggro.'

'Look,' Catfish put in, 'I don't want me 'ouse wrecked so just forget it.'

'I can't forget it,' Claire said, 'he's just insulted the Malcontents.'

'I'm gonna teach her that North London rules!' Jed screamed.

'Well,' Catfish looked from one to the other, 'if you must 'ave it out, then it should be just the two of you.'

Jed tried to hit Claire in the mouth.

'Hold on,' Catfish said placing himself between them. 'If you're gonna 'ave a fight, then you 'ave it in the garden.

176

And just to make it a bit more interesting let's say that the loser has to lick the winners arse.'

'Okay,' Claire replied. 'Only he should realise it's a privilege to lick my arse. I'll only let him do it because I'm so magnanimous.'

'I'll make you eat shit!' Jed spat.

Claire and Jed marched into the back yard. A circle of revellers gathered round and urged them on. Tracy remained inside. She didn't want to see any violence. She was deeply depressed. Things with Paul just got worse and worse. If she hassled him enough he'd leave her alone for a day or two. He claimed he understood her need for space, but any that she got she'd had to fight for.

The worst thing was the sex. She didn't find Paul physically attractive any more, she didn't want to screw him. Paul refused to understand this. He was always putting his hand up her skirt and grabbing a free feel. Suggesting they go to bed. When they did it was awful. She felt nothing and couldn't come. Then he'd get angry about her not having an orgasm. She knew how to get one so she'd imagine it was Edward on top of her rather than Paul. Then she'd find the pleasure almost unbearable. She wanted Case so much and she was trying so hard to be loyal to Paul.

Tracy drained her glass. She poured another Hundred Pipers. Alan was sitting across from her. He'd hardly said a word all evening. She knew he was in a bad way. The deaths at the cafe had really shaken him up. She was worried about the Dalston Three. She thought she ought tell the cops what had really happened. But she couldn't bring herself to drop the others in the shit.

She didn't want to see Case put inside. He'd be the one who suffered most. And he'd committed those murders because he loved her. She wanted to make a full confession, but couldn't. She drained her glass and poured another Hundred Pipers. As she did so she decided to get gloriously drunk. She needed some kind of release.

177

Jed's fighting technique was anything but subtle. He did not believe that Claire, a mere girl, could present a serious challenge to his supremacy. It was somewhat degrading to go through the motions of flattening her.

Jed charged. He was running at full speed intending to head butt his opponent. Claire sidestepped and swung out with her fist. There was the satisfying crunch of splintering bone as her knuckles connected with Jed's mouth. Even if she hadn't put considerable force into the punch, Jed's momentum would have made the blow devastating.

The Philistines' leader staggered backwards spitting out gouts of blood and the occasional piece of broken tooth. He stumbled and fell flat on his back. The impact of the fall was the straw that broke the camel's back for his reeling senses. He lay there unconscious.

Catfish disappeared into the house and the reappeared with a bucket of cold water, a bottle of Hundred Pipers and a clean white handkerchief. The guitarist splashed water onto the Philistine's face. Jed came round and took a slug from the proffered bottle of whisky. Taking the hand-kerchief from Catfish, he dabbed it against his bloodied mouth.

Wayne and Catfish helped Jed to his feet and led him through to the lounge. Claire was standing in the middle of the room with her trousers around her ankles. The lounge was filled with revellers and there was a burst of applause when Jed knelt in front of the proffered arse.

The Philistine licked. He liked the taste. Sex was all about sweat, shit, piss and come. Although on this occasion the rim job was a humiliation, he'd have really got into it if he'd been alone in his bedroom with Claire. She was a damned attractive woman on top of being able to get the better of him in a fight. They'd finally sorted things out between the Philistines and the Malcontents. The tension between the two groups had disappeared. It had been publicly accepted that South London ruled the roost.

As Jed licked he tried to force his hand between

Claire's legs, but she moved away. Claire pulled up her jeans. She looked Jed over. He didn't do badly in the beefcake stakes, had bulges in all the right places. She'd have his balls out very soon. But she would not make love to him now, or in public. Whatever else happened, Claire was determined to maintain her dominant position.

Sorts were dancing to **Chirpy Chirpy Cheep Cheep**, an anthem which summed up a decade. The song appeared at least once on each side of the tapes Chickenfeed had made for the party. Everyone was drunk. Chickenfeed had splashed out on booze – from band expenses, of course!

Tracy was virtually legless. She was sitting next to Claire, trying to explain to the Malcontent the problems she'd been having with her boyfriend. Claire couldn't hear what she was saying above the music and just looked bemused. Tracy didn't think about what she was doing. She put her arms around Claire and started kissing her.

Claire accepted the situation and enjoyed the sensation as Tracy's tongue probed her mouth. She put her arms around Tracy and closed her eyes.

Chickenfeed noticed the scene between Claire and Tracy. When Claire got up to get a drink he plonked himself down where the Malcontent had been sitting. Tracy put her arms around Chickenfeed and started kissing him. Chickenfeed couldn't believe it. This was what he'd been dreaming of for so long! A lot of people at the party knew he'd fancied Tracy for years and so his couch session with her did not pass unnoticed.

When Chickenfeed led Tracy out of the room most of those present assumed he was going to screw her. She was so drunk he was more or less carrying her. Alan, Wayne, Christine and many others did not approve. They didn't think very highly of Chickenfeed for taking advantage of the state she was in.

Chickenfeed had a hard time getting Tracy back to her flat. He carried her down to the bedroom and proceeded to undress her. Tracy was slurring words incoherently, could

179

hardly keep her head straight. Chickenfeed undressed himself. He got into bed with Tracy and began to kiss her. She kissed him back. Chickenfeed worked his thigh against her pubic mound. He reached down, found her clitoris and began to rub it with his index finger. Once she'd juiced up, he entered her. Tracy liked the feel as Chickenfeed's cock plumbed the depth of her mystery, but she was too drunk to actively contribute to their pleasure. Chickenfeed managed to come but there was no way he could bring his partner to orgasm.

Tracy fell asleep, Chickenfeed got up and dressed. He felt disgusted with himself. This had not been what he'd dreamed of for so long. He hoped Tracy was too drunk to remember what had happened. He'd claim he'd just taken her home and put her to bed.

Chickenfeed walked down to the taxi office on St Leonard's Road. His heart sank as he paid off the cab in Elgin Avenue. The lights were on, Elizabeth was awake. He didn't want any more sex tonight. . .

Twelve

THE LINE OF TEENAGE SORTS stretched several hundred yards down Tottenham Court Road. They were queuing to get into the Cyclops Club, a former strip joint which had taken to booking **Alienation** for weekly gigs. These were well attended and so having tested the atmosphere, the management announced a two-day event entitled **The Cyclops Club Déjà Vu Festival**.

This would be the biggest déjà vu rave up to date, if you didn't count the **First European Déjà Vu Festival** held in Arras, France. No self-respecting sort counted that event as anything more than a farce, since **Contradiction** were the nearest thing to real déjà vu the promoters had on offer. The rest of the bill was made up of tenth generation punk bands and dodgy French rockers. **Alienation** withdrew their services because they refused to share the stage with the **Judas Freaks**. KU 422 pulled out in solidarity with Alienation.

Inside the Cyclops Club, the soundchecks had finished. A bouncer padded up the stairs to the club's entrance and opened the doors. Teenage sorts streamed down the stairs and into the long and narrow basement which housed the club. Tracy and Christine huddled together, their body language warning anyone who might want to join them that theirs was a private conversation.

Frustration launched into the first number of the night. The verses were sung in French, the words lifted from an assortment of late romantic poets including **Baudelaire**, **Rimbaud** and **Verlaine**. During the chorus, lead singer Dick Frustration dropped his trousers and mooned the audience while repeating the words, 'Why don't you kiss my arse?'

After the band had been through eight verses, Dick

announced the group would keep playing the chorus until someone got up on stage and kissed his arse. After three minutes of chorus repeats a teenage sort gave Dick a rimjob.

Claire and Jed were in the ladies toilet working their bodies up and down to the primitive rhythm of the swamps, improvising their way through the hot melodies of lust and desire. They'd left the club, left the toilet. They imagined they were out on the mudflats. The smells of bleach and disinfectent had become a salty seabreeze wafted from a tropical shore.

They came together, imagining their orgasms to be genetically-encoded memories of the first star exploding or, at the very least, the sexual history of their race played through their veins in a rush of ecstasy. Flickering moments of pleasure/pain which had been programmed into the binary structure of the universe. And thus, once again, they reached that peak from which two sorts can never jointly return. . .

Frustration's second number was called 'Why Don't You Suck My Cock?' The chord sequence was identical to the one they'd used on their first song – only this time it was played backwards! The singer's German wasn't as polished as his French. The verse quotations from **Rilke** were virtually recognisable. The song went on and on until the same sort who'd rimmed Dick got up on stage and gave him a blowjob.

As the anonymous teenager sucked, chewed and then swallowed the member, Dick found it increasingly difficult to sing the words coherently. They became slurred, went out of time with the music and were eventually reduced to guttral utterances of pleasure. The band pumped up the volume.

Dick screamed pure ecstasy as liquid genetics boiled through his penis. He'd left the club and was out on the mudflats. There was a flash of light and Dick experienced orgasm as a genetically-encoded memory of teenage girls

182

mobbing him as he mimed to a hit record on a TV pop show. Dick's breathing was heavy. The band slowed and stopped playing.

The group walked off stage. There was some applause but it wasn't particularly enthusiastic, a few whistles but no foot stomping. There was a thirty second hush before the club DJ put on a record.

Le Pissoir had come from Paris and everyone wondered why they'd bothered. The girl singer had a fine voice but the band were out of tune and all their songs sounded the same. They whacked away for half an hour and then abused the audience for not applauding. This was greeted with chants of 'Hop Off Frogs'. Someone threw a glass which shattered against an amplifier. The band left the stage very quickly after that.

Erection Set, **Subversion** and **Death Squad** came and went. Each of these bands sounded reasonably polished and had stayed in time and in tune, but there was nothing to set them apart from the herd. They had speed and fury galore but lacked that extra something which would place them a cut above the rest. Their riffs weren't familiar enough. Each singer put a little too much expression into his voice.

Without doubt these three bands would be signed very soon. Their records would enjoy respectable sales. In the short term their music would be more popular than that made by the likes of Frustration. But Frustration would attain cult status and be remembered for years, whereas these groups would soon be forgotten. The last two bands of the night were in a different league entirely.

A horde of record company executives and music journalists swarmed around the bar as KU 422 launched their set with a savage rendition of **Organisation and Democracy**. The group had taken their name from the flight number of a hijacked plane. The singer, John Scat, had only recently parted company with a minor punk band. The rest of the group had virtually no musical experience at all.

183

They'd run into Scat on Stoke Newington High Street and told him that he was great but his group didn't cut it. He'd immediately formed KU 422 with them because he liked the way they dressed. That was three months ago. . .

'This one's for the freedom fighters who've taken the American Ambassador prisoner in Rome,' John announced.

There was frenzied cheering from the dance floor and the band went into **Death or Glory**. There were stage invasions during **Communism Forever** and **Kill A Cop For Jesus**. Bouncers kept the kids away from their heroes during **Platform and Manifesto** and **Theses On The Commune and its Time**. Towards the end of **Theoretical Coherence**, several sorts managed to evade the security and climb onto the stage. This select few became a flood as mates helped each other beat off the threat from the bouncers. The group ended their set with their sort supporters crowded around them as they stormed through **Origin and Function of the Party Form**, **Night Of The Proletariat** and **Eat The Rich**.

The stage was cleared of sorts before the band were allowed back on for the first encore of the night. As the group strummed the opening bars of their anthem **Red Menace**, the teenagers made another successful invasion.

Derek Jacobs was propping up the bar. He loved seeing teenagers crammed into a small club and fleeced of their money, liked it even more when his own company had a stake in the operation. If he hadn't known better he'd have thought KU 422 were the headlining band. God only knew what the sort reaction would be when Alienation came on.

Chickenfeed was one hell of a mean bastard. He'd insisted on a 12 per cent deal. It was unheard of for a new group. Only established superstars could demand such an outrageous royalty. And yet, Derek had a contract inside his pocket which his board had drawn up and signed. All that was needed were the signatures of the group and their manager. Derek had been forced into accepting the

12 per cent figure. There were too many other companies interested. He couldn't allow them to snap up such a hot property.

The Malcontents and Philistines shoved their way to the front of the crowd. Those sorts jammed against the stage were tilting at the waist, from the pressure of hundreds of teenagers pushing them forward. Three bouncers were unsuccessfully trying to force the crowd back.

Christine shouted 'One, two, three, four,' and Alienation stormed into 'My Baby's Got Syphilis':

> **The sun shines outta my arse,**
> **So let's not let the chance just pass,**
> **Ram your cock right up there baby,**
> **Those sphincter spasms drive me crazy.**
> **My baby's got syphilis,**
> **He's only three years old,**
> **I've no reason to mistrust him,**
> **He does what he is told.**

Christine chanted the words, Alan and Catfish backed her on the chorus:

> **I like playing with excrement,**
> **I like playing with excrement,**
> **I like playing with excrement,**
> **Anal electric current.**

Desmond Taylor, the sociologist, was standing at the back of the club. The phenomenon had got worse since he'd first seen the group. Alienation had added sexual perversion to their left communist stance. Kids were dancing on the stage, dancing with members of their own sex, dancing by themselves, pushing and shoving. Taylor noted signs of deep disturbance, of hysteria. Déjà vu and sorts had to be stopped before it was too late! Desmond's pen scampered across his note pad:

> **My baby's got herpes,**
> **And gonorrhea too,**

I gave them all to him,
He's gonna pass them on to you.

My baby likes to tango,
He likes to do the twist,
And when he's really good to me,
He gets an arse full of my fist.
I like playing with excrement!

Taylor was thinking about his column for next Sunday's paper. Alienation's music was a source of evil. He'd start a campaign to have déjà vu gigs banned. It was the only way to save the kids.

Desmond watched as a girl of sixteen pushed her way through the crowd. One of her nipples and the uppermost reaches of her pubic thatch were visible through her torn clothing. Christ, Desmond thought, that's an open invitation to sexual athletics.

Taylor remembered his wife and pretended he didn't have a hard-on. He decided to stop staring at the girl, but found he couldn't look away. She smiled at him. He was in two minds as to whether he should offer to buy her a drink. While he stood and convinced himself that she'd reached the age of consent, an acne-splattered youth put his arm around her shoulder. . .

Taylor decided to leave the club: he'd go home and write his column for the paper. This evil cult had to be stopped. He was in a position to save innocent teenagers from depravity and heartache. The kids gathered here tonight might not appreciate his concern now, but in the years to come they'd thank him!

DEREK JACOBS WAS A HAPPY man when he left the club. He had the necessary signatures on his contract. Chickenfeed struck a hard bargain but Derek would still make a great deal of money from the group. After all, once Alienation had been given 12 per cent of the profits from sales of their product it still left 88 per cent for Derek's company.

CHICKENFEED GOT BACK TO MAIDA Vale at 3.30am. He crept into the flat. He undressed in the hall and padded through to the bedroom.

'Hello love,' Elizabeth said as she snapped on the light. 'You undressed in the hall, you're such a dear, so considerate. You can make as much noise as you like when you come home, it won't make any difference. I just can't get to sleep until I've had a good fuck.'

'Your sexual appetites never cease to excite and amaze me!' Chickenfeed replied.

'What kept you out?' Elizabeth asked.

'We signed to IMC tonight, I had to take the group out to celebrate.'

'It's good to see you doing so well in the music business,' Elizabeth said as she stretched her arms out towards Chickenfeed, 'but don't forget that your writing should come first!'

'I know,' Chickenfeed said, climbing into her arms. 'But I've finished **Yo Boy** and I'm halfway through the first draft of **Swish**, I'll have another six books written before they get round to publishing my second novel.'

Chickenfeed pressed his mouth against Elizabeth's lips and that ended the conversation. Elizabeth took Chickenfeed's right hand and placed it against her left breast. The nipple was hard. Chickenfeed rubbed his fingers over it and Elizabeth moaned.

Chickenfeed closed his eyes. Tried to imagine it was Tracy who was holding him, the fantasy no longer

187

worked. He summoned up a mental picture of **Kim Wilde**, she never let him down. Elizabeth took his love stick and guided it into her cunt. Chickenfeed imagined it was Kim's hand that was holding his dick.

They pounded out the primitive rhythm of sex and imagined they were out on the mudflats where life's binary oppositions begin. Imagined that they could hear waves breaking on a beach as they pumped up the volume. Liquid genetics boiled through Chickenfeed's penis, Elizabeth was speaking in tongues. They both imagined their orgasms to be genetically-encoded memories of money, glamour and fame. Eliazbeth was still babbling incoherently as Chickenfeed fell asleep. 'You dirty bastard!' she repeated again and again. 'I love you, you dirty bastard!'

CHICKENFEED HAD BEEN ORGANISING GIGS. **The End Of Music Tour** would feature five bands – **Alienation**, KU **422, Contradiction, Frustration** and **Death Squad**. Thirty dates had been booked across the country, giving teenagers from outside London a chance to grab a slice of the déjà vu action.

Contradiction had a single out on the independent **Snuff** label. Alienation were hard at work cutting their first disc in a West London studio. Its release timed to coincide with the tour. The band had never recorded on anything larger than an eight track before. At **Discodrome**, they were forced to rely on the guidance of their producer because they didn't know their way around a thirty-two track studio.

IMC had picked **Seduced and Abandoned** as the A-side of their first release. It was slower and more melodic than most of the songs in Alienation's set. Chickenfeed had convinced the company to put **Say No To Democracy** on the other side of the disc.

'We'll just go through it without recording anything to see how it sounds,' Chris Davies the producer informed Christine over the set of headphones she was wearing.

Christine listened to the familiar chord sequence, E, A, G. It was the bass that made the song. The guitar was just a drone. Catfish played a short lead break during the middle eight, but other than this the only change he made was to drop a fifth for the chorus. Christine came in on the fourth bar:

There is no difference between the same and
                             the other,
Same and the other,
Seduced by my own reflection,
Seduced and abandoned,
Se-du-ced and a-band-oned.

There is no distance between the real and its
                              double,
The real and its double,
A mythic Narcissus,
Seduced and abandoned,
Se-du-ced and a-band-oned.

The frame and site of illusion have disappeared,
Frame and site disappeared,
Tiresias blinded,
Seduced and abandoned,
Se-du-ced and a-band-oned.

Ritualistic seduction,
Aesthetic seduction,
Political seduction,
The latter being the phase of its simulation,
The character of which resembles nothing,

Seduced and abandoned,
Se-du-ced and a-band-oned.

Seducers strategy is object and limitation,
Object and limitation,
The aesthetic and ethical,
Seduced and abandoned,
Se-du-ced and a-band-oned.

Seduction is destiny,
Se-duc-tion is des-tin-y!

Christine had never understood the words but felt they sounded right. When she'd asked Chickenfeed about them he'd mumbled that the group needed a 'post' lyric. 'It'll keep the critics guessing,' he'd said.

'Great!' The producer's voice cut through the headphones dispersing Christine's thoughts. 'I think that'll do.'

'But you said it was only a runthrough,' Christine protested.

'I know,' the producer replied, 'that was to put you at your ease. It's a technique I've used for years. I've found it's one of the best ways to get quick results from young musicians.'

PAUL WAS IN BED. TRACY got in beside him and he snuggled up against her. She turned over and pulled herself into a foetal position. Tracy was sick and tired of Paul's groping hands. Paul kissed the back of her neck and tried to force her legs apart.

They'd been going through this every night for weeks. Tracy wondered if she should end their relationship before things got any worse, so that when she thought of Paul she'd remember all the good times they'd had together and not the shit they'd been through. Tracy began to cry. Gently at first, a few tears rolling down her cheeks. Paul continued to paw at her body. The tears became sobs and water was flooding from her eyes. Her body was racked with spasmodic shudderings.

'What's the matter with you?' Paul demanded.

'Nothing,' Tracy choked out between her tears.

'I can't lie here with you crying like that,' Paul was insistant. 'I wanna know what's the matter with you.'

'Just let me get to sleep.' Tracy sobbed.

Paul yanked on Tracy's shoulder, pulled her round so that she was facing him. She put her hands over her face, Paul pulled them away.

'What's the matter with you?' Paul repeated.

Tracy put her hands back over her face. Paul pulled them away again and held them in a vicelike grip.

'You're not going to sleep until you tell me what's wrong.' Paul's voice was hard.

'I love you,' Tracy sniffed. 'But I can't handle a physical relationship at the moment.'

'Why not?' Paul wanted to know.

'I can't explain it. It's just the way my body reacts.'

'Have you been fucking someone else?' Paul asked.

'No.'

'Are you sure?' There was a note of menace in Paul's voice.

'Of course I'm bloody sure!' Tracy burst into a fresh wave of sobbing. 'If I'd seen Edward a few times, just to have a chat, I'd be a lot happier than I am now.'

'You bloody selfish cow!' Paul screamed.

He slapped Tracy across the cheek. Her sobs became hysterical. Paul ripped back the bedsheets and leapt out of bed.

'Edward can fuckin' 'ave you.' Paul swore at his ex-girlfriend as he dressed. 'I never wanna see you again.'

191

He threw his set of keys for Tracy's flat onto the floor, slammed the bedroom door, slammed the front door and was gone. Tracy lay naked and sobbing on the bed. She didn't even reach down and pull the sheets back over her body.

EDWARD WAS DELIGHTED WHEN TRACY phoned to say she was coming to see him. He opened the door and she flung her arms around him.

'I love you,' she whispered, and the words burnt into his ear.

'I love you too,' and he knew with Tracy it was the real thing.

Edward found it hard to believe that he could be so physically attracted to someone. Her body did things to him that it just wasn't possible to describe, and he was attracted to her mentally too. Chemical and electrical, the charges were flowing two ways. From Tracy to Edward, from Edward to Tracy.

Edward led Tracy into the living room. Their mouths met. Tracy's arms were wrapped around Edward's neck, Edward's around her waist. . .

Much later they were on the floor. Their twin bulks a single mass of flesh. Mudflats. Sea air. Genetic memories. The body a field of sense impressions. Consciousness of self abandoned in an entropic flow.

Tracy could feel the liquid genetics boiling through Edward's prick. But the penis was no longer Edward's. It belonged to Tracy and the cosmos. They'd momentarily abandoned the ego, dissolved their human frames of reference and taken the lefthand path to the Godhead.

Ascetics can never understand the joyous abandonment of fucking. If they knew how to go with the flow, they'd attain the enlightenment they seek pleasurably. Tracy and Edward believed the separations of this world

192

could be abandoned in the ecstasy of the sexual encounter. They knew that asceticism was a socially conditioned form of masochism and this led them to believe they could escape the cultural through dilligent pursuit of pleasure. . .

Supper was a beansprout salad which was continually interrupted for kisses and cuddles. When they'd finished the salad, Tracy made a tea from some powdered magic mushrooms she had in her bag.

Tracy had done hundreds of 'trips' in her time. She could sense the subtle changes coming on in her perception of the world. Case had always looked upon drugtaking as a degenerate habit. The mushrooms were a new experience. He didn't realise they took half an hour to hit. He was cuddling Tracy on the leather settee, thinking the mushrooms weren't much cop. He'd expected flashing lights and day-glo colours.

'I'm on the ultimate reality trip.' Edward announced.

Tracy kissed him and they both giggled. Case pretended he was on a 'trip'. The mushrooms hadn't affected him, he was just having some fun. He giggled some more, turned Tracy over and put an ear to her arse. 'The great seat of wisdom is speaking,' he announced solemnly. 'It says blue shoes is bad news. I'm glad my shoes are brown. Yours are black. We're both okay.'

Case thought his behaviour was becoming mildly silly. He wondered whether he should stop clowning around. Tracy was giggling. She seemed to be enjoying it. He was too. He'd carry on for another ten minutes and then pull himself together.

Tracy and Case were naked. Edward wasn't sure how it had happened. He seemed to have lost all sense of time's proportions. The two of them were beating out the primitive rhythm of the swamps. Edward could have sworn the last time he'd looked at Tracy's face it had been completely covered by flesh. He kissed it just to make sure his senses weren't deceiving him.

193

Tracy was grinning. Her skull was visible. The flesh that remained was covered by pastel swirls of green and red light. Case kissed her again. She was very pretty. He tried to remember what she'd looked like before her flesh had disappeared.

This time as they pumped up towards orgasm, Case saw their bulks below him. The spiritual side of Edward's being had risen above this vale of tears. He was looking down upon himself in voyeuristic fascination.

Their bodies experienced orgasm as a genetically-encoded memory of Hiroshima. Fire flooded their brains and Edward's spirit was once again banged up inside his bulk. He had reached that peak which marks the path of the eternal return. . .

Night was a blur of coloured lights and a marked absence of sleep. Case heard Tracy get out of bed and leave the room. He thought he could hear her crying. He pulled on his clothes and went to investigate. Tracy was lying face down on the living room floor. Edward pulled her up and held her tightly in his arms. 'It's alright,' he said.

'I want Paul,' Tracy sobbed. 'I want Paul.'

'You can have us both,' Edward reassured her.

'I can't,' Tracy sobbed. 'I want you both, but I want Paul more than you.'

'It's alright.'

'I want Paul,' Tracy sobbed. 'I won't be able to see you again.'

Thirteen

THE TOUR HAD BEEN EXHAUSTING, 30 dates in as many days, but the hard work paid off. **Seduced and Abandoned** nudged its way into the top 20 and stood at number 17, a climber from the position of 24 the previous week. Sacking Alan paid dividends in terms of music press coverage. He couldn't have timed his suicide better if Chickenfeed had told him when to do it. Exactly two weeks into the tour ensured maximum publicity. The group sent their condolences to his family, it was unfortunate their busy schedule prevented them attending the funeral!

There's nothing like playing in front of a live audience to sharpen the skills of a raw musician. Chickenfeed had learnt a great deal in a very short time. The tour increased the band's confidence and musically they were as tight as a duck's arse.

The crowd at the **Ritzy** in West London was the largest the group had ever played to. Over three thousand people were packed into the old cinema. The place was shaking as the band rocked out. Alienation were storming through 'Destroy The Family':

**Destroy the family, destroy the state,
Blow it up, burn it down, kick it till it breaks.**

The chords of the chorus were not dissimilar to the opening bars of the Sex Pistols' **Anarchy In The UK**. The words were pieced together from **Angry Brigade** communiques, **Situationist** texts and Deleuze and Guattari's **Anti-Oedipus**:

**The state intervenes in everyday life,
People don't live they just survive,**

From the cradle to the grave,
We're effectively kept asleep,
The soft cop psychiatrists,
Step in at the first sign of crisis,
There's no autonomy,
Outside of schizophrenia.

Teenage sorts were pushing and shoving each other, jumping up and down, but their efforts to get up on stage with the band were thwarted by bouncers who were not adverse to using fists and boots to enforce their employer's edict that the audience should not be allowed anywhere near Alienation's expensive musical equipment.

Peter Rogers had worked with the **St John's Ambulance Brigade** for many years. He'd given first aid to a score of teenagers who'd been beaten up by the security. Two of them had been so badly worked over he'd had to send them on to hospital. He didn't entirely blame the bouncers. They had a job to do and the kids were difficult to control. He'd caught the lyrics to several of the group's songs and could only conclude that whoever wrote them was driven by some evil force. The combination of such words and music had snapped the frail grip many of these teenagers had on reality. And as he listened to the song being played he had no doubt that this 'mind-snapping' was something the group deliberately set out to achieve:

Throw open the prisons, throw open the asylums,
Swarm out of the estates and kill the rich,
Practice free love in the parks and on public
                                    transport,
Accept nothing less than experience of the
                                    moment.

The concert hall was dripping with sweat, filled with the pungent aroma of teenage sex. Paul Johnson's naked figure was lit by a spotlight trained at the platform suspended high above the stage. Paul felt cool and calm. On every other date of the tour he'd sweated as he knelt blindfolded for the hour-plus length of Alienation's set. Tonight was different. It was the last night of the tour. The group were in the middle eight of the penultimate number:

No more leaders,
No more politicos,
No more superstars,
No more,
No more!

Tracy sent Paul several frantic letters. She loved him and wanted to sort out their relationship. Paul hadn't responded. He'd heard she'd split up with Case but didn't care. Tracy had abused him too many times in the past. . .The band played on:

We will fight the revolution of everyday life,
Smashing the spectacle and making truth burst
forth,
The subject-object duality will be abolished,
Only the present will survive.

Paul heard Catfish and Chickenfeed's voices come in behind Christine's. They did this on most of the choruses. It was a simple way of adding power and emphasis at a particular point in a song. The voices harmonised:

Destroy everything!

The song was over. Paul was about to die. He'd posted Tracy his suicide letter that afternoon. It was short and simple: 'My life is no longer worth living, your selfishness has killed me.' It was two months ago that he'd told Chickenfeed he was going to kill himself. Chickenfeed suggested he do it in a powerful way. He'd taken this advice seriously and knew his death would be the spectacular end he desired.

Catfish strummed the opening bars of **Sex, Shit and Death**. Paul reached out and grabbed the rope which was

197

dangling in front of him. He put the noose around his neck and stood up.

There was a gasp from the crowd. The band were still swaying to their music but the audience was still, mouths open. They'd never been to a concert like this. Paul walked out into thin air. The rope jolted as it took the full weight of his bulk.

Peter Rogers raced across the stage. The band played on. Paul felt dizzy, through the mists in his mind he imagined he was looking down on himself. His prick was stiff and there was a grin on his face. He'd read somewhere that when your neck snaps you ejaculate. His body was twitching but he hadn't come.

Rogers scrambled up the ropeladder which provided the only access to the platform slung high above the stage. His family had not been religious. His father had believed in UFOs but not God. Peter had been converted to the Catholic faith in his mid-twenties by the foreman at the factory where he'd worked for the past fifteen years. As he raced up the ladder he prayed he'd not be too late. Suicide was a cardinal sin.

Paul felt strong arms wrap themselves around him. Perhaps it was an angel who'd come to take him to heaven. He was unconscious by the time Rogers removed the rope from his neck. Peter put an ear to Paul's chest. He couldn't hear a thing over the racket the group were making:

'Blood!' Chickenfeed screamed.

'Orgasm!' Christine sang in reply.

'Death!' Catfish shouted.

The words were repeated another three times. The chorus finished, the group chanted over the two chords which served as introduction, middle eight and end:

The only things certain in life are sex, shit and death!

Alienation left the stage. Rogers was giving Paul heart massage and mouth to mouth resuscitation. The boy was

198

beginning to breathe normally again. Rogers wasn't happy about doing it but the only way he could get Paul to hospital was by putting him over his shoulder and carrying him down the rope ladder.

'Death, death, death!' the audience screamed, as they worked themselves into a frenzy.

Rogers lay Paul on a stretcher which two ambulance men had carried onto the stage. Journalists rushed to the foyer to use the pay phones.

Alienation were back on stage. The roar of the audience was drowned out as they stormed into **Refuse Any Dialogue**. Paul was carried into an ambulance. The band raced through the first chorus:

> **Refuse any dialogue,**
> **Don't fuck authority,**
> **Refuse any dialogue,**
> **Reject ideology.**

It wasn't a particularly strong number. The group had far better material. It didn't matter. Three thousand teenage sorts went apeshit. Fights broke out in the hall, chairs were trashed, pipes ripped from the wall.

> **It's time to break out,**
> **It's time for some action,**
> **Only communism gives unitary satisfaction.**

Christine's voice soared above the melee. Catfish and Chickenfeed came in on the chorus and stayed there for the middle eight:

> **Down with Big Brother,**
> **Down with anarchist ideology,**
> **Down with slogans,**
> **All power to the workers' councils!**

The sorts gathered at the front of the stage were splattered with blood. Teenage bodies swayed to the beat. Sexual organs were exposed through torn clothing, bruises making

199

the flesh all the more enticing. Kids who'd been fighting were now fucking. The song stopped but those having sex kept moving. Alienation stormed into another number:

Forget pleasure, forget desire,
Forget about setting yourself on fire,
Forget everything you've heard from those liars,
Take the present!

Christine wailed on like a banshee.

Tim Staines was a big man who'd worked as a bouncer for the past fifteen years. His wife had gone off sex after her second miscarriage. That was two long years ago. Staines didn't like to see kids half his age fucking in public when he wasn't getting his oats. The band played on as he waded in against their teenage fans:

Wrap me in plastic, dress me in lies,
Give me something I can fetishise,
Bind my hands and gag my mouth,
Give me a truth I cannot doubt.

Staines tried to eject a sex crazed teenager from the hall. A fist slammed into his mouth. The satisfying crunch of splintering bone was barely audible above the music. Staines staggered backwards spitting ou' gouts of blood and the occasional piece of broken tooth. A DM landed in the bouncer's stomach and his body doubled up as another teenager slammed a karate chop against the back of his neck. Staines crashed to the floor and sprawled with his face in the dirt. Then the boots went in – HARD. Muffled moans were lost beneath the deafening roar of Alienation's music.

Staines writhed in agony as teenagers pushed each other aside to give vent to their blood-lust. Blow after blow registered on his tortured consciousness. Then the light began to fade. Death came as a God-given mercy.

CHICKENFEED DIDN'T KNOW HOW LONG he'd been lying on the bunk. The cops had taken his watch, belt and shoes

200

before they'd banged him up in the cell. A WPC came in and laid down a tray of food. Chickenfeed didn't touch the meal, he suspected it was drugged. He heard keys jangle in the lock on his cell door. A policewoman had come to collect the tray and dishes. 'Not eaten any of it!' she exclaimed.

'I wasn't hungry,' Chickenfeed replied.

'You've not even drunk your tea!' she chided.

'I'm a vegan, I don't take milk,' Chickenfeed eyed the policewoman as he spoke. She wasn't bad looking for a pig. Reasonably skinny with honey-blonde hair.

'I could make you a cuppa without milk,' she offered, 'or are you one of those eco-extremists who won't drink tea or coffee?'

'You got it in one.'

'I can get you a glass of water.'

'I'm not thirsty.' Chickenfeed closed his eyes. He could hear the WPC moving towards him. A second later her hand was on his flies. She tugged on the zipper, undid the trouser button and rolled down Chickenfeed's briefs. She took his cock into her hand and squeezed it.

'Do you mind?' Chickenfeed complained.

'Don't resist,' the WPC instructed, 'you'll only make things worse for yourself.'

Chickenfeed knew the cops wanted to wear him down. Since he'd refused their drugged food, they'd concluded a hand job would make him more pliable. During orgasm chemicals called endorphines are released in the brain. They're similar in composition to opiates, only stronger. Police thinking was ridiculously logical. If Chickenfeed couldn't be persuaded to take drugs orally, they'd use sexual stimulation to induce brain flooding. Chickenfeed wondered why the pigs didn't just stick a needle into his arm. Then he realised he wasn't supposed to know he was being drugged. After that Chickenfeed stopped thinking because the WPC successfully activated the genetic code buried deep inside his cortex.

It was sunny out on the mudflats, rays of light bathed his skin. Chickenfeed's body was a pleasure field. His skull a blank screen. The WPC pumped him up towards orgasm. Her grip was tight and her hand moved with the ease of authority. She'd always enjoyed the power she felt when jacking off helpless prisoners. It was one of the many ways in which she confronted patriarchy and recruited sick and irrational males into the Men's Auxiliary of her SCUM cell.

There was an explosion of white across the movie screen which was Chickenfeed's skull. He'd reached that peak which marks the limit of the self and the point of its eternal return. He was hauled to his feet as the everyday experience of id, ego and superego once again took control of his bulk.

Chickenfeed wondered how long the interrogation would go on. The inspector interviewing him was repeating questions, trying twists on them, looking for ways to catch him out.

'I've told you,' Chickenfeed insisted, 'I had no idea Paul would attempt suicide.'

Chickfeed had drilled everyone on how to deal with the cops when questions were raised over Paul's death. He'd even briefed Paul on how to deal with the authorities in the eventuality of his surviving the suicide attempt.

'But tell me officer,' Chickenfeed made a point of being polite since he didn't want to give the cops anything on him. 'How is Paul? Has he survived?'

'His condition is critical, but the doctors reckon he'll pull through. Now tell me about the bouncer.'

'I don't know anything,' Chickenfeed replied. 'You told me he was murdered, I'm afraid I couldn't see a thing through the stage lights.'

'Take him back to his cell.' The inspector was speaking to the WPC who'd given Chickenfeed the hand job. 'I'm not satisfied with his answers. I'll call for you to bring him up again later. Get PC Allen to bring me the singer.'

THE POLICE SUMMONED TRACY. THE doctors thought the sound of her voice would pull Paul out of the coma. She'd been sitting at his bedside for three hours, telling him about the depth of her love.

A PC sat on the other side of the bed, a newspaper folded over his lap.

DALSTON THREE GET LIFE

screamed the front page headline in letters two inches high.

Tracy was prepared to go to jail if it meant freedom for the youths from E8, but she knew she couldn't make a similar decision for her friends. She'd spoken to Case, Chickenfeed and Christine. All three had told her to leave well alone. Edward and Chickenfeed had been particularly vehement about it.

'I love you Paul, I love you,' Tracy murmured as she held on to one of his hands.

Tracy was staring at Paul's face. She noticed him twitch. The copper clocked her excitement. Paul's eyelids fluttered. Tracy bent over and kissed him on the cheek. His eyes opened.

'Can, can I move in with you?' he asked Tracy in a whisper.

'Did the band know you were going to try and kill yourself?' the copper demanded before Tracy had a chance to reply.

'No,' Paul's response was automatic. Chickenfeed had trained him well.

The copper walked away a disappointed man. He'd wanted to nail these sort bastards. He didn't give a damn about their innocence. What fucked him off was the fact that there was too much media interest in the case for his inspector to run the risk of fitting people up.

'Don't speak,' Tracy said, bending over Paul and kissing him. 'Save all your energy for getting better. When you get out of hospital you can come and stay with me. I'll look after you until you've recovered. Then we'll see how things go and if they're good you can stay in my flat on a permanent basis.'

REPORTERS CROWDED AROUND ALIENATION AS the group left the police station. Photographers jostled each other, journalists fired questions at the band.

'Fuck off!' Wayne screamed at another bloated example of the vermin that pass themselves off as newshounds.

The words were scribbled on a dozen notepads. They'd be quoted in tomorrow's editions along with whatever string of lies each reporter decided to use as an embellishment to their story.

'I suppose even scum like you journalists have to earn a living,' Chickenfeed allowed generously in reply to a question. 'But in this instance you'll just have to wait until we issue a press statement.'

As Alienation were being pursued by the throng of pressmen and wimmin, Edward Case pulled up in a car. 'Get in,' he commanded.

All four musicians obeyed. They were sick of being hounded. They just wanted to get home, and as quickly as possible.

'You made the front pages of the nationals today,' Case announced as they sped off. 'Quite a story. You're all famous.'

'Where we going?' Chickenfeed enquired.

'I'm taking you all home,' Edward said with a grin. 'Have you all had a chance to discuss the proposal I put to Chickenfeed?'

'Yes,' came the unanimous reply.

'And what's your decision?' Case wanted to know.

'We were reluctant,' Wayne was speaking for Christine and Catfish as well as himself, 'but Chickenfeed won us round. This time we can't lose. If we're caught we'll become the most famous rock'n'roll band of all time. If we pull it off, it'll be a blow against ecocide and we'll make a packet at the same time.'

'We're going to demand the release of certain political prisoners too,' Case said smugly. 'I thought of it this evening. We'll demand that the Dalston Three are given safe passage to a country of their choice.'

'Good idea,' Chickenfeed said as he got out of the car. He was glad to be home.

Elizabeth was at her front door. She literally pulled Chickenfeed into the flat. He'd been hoping to get a solid meal and some sleep. Elizabeth had something else on her mind as she dragged him into the bedroom.

There was nothing subtle about what the two of them did. There didn't need to be. Both were admitted masters of the pornographic touch. Elizabeth's beautifully manicured nails drew blood as her hands clawed down Chickenfeed's back. Her teeth bit into his shoulder. The age old smells of piss, shit and sweat filled the room. Their bulks were no longer human, they'd become a mass of amphibious flesh.

They pumped, pumped up the volume. Chickenfeed raised his arms and Elizabeth pinned them behind his head in a vicelike grip. Her mouth bore down upon his armpit, her tongue lashed into a mass of sweat and tangled hair.

A thought flicked across the moviescreen in Elizabeth's skull. Then the screen went blank. Once again the

205

endorphins had taken control, demonstrating their superiority to any form of opposition human consciousness could marshal.

With Chickenfeed and Elizabeth there were a million and one positional variations, but basically sex was about annihilation. An imagined return to primitive unity, psuedo-escape from the alienated reality of the capitalist present, an act of universal (in)significance.

Orgasm was the point at which the soul was crucified so that the body might live on. They'd reached that peak from which mistress and slave could never jointly return.

'Don't pull yourself free,' Elizabeth commanded. 'Stay inside me.'

'But I've gone limp,' Chickenfeed protested.

'I don't care! Just do what I say.'

Chickenfeed obeyed. He wasn't in a position to argue, Elizabeth had him pinned down. She lifted her head, then brought it down on Chickenfeed's chest. Her teeth dug into his flesh. She chewed and sucked.

'What you doing?' Chickenfeed demanded.

'Giving you some lovebites,' Elizabeth replied, lifting her head.

'Why?' Chickenfeed wanted to know.

'It's a good way of staking out my territory,' came the reply.

'What does that mean?' Chickenfeed's curiosity had been aroused.

'I'm going to love bite my initials onto your chest.'

Elizabeth could feel Chickenfeed's love muscle hardening inside her. She wasn't going to talk any more. The idea had turned him on – and she was turned on too. She gurgled, put her head to his chest. Sucked and chewed. Chewed and sucked. It took an hour before she was finished and Chickenfeed stayed hard the entire time. Her handiwork completed, Elizabeth began to pump up the volume. . .

206

Fourteen

BACK IN THE OLD DAYS, everyone had geared up more or less as they liked. But now, as Claire and Jed strolled along Merton Road they were instantly recognisable as sorts, as followers of déjà vu rock groups such as **Alienation** and KU 422.

When Chickenfeed coined the term, it referred to the rainbow alliance of radical groups. But with the growing media interest in déjà vu, the term became associated with the uniform worn by Alienation's camp followers.

The clothes were cheap and conservative, the type of casual wear clerks and other junior office workers would buy off the peg from **C & A** or **Marks & Spencer**. What made sorts stand out was the unusual colour combinations they adopted, most typically black and red, the colours of anarcho-communism.

Girl sorts were more conservative in their choice of colours. Masculine clothing alone was enough to signify their fundamental disagreements with consensus reality. Being a fanatical female follower of Alienation, Claire dressed in grey. Her trousers had been bought off the peg at **Tesco Home & Wear**. Above them she wore a grey shirt, a grey jumper, and over these a grey anorak. Her shoes were black brogues.

Jed's trousers and shirt were black, his sweater and anorak red. Like Claire he was wearing black brogues. Both of them carried a black umbrella with a wooden tip which had been filed into a point.

The **Merton Marauders**, a fanatical firm of Wimbledon supporters, had just clocked the two sorts. The Marauders were hardcore **hicks**, dressed in flares and tie-dyed T–shirts. Their leader, Dave Cosgrove, was in his late twenties and had followed the Dons from their days as non-league outsiders to cup winning status. Until a few weeks ago, Dave and his firm of teenage hooligans had been **Casuals**. The change came after Dave read a novel about soccer crews by Kelvin Callahan. Once hacks started churning out paperbacks about hooligans in expensive casual wear, it was time for a change of gear.

The flares and tie-dyes had been chosen because they were cheap and out of fashion. However, despite its negative effect on Cosgrove's consumption of sportswear, the lurid paperback had other merits – like sex and violence galore. Before he'd read the book, Cosgrove had never heard of 'sorts'. He'd suspected the cult was just a figment of the author's overfertile imagination. The newspaper headlines of the last few days had put him straight about that.

Casuals and sorts were natural enemies. And despite their metamorphosis from casuals to hicks, the Marauders still perceived sorts as a vermin to be wiped from the face of the earth. Cosgrove had a feeling for violence. The thud of his boot in someone else's groin did something for his 'soul'. Cosgrove's bent for creating mayhem found a much-needed outlet in the Marauders, as did his Hitlerite belief that anyone who deviated from his own set of norms should be beaten to a pulp.

The boy and girl making their way towards him were sorts. He'd read in the papers, as well as in **Casual**, that members of this new cult were fanatical **Communists**. Cosgrove liked to frighten his victims before pulverising them. He began to goose-step and the rest of his crew followed suit. They raised their arms in Nazi salutes and chanted 'Sieg heil! Sieg heil!'

Claire and Jed had been in enough gang fights to resist the urge to run. They were not yellow cowards who shat their pants when superior odds were marshalled against them! They'd meet the enemy head-on, take out at least some of the opposition before the bastards got the chance to give them a kicking. Theirs was a new cult, they'd stand

and fight to establish its reputation.

Cosgrove knew something was wrong. He'd expected the sorts to flee when they clocked his firm advancing upon them. He broke into a run, his men behind him. The Marauders chanted their anthem as they closed the distance between themselves and their victims: 'Mindless aggression, mindless aggression, you're gonna get your fucking head kicked in!'

Claire and Jed stood firm, levelling the sharpened points of their umbrellas. Cosgrove was impaled on Claire's tool before he realised it had been a miscalculation on his part to make a running charge at the teenager. Jed took out a second Marauder.

Claire swung her fist. There was the satisfying crunch of splintering bone. A hick staggered backwards spitting out gouts of blood and the occasional piece of broken tooth. The remaining members of the gang were more careful. Whipping out their Stanley knives, they formed a circle around the two sorts.

A blade tore into Claire's cheek. She put a hand to her face and another blade slashed her fingers. The Marauders literally cut the two sorts into ribbons.

Claire and Jed were crawling in pools of their own blood. Steel toecaps smashed into their ribs, bruised their shins – and mercifully – brought about concussion when they were sent cracking first into Claire's, and then Jed's, skull.

The Marauders were singing a variation on a terrace standard. When **Gerry and the Pacemakers** had a hit with it back in the sixties, the words ran 'You'll never walk alone'. In the Marauders version 'alone' had been substituted with 'again'. Hearing police sirens, those Marauders who'd survived the ruck melted into Saturday shopping crowds.

RADIO AND TV BULLETINS BROADCAST news of the gang deaths in Merton to a horrified British nation. As Saturday morning became afternoon, and then night, gang warfare broke out in every city. Sorts, casuals and hicks were battling it out to avenge their dead. The disturbances were more serious than the punk v. ted outbreaks of the late-seventies, or – indeed – the mod v. rocker bank holiday clashes of the mid-sixties.

Bookshops found they had a sudden rush of orders for a paperback called **Casual**. Its publishers were making a few last minute changes to its follow up. Originally entitled **Yo Boy**, the novel had been renamed **Hick**. A typesetter was earning overtime pasting in changes to the camera-ready copy, changes which the author had not been consulted about. They'd massively increase sales but were virtually irrelevant from an artistic point of view. All references to sportswear were deleted and descriptions of flares and tie-dyed T-shirts substituted in their place. The original cover art was scrapped and a photographer was developing a series of colour prints of hicks he'd taken less than a hour before. He was making a small fortune from this rush job. **The Anglo-Saxon Press** had offered him four times the going rate if he got the work done within twenty-four hours.

THE PRIME MINISTER WAS WORRIED. When the Prime Minister worried the rest of the cabinet worried too. The PM had always been a hardliner, a firm believer in the creed which says the only way to deal with political opposition is to crush it before it has the chance to destroy you. The PM steadfastly refused to give in to the demands of terrorists, strikers, football hooligans, foreign powers, liberal sentiment.

The demands could not be met. **McDonalds** and **Burger King** could not be legislated out of existence. The Dalston Three could not be freed. Cars could not be banned from inner cities. Public transport could not be offered as a free service, subsidised entirely out of taxes!

The terrorists had taken control of the **National Gallery**. They were threatening to blow it up if their demands weren't met by midnight. The SAS would have to be sent in. Human lives didn't count. What mattered were the countless treasures inside the building. A few squaddies meant less than nothing when gambled against the nation's heritage. Soldiers were paid to risk their lives. If they didn't get killed in the line of duty then the taxpayer wasn't getting value for money.

The orders went through. The building had been surrounded for many hours. A military psychologist was using a telephone to communicate with those inside.

'It takes time to organise these things,' he was saying, 'can you extend your deadline?'

'No,' Case replied. 'We calculated the time these things should take, which is why we gave you until midnight tonight.'

Edward hadn't expected his demands to be met. He'd simply felt it necessary to make a stand. Eco-veganism needed martyrs. Case believed in fanaticism as an efficient means to an end. His life meant nothing when gambled against the fate of the earth. His death would give strength to the eco-vegan movement. Catfish, Christine and Wayne understood the risks they were taking. Chickenfeed too, which presumably explained why he'd slinked off instead of smuggling arms into the building.

It had been dark for several hours. The army had searchlights trained on the National Gallery. The SAS had orders to liberate the building. The terrorists' deadline would expire in one hour's time. Until the commandos moved in, the **Ronnie Lee Field Unit** had not been endangering anyone's life. The threat they posed was to the **cultural capital** of the ruling class, in this instance manifested in the form of several thousand paintings and other art treasures. The government would sacrifice a million lives if that was what it took to save canvasses by the likes of **Constable** and **Gainsborough**. As it turned out,

211

a commando of just thirty men was the optimum number to send in.

Case knew the SAS would be deployed against him. He held a plunger in his hands. He'd wait until he was sure they were in the building. He wanted to take a few of the bastards with him when he died. He could hear canvasses being slashed in an adjacent room. Christine, Catfish and Wayne were an asset when there was a task to be carried out. It was their help which had enabled Case to overpower the guards, but when it came to sitting tight the three sorts had no patience.

The SAS entered the museum by a rear window. Edward began to count backwards – 'Ten, nine,. . .'. The troops were fanning silently through the building, moving steathily and with great speed. They met no resistance. All staff had been ejected by the Ronnie Lee Field Unit as it seized control of the museum. The army knew there were no more than ten terrorists, and that possibly their strength was as low as five 'men'.

'Seven, six, five. . .' Case was muttering under his breath.

There were shots in the next room. Case didn't bother to complete his countdown. He pushed the plunger home.

The commandos were amazed at the ease with which they shot down three of the guerillas. They were advancing on the next room when the blast flung them back. The charges were wired in a sequence. Masonry was falling all around the SAS unit, crushing them. Their deaths would not worry the Prime Minister. They could be replaced! There were plenty of working class youngsters who'd beg for the chance of a place in the army rather than suffer the ignominy of life on the dole, YTS or the Enterprise Allowance Scheme.

What could not be replaced were the thousands of old masters which had just been destroyed. A human life was nothing. Even if you buried the soldiers with full military honours and granted the odd widow a pension, the cost to the state was minimal. Whereas the canvasses which had been lost were worth billions!

The **Election** loomed like an execution. The cabinet knew it had served its final term. The middle classes would never forgive those ministers responsible for the loss of the nation's heritage. All the polls showed a massive swing to the centre. For the first time in years it became fashionable to describe oneself as a **humanist**. The government had rigged the past three elections. This time the polls showed they'd lost the support of the ruling class and that not even cheating would keep them in power. . .

WHEN ONE OF THE TABLOIDS revealed that three of the terrorists who'd blown up the National Gallery were members of the déjà vu rock group **Alienation**, there was a massive demand for records and other memorabilia. Chickenfeed had planned carefully. He'd got four albums' worth of material down on tape before the raid took place. A lot of it still had to be mixed, but it was there. . .

Every date on the **End Of Music** tour had been documented using top quality gear. Chickenfeed intended to off-load as much live material as the market would take. The second single, **Smash The Individual**, was rush-released. It topped the charts within a week of being issued. Chickenfeed had negotiated a massive advance on a book about Alienation. Meanwhile, his fiction had topped the bestseller lists. With all the royalties he was due, he would soon be one of the world's richest men.

Part of the contract Chickenfeed had drawn up with the group stipulated that in the event of their deaths any royalties which hadn't been paid were the property of his management company. The authorities suspected Chickenfeed had a hand in the National Gallery affair but decided that this particular stone was best left unturned.

Elizabeth was surprised when she discovered that Chickenfeed had never made a will. She had one drawn up in which he left everything to her. It was not even difficult getting him to sign it! She'd simply said it was necessary to take these precautions. After all, no one wanted the taxman to get a king-sized slice of their assets. . .

After Chickenfeed signed the will, Elizabeth dragged him into their bedroom. They took off their clothes. Chickenfeed lay on the bed.

'Wanna use the noose?' she asked.

'Yeah!' Chickenfeed replied.

Elizabeth took the rope from under the bed. She put it around Chickenfeed's neck and tied the other end to a ring in the wall. Their sex-life had been transformed since they'd started using the noose. Chickenfeed no longer relied on his **Kim Wilde** fantasies to see him through the fucks with Liz. It's well known that mild strangulation gives men a better orgasm, and that a full hanging is the ultimate in come culture.

Elizabeth got on top of Chickenfeed and yanked on his shoulders. His cock stiffened as the rope bit into his neck. Liz eased herself onto his rigid member. Eventually it was sucked into her snatch. They began to pump up the volume. Chickenfeed had his arms around Elizabeth's waist. Her arms were tucked along his body, her hands curled round his shoulders. She was applying a gentle downward pressure which kept the rope biting into Chickenfeed's neck.

They pumped up towards orgasm. Chickenfeed was intent on taking Elizabeth as hard and fast as possible, determined to plumb the furthest recess of her mystery. His body shuddered as the rope bit into his neck and then

214

the pressure eased as he thrust his cock deep into Elizabeth's cunt.

Elizabeth timed it perfectly. As Chickenfeed withdrew, she yanked as hard as she could on his shoulders. The pressure snapped his neck. Jism spurted from his cock and Elizabeth could feel it flooding her insides. It was the best fuck she'd ever had! Chickenfeed experienced death as a genetically-encoded memory of the first star exploding. They had reached that peak from which man and woman can never jointly return. . .

WHEN TRACY HEARD THE JUDGE announce the sentence she could hardly believe it. Strong hands grasped her and she was led away to the cells. 'Two years,' she mumbled, 'two fucking years.'

'That's nothing,' the WPC who was locking her up replied. 'You deserve more than that for trying to pervert the course of justice. In my book you're as bad as the terrorists who blew up the National Gallery. Thank God none of you succeeded in your aims. The Dalston Three will rot in jail. Personally, I'd like to see them swing from a rope.'

'But they didn't take part in the raid on Enrico's!'

'Keep that up and you'll get yourself certified!'

Tracy couldn't credit it. Paul had warned her not to go to the cops. She'd said she didn't mind going to jail if the Dalston Three were freed.

After Tracy had come forward the Crown had reopened the case. They'd been sceptical about her story from the beginning. It was too convenient that none of her cell had survived to corroborate the tale. In the end it had been decided she was just another eco-activist trying to take a short rap so that dangerous 'comrades' would be freed from jail. The British police did not fabricate evidence! Tracy Smith was simply a communist militant out to discredit the best judicial system in the world! The Crown decided to try her for attempting to pervert the course of justice. . .

PAUL STARED DESPAIRINGLY INTO HIS coffee. Nothing ever went right in his life. Tracy would kill him if she discovered what he'd been drinking. The coffee in front of him had gone cold so he ordered another.

After the suicide attempt he'd assumed Tracy would let him move in with her and that they'd finally settle down to a lifetime of loving each other. Then she got two years inside. Fortunately she'd been paroled after eight months. Paul had stopped over at her council flat while she was in nick so that there was someone to pay the rent. The tenancy was still in her name.

Tracy had been out two weeks. She'd told him she couldn't possibly ask him to leave the flat. No, he could have the masionette – she was going to find somewhere else to live. She was so fucking selfish he couldn't believe it.

Oliver Baker sat down opposite Paul. Years ago they'd both been members of a fanatical punk crew called the **Surrey Scum**.

'Haven't seen you for a long time Paul,' Oliver observed. 'What you doing in this neck of the woods?'

'I'm living on the Teviot.'

'Funny you should end up there,' Oliver replied. 'I'm living the other side of the East India Dock Road. I've a flat above a shop on the High Street.'

'I'm depressed!' Paul moaned.

'What is it?' Oliver enquired.

'A woman,' Paul replied.

'They always were your downfall. You still a militant heterosexual?'

'Yes.'

'You should try a man, it would do you good!'

'Is that a propostion?'

216

'If you want it to be.'

'Okay, let's go back to your place.'

Paul was becoming expert at pretending he'd never had sex with a man. After it was over he told Oliver he still preferred girls.

'It was nice to try it once, just to see what I've been missing. But I'll not do it again. I'm a confirmed heterosexual.'

And then he walked back to the Teviot and to Tracy. . .